PBK
L   LeBeau, Roy.
                Rifle river

DATE DUE

DATE DUE	
APR 2 8 2014	
MAY 2 0 2016	
MAY 1 6 2016	
JUL 2 4 2016	

29

PRINTED IN U.S.A.

Also in the *Buckskin* Series:

BUCKSKIN #2: GUNSTOCK

BUCKSKIN #1

RIFLE RIVER

ROY LeBeau

LEISURE BOOKS NEW YORK CITY

To the Whitesburg gang . . .

A LEISURE BOOK®

May 2003

Published by

Dorchester Publishing Co., Inc.
276 Fifth Avenue
New York, NY 10001

ISBN 0-8439-2066-1

The name "Leisure Books" and the stylized "L" with design are trademarks of Dorchester Publishing Co., Inc.

Printed in the United States of America.

Visit us on the web at www.dorchesterpub.com.

RIFLE RIVER

PROLOGUE

In the early 1880's, throughout the whole West, perhaps only a dozen men were known as truly supreme gunfighters—the deadly best of the thousands of tough, gunwise frontiersmen who made their livings by violence: manhunters, Indian fighters, lawmen and bandits. The names of these top guns were known to everyone, and one of the most infamous was Buckskin Frank Leslie.

Gambler, killer-for-hire, ladies' man and mad dog—he had been called them all. Friend to Doc Holliday and the Earps, deadly enemy of the Texan killers, Ben Thompson and Clay Allison, Buckskin Frank Leslie had killed twenty-seven men with knife and gun by the time he was thirty. Doc Holliday called him "the fastest gun I ever saw."

Then one night in a savage, booming trail town, the legend of Frank Leslie came to an end. In a blaze of gunfire, provoked by Leslie himself in a drunken rage, a young girl was accidently shot to death by a terrified tinhorn gambler. The girl, a young dance hall singer, had loved Frank Leslie. And he had loved her.

Within hours of the girl's funeral, Buckskin Frank Leslie had ridden out of town. And out of history. He was never heard of again.

CHAPTER ONE

Fred Lee reined the big dun in and sat back easy in the saddle to take a long look down Rifle River. The narrow, brawling mountain stream raced straight down the mountain slopes to the broad green valley beyond. On the skyline, the *cordillera* of the Rockies rose, granite-gray and snow-peak white against the clear, vacant blue of the Montana sky.

It was a perfect spring day. The kind of day when most men are happy to be alive.

The big dun, catching the scent of spring grass from the rich valley below, snorted and shook its head, shifting under Lee's calming hand.

Lee was a man in his thirties, lean, wire muscled, a shade under six feet tall. His face, high cheekboned, almost gaunt, was sunburned into a deep mahogany, scored by squint and weather lines about the dark, gray eyes and thin, drawn lips.

He might have been a ranch foreman, or small ranch owner, judging by his fine horse and neat woolen trousers, tooled leather boots, and pale gray Stetson. He wore a Colt .45 Peacemaker, as many of those men did. But his rig was a little different from most. The .45's barrel had been cut down short, to about five inches, and he wore his gun rather high, the walnut butt at his right hipbone, the barrel slanting down and in across the crease of his thigh, almost to his groin. It looked a little odd, but handy.

The only decoration Lee wore was a silver watch chain, and a very handsome fringed vest, decorated along its stitching with tiny turquoise beads. It looked like fine Indian work.

The vest was buckskin.

Lee pulled one foot out of a stirrup, leaned back, and crossed his leg over the saddle bow. He reached into his vest pocket and extracted the fair butt of a black cheroot. He'd smoked most of the cigar that morning.

He struck a lucifer against his saddle, lit up, and sat the dun relaxed as any kid cowpoker, taking a long, long look at the valley below.

It was a pretty big stretch, maybe sixteen or eighteen miles long from where he sat out to the sudden steep foothills rising fast into the Rockies. And about eight or nine miles wide. A big stretch. And probably cold as Belaam's Balls, come winter!

It might become a man's home, a valley like this. Cree Valley, it was called. And it looked good. It looked rich as Greenback Heaven.

Even from this distance, Lee could make out the buildings and smoke of three or four ranches. And he could see the town plain. It sat down square in the middle of the valley, just at the place where the river took its first bend. Up to there, Lee saw that the river did indeed run straight as a rifle shot, but right at the town it took its first bend, and then broke into two branches.

Lee could follow one branch curving off to the left and out of sight beyond a distant hill. The other branch ran on out into the valley's distance. It gleamed like silver under the morning sun.

Lee couldn't make out the number of buildings in the town; it looked to be quite a few. "A fair-sized town," he remembered McGee having said. He'd been leaning on the bar in the Alten House in Helena at the time. "A fair-sized town, Mr. Lee," McGee repeated, "in one of the most goddamned beauties of a valley you ever saw! Now, I warn you, the winters are pure refined pissers up there! But your northern ranchers are a sight smarter than your scrubcattle southerners. Up there, the men put up hay for their beasts instead of leaving them in the snow to scratch or starve! There're no fools up in Cree valley." He'd given Lee a shrewd glance. "But I won't say they're all perfectly peaceful men, either . . ."

"I'm intending to mind my own business wherever I go," Lee had replied.

"So I'm sure you are," said McGee. "Still, it's only fair you should know that there's some of the same small-ranch and big-ranch trouble you find everywhere now." He heaved a sigh and took a big bite of his beef sandwich. "There's a little trouble in every paradise," he'd mumbled through the meat. Some bits of beef fat clung to his ginger whiskers. "No heaven without it."

Lee ground the cigar stub out on the sole of his boot, sat up, and slid his boot toe back into the stirrup. He touched the horse with his spurs, and the big dun, happy to be moving, took off down the long slope in easy swinging strides, single-footing fast along the broken ground beside the steep river bank.

It was a long way down to the valley floor, perhaps a one- or two- thousand-foot drop; it would take most of the day to reach it. And Lee had a stop to make along the way.

Early in the afternoon, after a cold meal of jerky and one of last night's campfire-baked potatoes, Lee pulled the dun up at the edge of a small meadow. Across a stretch of high buffalo grass, the river ran wide over a series of broad rock shelves, bubbling and brawling in the bright mountain sunlight, but running shallow over the stones.

Lee tugged a folded sheet of paper from his vest pocket and unfolded it across his saddle bow.

It was a rough map of the valley and surrounding range. One small section of those hundreds of square miles was outlined in heavy ink. Lee traced it carefully with his finger, looked across the river again, then folded the map and put it away.

He spurred the big horse out across the meadow, breasting through the tall grass to the edge of the river's shallow rapids, on into the racing current without a pause, the dun lunging out into the foaming rapids, plunging and high-stepping through the low, swirling water, its hoofs slipping and clattering on the wet rock shelves drenched with spray.

The dun reached the far bank and lunged up into the thin beech scrub that lined the stream. Lee pulled his Stetson low over his eyes and bent in the saddle as the whippy branches lashed back at him.

"Hold up a little, dammit!" He gathered the reins and slowed the big horse down. The dun's sire had been a Morgan, the dam, some Texan's cross of a mustang Barb and Louisiana Thoroughbred. It made for a restless, shifty horse; but a strong one, and fast enough to win some country races, if Lee had still been interested in that.

He rode cross-country for almost an hour by the big silver hunter on his watch chain. Then he saw the house lower down on the long, gentle mountain slope.

He was still at least a thousand feet above the valley, but the house and some outbuildings rested in a little hollow of their own, overlooking the final, slow fall of the mountainside into Cree Valley.

Two low ridges guarded the ranch buildings on either side, and both ridges were rich with thickly clustered beech and pine.

Lee rode on down.

A few hundred yards out, he saw a man walk out from behind a shed, carrying a sack of something over his shoulder. It looked like feed or seed.

11

Lee could see a twinkle of steel. The man had a pistol stuck in the belt of his pants. He was walking on his way, doing his work. Either he hadn't seen Lee coming down the near side of the ridge or he was pretending so.

Lee stretched back for the Henry carbine in its saddle boot and lifted it out. He didn't care for the Henry much; its short cartridges were short-ranged as well. If he were going to stay in this mountain country, he would need more gun.

The man had seen him now. He'd let the sack down and was standing by the corral fence, waiting.

He was an old man, sixty at least, had a big gray beard, like old Saint Nick, and rusty, tore-up, old cowboy clothes and split boots. He was also bowlegged to a considerable degree.

Lee rode right down to him.

The pistol was a Colt .38 Parrot grip. Clean and oiled.

The old man kept his hands away from it.

"My name's Tim Bupp!" the old man yelled to him. "What the hell is yours?"

Lee waited until he was upon him. He kept the old man in the corner of his eye and watched the windows of the house.

"There's nobody up there, Mr. Nosy!" the old man said. "And I would like to know your name . . ."

"My name's Lee."

"Named after that fancy general, I suppose." The old man was eyeing the dun.

"No, I wasn't."

"Well, whoever, you don't belong on this land, mister! This is the property of the Chicago Union and Development Corporation. And I'm the caretaker, signed on and paid."

"That's all right," said Lee. "Why don't you get a horse saddled and come on down to town with me?"

"Where did you get that horse? It looks to me like

12

he's got a funny-lookin' back." The old man jerked up his head. "And what the hell do you mean come to town with you?"

"I own this ranch now," Lee said. "And the horse is short one of his backbones; he's part Barb."

"That's it . . . that's it," the old man said, and he slowly walked around the dun, looking it over. "Some horse," he said. He went back to where he'd been standing and bent down to pick up the feed sack. "Shit," he said. "So you bought this ranch, did you? Well, that's bad news for me, if true!"

He walked off with the feed sack, and Lee rode the dun along beside him.

"Why bad news?" said Lee.

"Because I'm too old to be a cowpoker, that's why. And I can't cook worth a damn."

"Is there a woman in town who can cook?"

"Hell yes, and so what?" Bupp dumped the feed out into a trough under the corral fence rails.

"Then you work for her for a few days until you learn something of simple cooking from her—and I'll hire you on."

They both watched the horses come up to the trough to nuzzle the feed. There were two good *grulla* mares, one in foal, and a strong old cob, too slow for working cattle.

"Where are the ranch horses? Where's the cavvy?"

"Sold off," Bupp said. "All sold off when the cattle were." He watched to make sure the pregnant mare was eating well. "These are mine."

"Well, when that cob's fed up, saddle him. I want to get into town and do some business."

When Bupp led the cob off to the stable to saddle him, Lee rode slowly around through the cluster of ranch buildings, getting the feel of the place. The sheds were old, but in good enough shape; the barn was almost new, and bigger than most ranch barns that Lee had seen. Probably for that winter hay. And all the buildings were built solid of heavy, fat, split logs, with fieldstone foundations. They looked crouched down into the ground, braced for a storm—or for a rough mountain winter.

He looked at the house last. He rode the dun up to one of the side windows, bent in the saddle, and peered in. It was dim inside the house. Most of the windows had been left shuttered. The rooms, low-ceilinged and whitewashed, were clean and bare of all but a few pieces of rough furniture: rawhide chairs and a long rawhide sofa too, with feedsack cushions. There was also a long pine-plank table with pine-slat chairs set around it. The room was intended for some sort of parlor; and in fact the whole house was bigger, with more rooms—at least four—than most ranch houses boasted. Lee had known men who owned whole counties, who had started running their empires from a one-room, dirt-floor shanty no more than eight feet by eight and not six feet high at the roof, either. This was a pretty fancy setup and would look odd with just a lone man living in it.

Lee slid the Henry into its saddle scabbard. The house was certainly empty.

He heard the cob's heavy hoofs thumping up behind him.

"Why the hell don't you get down and go in? It's your damned house, isn't it?"

Without answering the old man, Lee turned the dun down the path worn alongside the corral. It looked to lead off down to the valley.

Past the meadows, over the thick green of the ridge woods, he could see the afternoon sun low over the hills to the east. Night would come fast to a valley set this deep.

Bupp kept his peace for the first few miles of their riding, jogging along beside Lee on his stocky cob, occasionally moving ahead on a new lead when the path thinned away under the spring grass. Lee was content to follow him, marking the landscape as they went, so that he'd know how to go the next time.

At a broad meadow, Bupp pulled up and pointed off to the right and broke his silence.

"There's your bad luck over there, Mr. Lee." He said it with a certain satisfaction.

"That so?"

"That it is. Over there, just past that meadow, is your line. And on the other side is Fishhook."

"Is what?"

"Fishhook! Mr. Ashton's place. Everything past there to the mountains is all his. Ashton owns every damn square foot by legal deed, bought and paid for!"

"I won't bother him," Lee said, "if he doesn't bother me."

Bupp turned in his saddle to look back at Lee.

"Doesn't bother you, huh? You talk more like a sport than a cowman, Mr. Lee!"

"I've done some gambling," Lee said.

"You better have," Bupp said, and he spurred the cob on down the trail. "Because you're gambling now, that's for sure!"

They reached the valley an hour later and were combing their way through a thick patch of scrub. Rifle River had curved down the mountain to run beside the narrow trail for a little way, and the scrub growth had taken heart from the flood of water and grown thick enough so that even the dun had to shove and lunge his way through.

"We've got to clear this out down here, burn it out, maybe, or we'll lose some colts."

"Are you planning to raise horses?" Bupp said, and he gave Lee a quick, sidelong glance.

"Yes, I am. Mountain appaloosas, if I can settle a good-enough stud on the place . . . ."

"No cows?"

15

"No," Lee said, guarding his face against a low branch. "I don't know cattle well enough."

Bupp rode along for a few minutes, muttering at the dwarf birch that tripped their horses and tugged at their shirts as they rode through.

"Listen," he said. "Mrs. Boltwith runs the hotel in town, though Christ knows it's not much of a hotel. A road inn is more like it! But she is a fair cook; nobody in town will say she isn't."

He didn't say anything more for a while. They were almost out of the scrub. Lee could see the river water flashing in the sunlight through the last of the brush in front of them.

"Well," said Bupp, "I suppose she'd teach me some cooking, if I was to wash up and swamp for her for a week or two."

"Then you'd have a job with me," Lee said to him. They rode out of the brush, Bupp leading.

A shot cracked past Lee's head and flicked the old man's shirt sleeve as it went on its way.

"Jesus Christ!"

Bupp kicked the spurs to his cob, and took off out into the river meadow at a stiff gallop. It was the wrong thing to do. Any man shooting at them had to be concealed in the scrub they'd just worked through. Out in the open, old Bupp would be dead meat.

Lee hauled the big dun up on his hind legs, turned him, and spurred him back into the tangle of dwarf willow and birch. The big horse squealed at the rake of the spurs and lunged and heaved its way back into the brush like a steam locomotive. It was the kind of fast, rough going the dun was made for.

Lee ignored the willow branches lashing across his face and reached back for the Henry. The light rifle was fine for this close work. Lee felt his heart pounding as the dun battered through the scrub; he'd always hated rifle fights. He worried for years that some man who wanted to kill him would be wise enough, some day, to come after him with a rifle and catch him well out in open country where only long-distance shooting would matter and nothing else.

But this wasn't such a long distance, after all.

Lee rode the bucketing dun like a sailor on a skiff in a stormy sea, watching the willow thickets ahead for the heaving motion that would betray a horse plowing through them, trying to get away. The shooter wouldn't have expected this kind of charge.

For a few moments, Lee thought he might have misjudged his direction and faulted on calculating the angle the bullet had come from. Then he saw the brush shudder and bend suddenly a hundred yards before him. In front, and a little to the left.

The shooter was running.

Lee steadied himself on the galloping dun, eared back the hammer on the Henry, then raised up in the stirrups, and began to shoot, ignoring the branches whipping at him.

He levered the Henry as fast as he could, cracking out the whole magazine into the low center of the heaving clump of brush in front of him.

It was scattergun shooting, nothing to be proud of; and it was a horse-shooting too. There was no use shooting for the rider in that green flurry of scrub.

And he missed—or thought he had.

Then a branch kicked back not thirty yards ahead of the dun's nose, and Lee saw a black and white spotted horse's leg—a pinto—and then the animal's muzzle as it reared up out of the brush.

It was hit hard; blood was pouring from its mouth.

Lee kicked the dun on in, driving it down on the thrashing pinto, searching the brush for the rider.

He dropped the Henry, swung off the dun, and dove into the scrub, falling and rolling into the thick greenery, the small branches catching at him, splintering

17

and breaking as he rolled.

No rider showed.

Lee rolled to his feet and lunged past a low, dwarf birch near where the pinto lay. It was in plain sight now, kicking and thrashing. Lee hadn't drawn his gun; he never had to draw his gun to make it more handy.

The dun was bucking and snorting away. Lee could hear the brush crashing under its hoofs a few yards further on.

Then he saw the rider.

The shooter.

He was standing, past the downed pinto, hanging on to a bent box elder as if he were hurt. Dirty canvas pants, dirty brown homespun shirt. No gun showing.

Lee considered killing him, and would have, except there was no gun showing.

He walked over toward the man, watching his footing amid the tangle of branches and bush roots. The pinto was dying, coughing out great blurts of bright-red, foamy blood. One of the Henry rounds had caught it in the lungs.

"Turn around, you son-of-a-bitch!"

The man started to turn, then stumbled, tripped on something, and fell over on his face.

Lee thought he must have shot the son-of-a-bitch, after all.

"Oh, Mr. Lee!" It was Bupp, calling through the brush. The old man's voice was quavering, scared.

Lee walked to the fallen man. As he did, the man stirred. Lee strode over, kicked him in the side of the head, and set his boot down hard onto the man's right arm.

It was an Indian. A young one, a boy maybe fifteen or sixteen years old. Tall, skinny, and ugly as sin.

The boy lay back under Lee's boot, staring up at him, blinking his eyes, still stunned by the kick.

He was a really ugly boy. His face was blackened by

the sun and dirt and pitted by old smallpox scars. His eyes were Indian-black and slanted as a Chinaman's. He had a big, broken nose like one of General Miles's pack camels.

Lee looked around for the boy's rifle and couldn't find it in the underbrush. Suddenly, the Indian turned under his boot, and Lee stepped back to kick him again. The boy began to vomit, heaving and spewing his guts out into the branches and leaves beside him.

Lee smelled the sour stink of whiskey from the vomit, and stood watching while the boy threw it up, groaning and gasping for breath.

A drunk Indian. And a boy at that.

"Mr. Lee?" Lee heard the old man kicking his cob into the brush toward him.

"Over here!"

"Did you get him?" Lee heard the cob stumble over a root.

"I got something, Mr. Bupp!"

Bupp rode the cob through the scrub into the small clearing the pinto had made in its death throes.

"Why you little red-nigger bastard!" Bupp said, staring down at the boy. His face was still pale with fright over his frizzy gray beard.

"Do you know him?" Lee asked, watching the boy still gagging, retching on an empty stomach now.

"Hell, yes, I know him! That's Tom Cooke. The son-of-a-bitch worked for me for two years, and this is the thanks I get, a goddamned bushwack murder!"

The old man was shaking like a leaf.

Lee left the boy and walked around the little clearing, looking for the rifle.

"I had to let the bastard go because the company wouldn't pay extra for his keep. Hell, they don't pay me enough to stay alive, as it is!" Bupp leaned down to shake his fist at the Indian. "And this is what you do, is it, you little son-of-a-bitch!"

Lee found the rifle under a broken birch sapling. It was an old Spencer with a split stock.

He walked back to where the Indian boy was lying.

"Is that so?" he asked him. "You were aiming to kill Mr. Bupp here?"

"Yes," the boy said, spitting some phlegm out and lying back in the brush. He looked sick. "Bupp made me go from the place . . ." He spoke good Mission English, and his voice was as deep as a man's.

"I didn't have the goddamned money to pay you, you dirty pissant!"

The Indian boy tried to sit up. He was still drunk. His eyes rolled and he slumped back into the brush.

"And that was a month ago, too!" Bupp continued. "This little bastard has been plotting to murder me!"

"What would the sheriff of this county do to him?" Lee asked, "if we took him in?"

"The sheriff wouldn't do shit! He's in Caswell, anyway, and that's forty miles away. But the town marshal will sure as shit hang his ass. He don't like Indians, anyway—and especially not a Blackfoot."

"You do what you want," the Indian boy said. And he lay back and closed his eyes.

"Now, how do you like that?" said Bupp. "The little red bastard damn near kills us and just don't give a shit!"

"It's not that easy, boy," Lee said to the young Indian.

"You giving him to the marshal?"

"No," Lee said, "I'm not. Lend me your belt."

"Say what?"

"Your belt."

The old man stripped off his wide leather belt and leaned off the cob to hand it to Lee.

The Blackfoot boy had sat up.

"You don't hit me with that!"

"Yes, I am," said Lee. "I'm going to beat the hell out of you."

CHAPTER TWO

The young Blackfoot raised his arms to ward off the blow as Lee stepped up to him, the heavy belt swinging. When the heavy leather struck him, the boy kicked out, trying to catch Lee in the knee.

It did no good. Lee kicked the boy's foot aside and brought the belt down again and again, lashing the boy as if he'd been a vicious horse, the belt leather cracking home like a coachman's whip.

The Blackfoot tried to roll away, scramble to his feet, anything to escape the searing fire of that hissing length of half-tanned rawhide. But Lee kept after him, kicking his feet out from under him when he tried to get up, swinging the heavy belt down with all his strength.

The Blackfoot was tough, but he was only a boy, and drunk. The pain finally became too great for him, and he lay huddled in the brush, vainly trying to protect himself with his raised hands as the belt sliced into his skin, leaving long, scarlet welts where it struck. His homespun shirt was torn to strips by the leather, stained with blood where the belt had cut deep. The boy's face was a mask of pain. But he didn't cry. The heavy crack of leather striking flesh sounded through the surrounding scrub.

"Mr. . . . say, Mr. Lee . . ." Tim Bupp shifted uneasily on the cob. "Don't you think he's had enough now?" he said, raising his voice above the hiss and snap of the belt.

Lee struck the boy three more times, grunting with the effort, the leather slashing into the boy's back when he turned on his belly, writhing from the pain.

Then Lee straightened up and tossed the belt to Bupp, its leather spattered with blood.

He reached down, gripped the boy's shoulder, and turned him over.

The Blackfoot was pale under the dirt on his face, and his narrow black eyes were brimming with unshed tears. He looked sober enough now.

"Listen to me, boy," Lee said. "You tried to kill a man—murder him from cover—and you got a good beating for trying it! Now, there's just two things you can do: you can get out of this valley and stay out of it or, if you want, you can come back to work at the ranch."

"Mr. Lee owns the River now, Tom." Bupp sounded sorry to see the boy hurt. "He can hire you back."

The boy said nothing. He lay staring up at the two of them.

Lee whistled for his dun, picked up the old Spencer, and walked off into the scrub to bring the animal in.

"Why don't you do that, Tom," Bupp said. "You know that man could take you to Marshal Phipps if he wanted to; and what the hell would happen to you then?"

Lee rode his dun back into the little clearing.

"I'll see you up at the ranch, Tom Cooke," he said. "You can walk up there by morning." He turned the dun to spur away. "I'll see you there tomorrow—or I'd better not see you anywhere!"

"You do that, now, Tom," Bupp said, as he turned the cob to follow. "That man just gave you a break, as well as a goddamned good beating you deserved, you pup!"

The boy said nothing. He lay still, listening, as the riders prodded their horses away through the brush.

22

When the scrub was quiet again, except for the gentle sighing of wind combing softly through the willows, Tom Cooke sat up and held his face in his hands and began to cry.

"I thought this was Cree country," Lee said, when the old man caught up with him. They were leading out across river meadows, striking along the stream's course for the trail to town.

"It is," Bupp said, bouncing a little to the cob's rough jog. "Young Tom there is the last of the Mohicans—the last of the Blackfoot around here, anyway. And those Crees don't like him any better than white people do."

"Why did he stay here then?"

"Hell, his ma's buried here! She was a whore at Rebecca's. Or a laundry girl, anyway. She was damn near as ugly as Tom is. He sure is an ugly Indian!"

"Here." Lee swung the boy's old Spencer off his saddlebow and handed it across to the old man. "You can give it to him if he shows up on the place."

"Oh, I don't know if he'll show up." The old man hesitated. "You gave him a real larrupin'."

Lee didn't say anything to answer him, and they rode in silence for a while. The valley branch of Rifle River ran clear as fine glass off to their right. It looked like good swimming water. Good fishing water, too. Good for everything.

"No," the old man said. "I don't think he'll show back at the ranch."

"Then he'd better not show at all," said Lee. "Anywhere in this valley."

Bupp glanced over at him, but said nothing.

It was after dark when they reached the town.

They'd stopped just once, to water and rest the horses, and Bupp had asked if he could try the dun out. Lee had let him, and the old man had done quite well, sticking for a good while before the dun had suddenly sunfished and dumped him. The old man had hobbled around, cursing, "You fuckin' reprobate, you!" until he felt better. The dun had dropped him hard.

Lee pulled up on a little rise just to the south of town and sat quiet for a few moments looking it over.

Cree was a fair-sized settlement, pretty easy to see under a rising moon, its windows shining yellow with lantern light. There were about thirty buildings—log and shingle or dressed planks—and three or four of them were substantial, two-story affairs. And there was a scattering of shacks on the outskirts, one just below the rise.

There were people in the streets down there, and some fair action too, by the sound of it. Lee heard a piano and a concertina playing somewhere else and women laughing.

"It's bigger than I thought."

"Oh, there's about one or two thousand going in and out most times. Cowpokers, mostly, from Fishhook or Bent Iron or one of the small spreads. And some lumberjacks too from the logging camp over the mountain."

"A lumber camp? Where do they raft their wood?"

"There's a lake over there—about a two-day ride—and they got a train spur out to Helena. Just a one-horse line."

"Could that line take stock as well?"

Bupp threw him one of his sly glances, his eyes gleaming in the moonlight.

"I'm glad to hear a man that can ask a smart question! The answer is yes, the line will take stock into Helena for you. But it costs."

"Let's go," Lee said, and he heeled the dun into a trot.

For a Friday night, the town was full of life.

24

The main street was dirt, with a careless layer of rock and gravel strewn across it, and it was fairly crowded with supply wagons and buggies and tied horses.

The raised plank sidewalks on both sides of the street were thronged with cowboys marching along arm in arm, shouting and laughing, already drunk. There were a few women walking with them, fat, ugly girls, for the most part, as drunk as the cowmen.

Lee saw only a few lumberjacks. Big men with full beards, wearing blanket jackets and heavy, hobnailed boots. He noticed that they and the cowmen stayed out of each other's way.

Lee felt good being in a town again. It had been three weeks since Helena, six weeks since Denver. And that had been a sad time, anyway, except for buying the ranch. It was never a pleasure saying goodbye to a friend.

"There's Mrs. Boltwith's," the old man said, pointing to a small two-story building standing beside what looked like a bank.

"Where would I find the land office?" Lee asked, raising his voice as four cowboys stumbled past them in the street, singing "*Lorena*."

"In the bank," Bupp said, nodding at the brick building. "And, say, Mr. Lee, I could use some kind of an advance on my wages if you could see your way clear . . ."

The dun was shifting restlessly, not liking the crowds.

"Let's get out of this," Lee said, and he turned the dun to a hitching rail in front of the bank building.

They crowded the horses in beside a weary row of cow ponies and tied off the reins.

They stood on the high plank sidewalk while Lee dug his purse out of his vest pocket, counted out five silver dollars, and put them in Bupp's hand.

"That's five out of your month's thirty," Lee said, and Bupp nodded and sighed.

"Listen," he said. "What do you want me to learn to cook, Mr. Lee?"

"Eggs, bacon, biscuits, steak, potatoes, and pie."

"Oh, my God Almighty! It'll take me a year to learn all that!"

"And stew, too. You learn those things, I'll have no complaint."

"I should think to hell you wouldn't!   Pie too?"

"Any kind you can."

Two fat men, who looked like sharpers or cattle buyers, jostled them as they went by, arguing about the price of something. —Yearlings. Cattle buyers.

"I'll do my damnedest, but I don't know." Bupp wandered away toward Mrs. Boltwith's. "Pie . . ." he muttered.

Lee walked down the sidewalk to the double door of the bank. It was a heavy door, banded with iron, and there was a small barred rifle slit high up on the right side. It was more like a jail door than a bank door. The town of Cree must see some lively times.

Lee looked for some sign saying when the land office would be open, but there was no sign at all. He tried the door; it was open.

The place was empty except for a pimpled kid wearing a clerk's eyeshade. The kid was perched on a high stool behind an oak desk, writing in a ledger. The oil lamp hanging over his head threw shadows around the empty counters and tellers' cages.

"What do you want, mister? Banking hours are from eight to six . . ."

"What time does the land office open?"

A door opened behind the clerk.

"Banking hours," a man's voice said. He stood framed in the doorway, outlined by the lamplight behind him. "You have a transaction to register, mister?"

"You the land agent?" Lee asked.

"I am."

"I've bought a ranch in the valley. I want to get the title registered."

"Have you, by God!" the man said. "Well, it's after closing, but what the hell. Come on in."

Lee walked back into the office and found the man already sitting at a rolltop desk, looking up at him. He leaned forward to offer his hand.

"Bill Calthrop, Mr.—?"

"Lee, Frederick Lee."

"Well now, what property is it that you've bought, Mr. Lee?" Calthrop was a big, beefy man, with shaggy black hair and thick eyebrows that ran in a straight black bar over his nose. His eyes were brown and small, watchful, like a bear's.

"River Ranch," Lee said.

Calthrop didn't say anything for a moment. He sat staring at Lee as if he hadn't heard what he'd said. Then he leaned forward.

"You say River Ranch?"

"That's right."

Calthrop pursed his lips, considering.

"Well, well, that's some news, all right. May I ask who you bought the ranch from?"

"Phillip McGee, in Helena."

"Phillip McGee. Let me see the papers, please."

Lee pulled the long oilcloth envelope from his shirt and handed it over to the land agent.

"Sit down—please sit down, Mr. Lee. I've forgotten my manners." He unfolded the papers and checked through them. He sorted them out onto his desktop and then slowly read them through.

"Jumpin' Jesus Christ . . ." he muttered.

"Is there any problem, Mr. Calthrop?"

The land agent looked up at Lee with a sigh. He slowly folded the papers, put them to one side, and dug into one of his desk drawers for a stack of registration forms.

"There is no problem with the sale, Mr. Lee. It looks

legal, all right. You paid $27,500 for the property?"

"Yes."

"Well," he sighed again, "you weren't taken on the price; that's fair enough . . ."

"Then where's the difficulty, Mr. Calthrop?"

The land agent paused in filling out his forms.

"The difficulty, Mr. Lee, the possible difficulty is that someone else was intending to buy that land for himself. In fact, that somebody else had already sent a hard offer to the Chicago Union people for it!"

"How is that my business?"

"It isn't, really. You just had the luck to run into McGee in Helena and were able to close the deal with their agent right there. It was lucky for you, I think." Calthrop didn't look as if he thought it was lucky.

"Nothing wrong with the property?"

"Oh, hell no, nothing wrong with that property! You've got good buildings up there—better than average, I'd say—and you've got three thousand acres of prime land to go with them. Of course, its not a big ranch as stocklands go, but still prime land . . ."

"So?" Lee sat relaxed, watching the land agent's face. The agent had something more to say.

"The thing is, Mr. Lee, that your place is called River Ranch because it straddles the north branch of Rifle River, right on up to the falls . . ."

Lee said nothing, just sat, listening.

"Well, dammit, you see you control that river! You own the water rights on it! Hell, if you decided to dam it up—well, there's not a damn thing the other ranchers could do about it—legally, anyway."

Lee sat forward a little, his dark gray eyes looking almost black in the lamplight.

"And what about the previous owner? Anybody scared over him having the water rights?"

"Well, no. But Thompkins was an old man. All his family was gone or dead and buried. He was a gentle man. He wasn't about to make trouble for anybody. And everybody knew it . . ."

"And how did the Chicago people get the property then?"

"Thompkins owed money in Chicago. He'd gambled on the corn exchange, the old fool, and those boys took him and took title to the ranch after he died."

Lee stood up. The agent, like most land agents, was quite a talker.

"I'm obliged for the news. What do I owe you for the registration?"

Calthrop stood up with him, handing the papers back across the desk.

"That'll be $15.00. And I want you to know, Mr. Lee, that you should be able to work that water rights business out with your neighbors. They're a good set of men, by and large."

Lee took the deed copies and registration, slid them back into the envelope, and tucked them into his shirt.

"A couple more things," he said.

"Yes?" Calthrop led him to the office door.

"First, who was the man who tried to buy the place?"

Calthrop hesitated. Lee stood silent, looking at him.

"I—it was Ashton, I believe. He owns the Fishhook Ranch. The line runs down your east boundary, Mr. Lee."

Lee nodded.

"And one more thing," he said to the agent. "I don't want you to talk of my business to other men, the way you've spoken of their's to me."

The big land agent flushed scarlet, looked as though he were going to say something, then didn't.

When Lee held out his hand, the agent took it without a word, then turned, walked back into his office, and shut the door.

The pimply clerk was still scribbling away on his high stool.

"Say, boy . . ."

He looked up.

"Tell me where I can find the cleanest bed and the best supper in town."

The clerk thought a minute, considering, sucking on the tip of his pen.

"Now, the best place to sleep is over at Mrs. Boltwith's hotel. And she's a good cook, too. Or you could try the Arcady. They do a good dinner . . ." He smiled slyly. "And they got the prettiest girls in town, too."

Lee strolled down from the bank building to Mrs. Boltwith's. Some men, they looked like hostlers and dry-goods clerks, were sitting out on the steps in the dark, smoking pipes and cigars and watching the occasional bunch of drovers go singing by.

Lee climbed up the steps past them and went through the whitewashed front door. The lobby of the little hotel was only a desk and an old bench set beside a steep, narrow flight of stairs. It was empty. Lee could smell meat pan-frying in the kitchen in back.

He walked on down the hall.

"It's got to be dry!" a woman's voice—a big woman, by the sound of her—rang out. "Dry!"

"All right, all right!" That was Tim Bupp. It sounded as though the old man was getting his first cooking lesson.

"Now, what in the world do you want?" A big, horsy, ugly woman with cold light-gray eyes turned to stare at Lee when he walked into the long kitchen. A pan of breaded steaks was sizzling on the broad black range.

"If you want a room, Abel will check you in out front, and if you want dinner, you're too late!"

"Hello, Mr. Lee," Bupp said.

"Oh," said the big woman. "You're the fella that

30

dropped this old fool in on me! Well, I'm damned if he can cut enough firewood to make it worth my while to teach him a thing!"

She had a harsh Kansas accent. Lee had heard it many times before. And she had a rough way of speaking, too. Lee had the feeling she'd seen darker days; she had that hard, grim air about her. A right old whore gone straight.

"Then put him to scrubbing pots as well," Lee said. And he walked to the kitchen table and sat down.

"Meanwhile, Mrs. Boltwith, I'll try one of those steaks he's done, by way of an experiment . . ."

For a moment, the big woman seemed near to exploding with anger. Then she paused and gave Lee a hard, searching look.

"Who the hell are you?" she said.

"A new landowner in the valley, Mrs. Boltwith. And a hungry one."

She gave him another slow, examining look, then grunted a grudging acceptance.

"Feed him," she said to Bupp. "And for the Lord's sake, next time dry a steak before you sear it!" And she stomped out of the kitchen.

"You sure have given me holy hell to go through, Mr. Lee," Bupp said, tinkering and clinking at the stove. He was dabbing at the frying steaks with a long-handled fork. "That old dragon's a pure pain in the ass—and no salve for it!"

"The steak's done, Bupp. And you can just call me Lee. The 'mister' isn't necessary. And by the way, you could take the horses over to the livery. Tonight."

"All right, all right." The old man was looking hot and harassed. He gingerly forked up one of the sputtering steaks, flopped it down onto a chipped platter, and brought it over to Lee, holding the plate in both hands like a new father with his first baby.

The steak was as tough as whang leather.

Lee was half through it, and chewing hard, when the horsy head of Mrs. Boltwith appeared around the kitchen door.

"Tough, ain't it?" she said, with some satisfaction.

"Not bad," said Lee.

"Not bad!" she laughed a hoarse, rumbling laugh. "I'll bet!"

"Tasty though?" old Bupp said hopefully.

"Tasty as horseshit," Mrs. Boltwith chuckled. She appeared to have a rough sense of humor. "As for you, Mr. Lee, if you want a room, you got one: 2-E, second-floor back." She pulled her head out of the doorway and was gone.

"Damned old dragon," Bupp said.

After the steak and a cup of Bupp's coffee—which was better than the steak—Lee had had a wedge of Mrs. Boltwith's peach pie. A tough old piece she might well be, but she could cook. Then he'd strolled out of the hotel, past the smokers on the steps—they'd stared at him, curious, as he went by—and out on down the street.

The Arcady was the biggest saloon on the strip, and it looked to be doing a land-office business. Lee took a slow stroll around the building, working the last of the trail cramps out of his butt and legs. He checked the back door and stairs. It was an old habit he had. It often helped to know the back way out, particularly in a place where there was heavy action.

When Lee climbed the front steps and pushed his way through the batwing doors, he was jostled hard by three lumberjacks coming out. The place was packed, heavy with the shouting and uproar of a jammed crowd of men and women, the broad, low-ceilinged room thick with the smells of spilled whiskey, stale sweat, vomit, beer and cheap perfume.

Lee stepped aside from the doorway and stood looking the place over.

There was a piano player and a man with a military drum pounding out some tune from the back, the music lost in the yells and arguments, the clatter and stomp of boots on the hardwood floor, as dozens of couples danced and whirled in the center of the room, knocking into each other, shoving each other aside as they spun around and around.

The faro tables were along the left side of the room. There were poker tables, too, further back. The bar ran down the right.

As Lee watched, two girls headed up the rough-sawn staircase at the back, each with a drunken jack on her arm. A bully stopped them on the landing, took the two bucks from the men, and pointed them to one of the corridor rooms beyond.

It was a prosperous place, as rich as any in Dodge City or Ft. Smith. Lee was impressed. And he saw that it was the lumbermen who kept the extra suckers coming in. The cowpokers alone wouldn't have been enough to support all this action. It was a first-class joint.

He didn't see anybody he knew.

Lee shoved his way toward the bar, found a place, and squeezed into it. The bartender picked him out right away.

"What'll it be?"

"Martini."

The bartender didn't blink an eye. He stepped over to his wet-bar, dipped up the ice, slid in the gin, dropped the vermouth in after it, and did a nice easy shake.

Lee knew it would be good before he got it; it confirmed what he'd already seen. Most cowtown bartenders couldn't make any kind of mixed drink—let alone a fancy cocktail—and if they tried, they ruined them. But this was a damned good Waldorf martini.

"Make me another one." The bartender heard him

33

and nodded while heading three beers down to some jacks twenty feet further down the bar. A real professional.

Lee finished his second drink, paid up—four bits each—and felt the gin settle in his belly. It mixed well with Mrs. Boltwith's peach pie. Then he left the bar and moved through the crowd toward the back of the room. There was another bully with a Greener shotgun leaning against the stair rail, watching the dancers.

Lee saw two girls, flushed and sweaty from dancing, standing off together, talking. They were holding hands.

He walked up to them to get a better look.

One was an older woman in her early forties. A beauty once, probably, and still not bad. She had a long jaw, and big blue-green eyes. Certainly a beauty—once. When she turned to look at Lee, she was still talking to the girl with her. Several of her front teeth were missing from her lower jaw.

The girl with her was a younger piece—half Indian by the look of her,—with a dark, broad face, big nose, and narrow black eyes. She had a squint in her left eye, not bad, but bad enough to keep her from being pretty. She had wide, heavy hips, and short stocky legs in high-laced, red-leather boots.

She looked as round and ready as a mare in season.

"How much are you charging, handsome?" Lee asked her.

The older woman made a face and turned away, letting go of the girl's hand. They were sweethearts, no doubt.

"I cost house rate," the half-breed said. "Two bucks for quarter, five for hour." She looked him over—from boots to trousers, from belt to gun to vest, from shirt to hat. It was a quick, squint-eyed glance, and she missed nothing.

Lee saw her glance down to his left boot again. She

34

was a very sharp whore. She'd seen the long, slight bulge in the boot leather where the six-inch toothpick he carried was sheathed. A sharp whore.

Lee made up his mind.

"I'll go for you both. Seven each for the hour."

The older woman made a disgusted noise, and the young girl said, "Not enough."

Lee shrugged and turned away.

They let him get a few steps, till they saw he meant it. Then they came after him and said all right.

CHAPTER THREE

Lee handed his fourteen dollars to the bully on the stair landing, a thick-necked thug in a cheap black suit, and followed the two women up the steps to the narrow corridor running the length of the building's back wall.

The women stopped at a pine plank door with the number twelve stenciled across it in white paint, opened it, and gestured Lee in.

He stepped in fast, his glance cutting through the room, checking for hide-holes, trick closets, trap-doors—all the stunts that grifters used. But the room looked clean, a small whitewashed bedroom with a few doodads, a long mirror, and a red-shaded oil lamp on a table beside the double brass bed.

A nice, hometown whorehouse with nothing shady. Except the mirror, maybe.

"This room all right by you, mister?" The older woman looked impatient to get down to business.

"Don't hustle me, sister. We've got a nice hour to do." Lee smiled at them. "Now, why don't you ring down for a bottle of champagne and tell the bartender to go easy on the gas." He wanted to see where the bell-pull was.

It was behind the thin yellow curtain drawn over the room's single window. The half-breed girl stepped over, found the cord, and gave it three short pulls. Signal for service. One sharp yank probably meant trouble.

Lee took off his clothes, hanging his vest and shirt over the top of the long mirror, draping them down to cover the glass.

"I don't like putting on a show for jerkers," he said. He noticed the quick flick of a look the two women exchanged. The mirror had been a two-way trick, a courtesy and pleasure for regular customers with the gazing inclination.

"Get your clothes off, ladies."

"It's extra if we take everything off, mister," the older one said.

"No, it isn't," Lee said, still smiling. "Are you two looking for trouble with me?" He was standing naked, with his gunbelt and purse in his hand. Still smiling, but the smile looked a little strange. His eyes were as cold as gray ice.

Lee had always liked to get value for what he paid.

The older one lowered her eyes, biting her lip nervously. "No, we're not . . ."

"Come on then, pretty," Lee said to her. The smile was warm again. "I'm not rough . . ."

The older whore sighed and started to take off her clothes, and the half-breed did too. Lee crossed to the wall side of the brass bed and draped his gunbelt over the knob on the bedpost—just to keep the Colt handy. He dropped the purse on the table. In plain sight.

Then he stretched out on the bed—and a nice soft feather bed it was—and watched the two women undress.

They'd gotten down to their corsets, when there was a knock on the door. The Indian girl went to open it, and Lee saw a fat old Indian woman in a greasy buckskin dress waiting there for the order.

"Champagne, Grace, and tell Harry easy on gas."

She'd remembered. A sharp whore.

Then they finished undressing.

The Indian girl was short and thick through the body,

37

with round, fat, full thighs running up into a butt like a soft, shining pair of brown balloons. Not much hair on her Jane, it was sparse, like most Indian women. A sweet round belly on her and full, hard-thrusting tits with nipples dark as plums. Lee could smell her across the room, his nose sharpened by weeks out on the trail away from city stinks.

She smelled smoky—rich and smoky—and dark. She smelled like campfire ashes after a rain. His cock came up full, just lying there, smelling her, and looking at her.

The girl must like him, or something about him, anyway—maybe the seven bucks—because she smiled shyly as he looked at her.

When Lee glanced over at the other whore, he chuckled out loud, because she was staring at the Indian girl as hard as he was—maybe harder. Her blue eyes were bright, looking at the girl.

Sweethearts, sure enough.

"She's beautiful, isn't she?" Lee said to the older one. He said it nicely, with nothing ugly in his voice.

The woman flushed and didn't say anything. She was something of a beauty herself. Tall, rangy as a hard-run deer, her stone-white skin was very smooth, but marked a little here and there with the slight scars, the soft puckering, and faint blue veins that a woman's body gathers in years of work, and babies, and fucking.

Lee never disliked those marks on a woman. They were what life had done to her, going along; nothing wrong with them. He liked the long legs she had, and the fine, narrow bones in her feet. Her cunt was furred with a thick coat of light brown hair, like an otter's belly.

Lee could smell her, too. Perfume, something like the smell of violets. And sweat, just a touch of sweat. She smelled just fine.

"But you're a beauty too, aren't you, darling?" She

38

gave him a grudging smile. "You think between us we can make your pretty dark-eyed girl here happy?"

She blushed at that. It was surprising how shy some whores were about some things.

Lee held out his hands. "Come on, come on over here, sweethearts." The Indian girl came romping and giggling over to the bed, bounced on it, her big breasts shaking. She reached out to give Lee's cock a friendly squeeze.

She had a soft, hot little hand.

Lee gathered her in in a hug. It was odd how few men took the time to give women a little cuddling, when there wasn't much that a woman liked more. He squeezed the plump Indian girl till she grunted with pleasure, and he reached up to pull the older woman into bed with them.

He felt how awkward she was in his arms, probably upset at having her Sappho-loving talked about.

Lee turned her, cradled her in his arms like a newborn colt, and kissed her on the ear. Then he nibbled on her earlobe, making hungry sounds. She giggled and struggled to get away—but not too hard.

"What's your name, beautiful?" he asked, still nibbling.

"Phyllis . . ."

"It suits you. An elegant name . . ."

"Oh, God. A lover boy," she said, but was not displeased.

There was a knock on the door.

The Indian girl rolled out of bed to answer it. It was the old woman again with the champagne and three glasses.

The girl came back to the bed with it. "That is ten dollar," she said.

Lee reached for his purse. "Here. Eight bucks for the champagne and one buck for the old lady."

The girl hesitated, then shrugged and went back to the

door to give the old woman the money.

Phyllis giggled in Lee's ear. "You do know the game, sugar! You're a sport, aren't you? You been to see the elephant!"

"I've seen it, and I've painted it, and I've left it with child!" Lee said, and he leaned over to kiss the Indian girl's nipples.

He'd learned long ago not to try to fool whores about being green. They didn't fool—and they didn't like the try.

Lee left the girl's breasts for a moment and caught Phyllis's head and drew it down so that he could whisper in her ear.

"And what's your pretty's name, Phyllis?"

Phyllis nuzzled into his throat, nipping and licking at him there. "Her name's Sarah Talltree . . ."

"So," Lee reached down to cup the woman's Jane and run his finger gently up and down her soft crease there, "so what does she like, hmmm?"

The Indian girl was cuddled against his side, while he stroked the cheek of her butt. She was wonderfully soft. He slid his fingers down into the crack of her ass. She was even softer there—and moist.

Lee put his tongue into Phyllis's ear blew gently into it, and said, "Tell me, sweetheart, what does she like? What would make her happy?"

"Oh, God," Phyllis murmured. He had managed to spread her and ease a finger up into her. "That's dirty talk . . ."

"What does she like?" He thrust another finger up into her and turned and turned his wrist back and forth. She was oiling, getting wetter and wetter. Now he could smell her cunt, the odor mingling with the violet perfume. A sea smell, like a dish of fresh oysters served beside a restaurant garden.

"She likes . . ." Phyllis started to whisper in Lee's ear. "She likes . . ." Then she began to giggle.

40

"What you say, Phyllis?" asked the Indian girl, looking annoyed.

"I'm just—I'm just telling him what you—you like!" And she collapsed across Lee's chest in a gale of giggles. She sounded more like a schoolgirl than a whore.

"Oh, Phyllis, you bad!" the Indian girl pouted.

"She likes to—to have her bottom licked!" And Phyllis went off in shrieks of laughter, her face as red as a beet.

Lee laughed along with her and rolled her over on top of the Indian.

"Then do it," he said. But she was embarrassed and shook her head. "Come on, sweetheart," Lee whispered in her ear. He gently gripped the back of her neck and guided her face down to the soft rounds of the half-breed's ass.

Phyllis resisted, struggling against him—but not much.

Lee pushed her face firmly deep into the crease of the girl's buttocks, holding her there, and, with his other hand, he stroked the Indian girl's long, strong back, soothing her like a fractious horse.

He felt the women's resistence a few moments more. Then the tension slowly went out of the smooth muscles of the girl's back, replaced by a kind of movement, a slight rhythmic motion.

He glanced down. Phyllis lay quiet, her face still pressed against the girl's ass. Her head was moving, slowly nodding, burrowing deeper into the girl's soft crotch. Lee saw her jaw move, working as she licked at the girl there.

He leaned over the Indian girl, gripped the cheeks of her ass, and gently spread them apart, opening her up so that the older woman could get at her.

Now he could see what she was doing, see the slim pink tongue sliding down into the girl's dark cunt, licking at it like a cat. She then went slowly back up to

41

the small brown bud of the girl's ass. She lapped at it wetly. Phyllis was groaning with pleasure from what she was doing. The Indian girl lay silent, her eyes shut, only moving a little, sometimes arching her back under the delicate probing of the woman's tongue.

Lee took his hands from the girl's big soft buttocks and got up on his hands and knees to slide behind the two of them. As he did, Phyllis reached up herself to force the girl's ass-cheeks wide apart again. She seemed to bite into the girl, groaning, burying her face in her. Lee saw her throat work as she sucked the girl's ass hard.

He was up on his knees behind the woman now, and he reached down and lifted her hips high in the air. He searched with his fingers, found her cunt running with juice in the tangle of her fur, propped the end of his cock up to her hole, set himself, and shoved it up her all the way.

She moaned into the girl's meat as the cock went into her, but she didn't stop what she was doing. She grunted as Lee drove it into her again.

Her pale back was slippery, running with sweat, as Lee worked on her. He ran his hands down to her small, dangling breasts, and gently squeezed and tugged at her nipples. He had thought it was the Indian girl he had wanted, but there was more to Phyllis, more person there to fuck with . . .

She struggled under him, bucking back up into his cock as he drove it into her, faster now. She was soaking wet there. It made a liquid, sucking sound each time he shoved it in—and she was at the girl all the time, her mouth working and lapping at her.

And the girl came, silently, suddenly heaving up under them, twisting, reaching back with both hands to clutch Phyllis' hair, to pull her deeper in. The girl's legs kicked out to the side in spasms of pleasure. Lee felt himself coming too, felt the semen surging up. He slid

42

his hands down Phyllis's wet flanks to the long slim muscles of her thighs. He rode her like a mare.

She screamed into the girl's trembling softness, and he came and came and came into her, as if he were coming into both of them at once. It was so good that it hurt. He gritted his teeth with the pleasure of it.

And then it was over, ebbing away . . .

Lee sagged down across both women, getting his arms around them, hugging them to him. The smells of sweat and perfume, semen, and the salty fish-smell of well-used cunt—all mingled together.

A few minutes later, Lee was propped up on pillows between the two women, drinking down a glass of champagne. As champagne goes, it wasn't much—just thin wine with bubbles blown into it from a bartender's gas-charger—and it had warmed up considerably waiting for them to get to it. But it tasted damn good nonetheless.

"You're a bad man," Phyllis said to him, murmuring cosily as she cuddled into his right shoulder.

"No," Lee said, "I'm not, not any more."

"You are very bad," said the half-breed from his other side. She bent down and bit him on the shoulder—not lightly, either. She had strong white teeth.

So Lee had two contented whores with him. Only a fool became sentimental about whores; but it was a sad man who couldn't play the fool, at least sometimes.

He sighed and wriggled out from in between them.

"Where's the pot?"

"Under the bed," Phyllis said.

Lee reached under, got the chamber pot out, and turned his back to the women to take a piss.

"A real gent," Phyllis giggled to the half-breed, who giggled back.

Lee finished his pee, gave his cock a flip for the last drop, and stooped to slide the pot back under the bed.

It was right then that the girl began to scream.

It came from next door.

Lee was already standing beside the bedstead with the Colt in his hand and cocked before the second scream came.

The two women lay frozen on the bed.

The scream rang out again; not the furious yell of a drunken whore. It was a shriek of terror. Lee had heard a girl scream like that before in Old Mexico. Her throat had been cut a moment later.

He started around the bed without thinking—then he thought. And stopped. He was in this valley to make a home—not more trouble.

Then he heard the clatter of boots on the stairs, coming up fast. The girl started to scream again, just out in the hall, but the cry was cut short.

Phyllis was lying in the bed as white as the sheets. She was crying without making a sound. The Indian girl was stroking her hair to comfort her.

There was a shout out in the hall. Lee couldn't make out the words. He heard some kind of swift scuffle and then the sudden, cracking blast of a shotgun.

It sounded like a stick of dynamite going off just outside the door. Phyllis screamed and covered her face with her hands.

Lee jumped to his clothes and started jamming them on as fast as he could. There was going to be trouble in the damn place, top to bottom. No use being naked in it.

He buttoned up his pants, shoved his shirt tails in, and shrugged into his vest. Then back across the bed and into his socks and boots. He scooped his purse off the bedside table, stuck it into the pocket of his vest, buckled his gunbelt on, and bent to give the weeping Phyllis a quick kiss on the cheek.

"Don't worry, sweety. Whatever, it's all over."

He headed for the door. The sooner he was out of the

Arcady and back in Mrs. Boltwith's hotel, the happier he'd be. He'd already scouted the back way out, thank God.

He stepped into the corridor—and there was trouble, right there. Trouble in a haze of left-over gunsmoke.

The bully-boy, the beefy one who'd been on the stair landing, was lying half propped up against the opposite wall. He appeared to be dying. The right side of his face was broken in as if he'd been struck with a blacksmith's maul. There was not much blood at all, which somehow made the injury look worse. Just that bashed-in wound. His right eye looked to be broken by the same blow. The shotgun was on the floor beside him. He'd been too slow with it.

Lee heard the girl again, her voice crying from downstairs from the big front room. She seemed to be begging, pleading about something. She sounded very young, no more than a kid.

He knew it was a mistake when he did it. He knew damn well he shouldn't. *Knew it damn well.*

He walked to the head of the front stairs, to the landing. Then he started down the steps.

For a few moments, nobody looked up at him.

They were looking at something else.

A young girl wearing a whore's shift and red boots lay sprawled on the splintered wood of the dance floor, blood running from her nose and mouth.

The whole crowd of people had fallen back to the edges of the big room, packed along the walls and in among the faro tables, watching in dead silence.

The girl cried out and tried to crawl away, but she couldn't. A man had hold of her wrist.

A bad one.

A very bad one.

Lee was surprised. It was true that almost any town or county had its hardcases, some of them considerably tough, too. And it was also true that Cree appeared to

45

be a nice little boomtown for the lumbermen working up in the mountains, and so might draw some badmen to it.

But this one seemed like something special.

He looked deformed at first, his short, thick legs as squat as a dwarf's, his hands broad, hairy paddles of bone and muscle. But he wasn't misshappen; only the immense width of his shoulders made him look it. He was dressed like a cattleman, except for a narrow-brimmed plug hat. He held the girl's arm with his left hand.

The girl's thin white wrist seemed to disappear in that massive grip.

Lee had stopped on the tenth step down from the landing: it put him above and about fifteen feet from them. There was still nothing that said he had to butt in. The man was facing away, looking around at the crowd. Lee could tell where he was looking by the lowered eyes around the room. The other bully was not to be seen; he'd skedaddled fast.

The man yanked at the girl's arm, dragging her a few feet along the floor. She shrieked with the pain from her twisted wrist and, weeping, tried to hit out at him.

"Don't you make me angry now, girlie!" He had a high, rather sweet voice, like an Irish tenor's.

He hauled her up to her feet.

"Don't you want to be with old Mickey, now?"

"Please help me!" she screamed, to the people standing round.

"Jesus!" said a woman's voice. "Where in hell is Phipps?"

The man started toward the front door, hauling the struggling girl along.

"Where do you think you're going, fatty?"

The words had come out of Lee's mouth despite himself.

You fucking fool, he thought. Now you've ruined everything.

46

The man in the plug hat seemed surprised. He slowly turned back to look up the stairs at Lee as if he weren't sure that Lee had been speaking to him.

"That's right, fatty; it's you I was talking to . . ." In all the way now.

A huge, round head rolled back on those massive shoulders, getting a good look up at Lee. His eyes were very blue, the wide, innocent blue eyes of a child. They looked strange, staring out of that murderous face. The man looked like a vicious dog, a huge bulldog with brutal, meaty jowls.

He carried a big old Colt dragoon .44 for a right-hand cross-draw. It looked slow, but Lee had known big men who were fast, and fast cross-draws, too.

"You was talkin' to me, wasn't you?" he said in that high, sweet voice, some Irish accent still in it. A city man, originally, Lee thought. A thug out of Hell's Kitchen, or maybe Chicago.

"Let the girl go," Lee said. "Just let her go, and walk away . . ."

"Oh, sure," the man said. "Why not?"

And he smiled an oddly charming smile, for all his brutal ugliness, and let go of the girl and reached for his gun.

He was very fast.

Extraordinarily fast for his size; he must have been a dreadful opponent in a fist fight.

The huge hand snapped across his broad belly to the Dragoon's butt. The gun was coming out in a blur.

Very fast.

Lee drew and shot him in the chest.

The man staggered back a swift step, his round face frowning, preoccupied. The dragoon was sweeping up, coming level.

Lee shot him again, firing through a haze of gunsmoke. Center chest, an inch or two to the right of the first slug.

The man's plug hat fell off; he had short red hair. He

staggered left for a step or two, still trying to level the dragoon.

Lee stepped sideways to clear himself of the smoke, being careful not to trip on the steps. He shot the man again.

His childlike eyes wide in agony, the big man stumbled and fell to one knee. The dragoon went off with a loud, flat bang, and Lee heard the bullet slam into the saloon's back wall.

The man heaved himself up and lurched forward, the big pistol wavering in his hand. But he couldn't seem to see Lee; he stumbled again, and went crashing into a faro table, knocking it over on its side. On his hands and knees now, he thrashed and struggled in the tangle of table legs and chairs, dying, his boots scraping and kicking along the rough flooring.

The blood was running out in a wide puddle around him. He was still heaving and rolling in it, but less and less.

For the first time, Lee heard the women screaming and the shouts of the men. All the light and color and noise of the place came rushing back in on him.

Now you've done it. Now you've done it, sure as hell . . .

"Mister, allow me to congratulate you!" Some jackass of a drummer in a yellow suit. Whores had gathered around the young girl now, lifting her up off the floor, cooing to her and taking her up the stairs. Lee glimpsed her face as they went up past him. It was dead white, blank with shock.

People were crowding all around him now. That damn drummer and a lot of others, all shouting and yelling in his face.

He needed to be alone for a minute. You always need that when you've had a faceoff with a man and killed him. Lee had the odd thought that the man in the plug hat had probably been a rough prankster when he was in good humor, an amusing man to get drunk with—sometimes.

He always had these thoughts about people when he'd killed them. And thinking that way always made the killings worse.

He had to get outside the noisy hole!

But as he pushed his way through the crowd, heading for the batwing doors, they were suddenly shoved open, and a tall man with long blond hair down to his shoulders stepped into the saloon. He looked flushed from running, and there was a long-barreled Remington .44 in his left hand. Another revolver was tucked into the left side of his wide sash.

For an instant—just for an instant—Lee thought it was Bill Hickok.

Then he saw that it wasn't. This man looked like Bill, and wore his guns Hickok's way, but he was younger and not as tall.

The man wore a long cream-linen frock coat, hanging open. There was a badge pinned on the left lapel.

The marshal had eyes the color of water, and they picked Lee out of the crowd with no trouble at all. Men were all around him now, busy telling the lawman the tale of the shooting, wanting some small part in it. But he sliced through the crowd right toward Lee, the Remington swinging easily at his side.

Another one, Lee thought wearily. Two fast guns in a little town like this . . .

A tall, well-dressed woman, who looked like a lady, had come through the batwings behind the marshal, and Lee could see her now, struggling through the crowd after him. She looked familiar; Lee wondered if he'd ever seen her before.

"What's your name?" The marshal had a deep voice for a slim man. He was standing in front of Lee, but not too close. The Remington was still in his hand, hanging idly at his side.

It was a nice trick, that. You held a bare gun in your hand, but held it down, casually, out of action. Then, if there was trouble, and knowing your man's eye would be on *that* pistol, you simply drew and shot him with the other.

One of Hickok's tricks.

"I said, what's your name?"

"Frederick Lee, Marshal." Lee stammered a little, trying his damnedest to look like a nervous citizen who'd just gotten damn lucky. "I don't even know why he did it! He just drew on me just like that, and all I did was ask him to leave that poor girl alone!"

"You outdrew Mick Slawson face-to-face?" Those water-pale eyes drilled into Lee's. "Mister, if you did, then you're either a fool for luck or you're a very quick gun." He looked as if he'd decided which.

CHAPTER FOUR

The tall woman had made her way to them by that time. She seemed worried that there might be more trouble.

"Tod . . Tod, is everything all right?" She gave Lee a quick glance. "I heard this man has killed Slawson . . ."

"He sure as hell did!" a lumberjack standing near them said. "He blew his buttons off! And Slawson drew first on him, too . . ."

"You sure of that?" the marshal said to him.

"Hell, yes, it was fair and square." And two other men, listening, agreed that it sure as hell had been fair and square.

"Well, you stick around here for a while, just the same," the marshal said to Lee.

"Not for long. I've got a place to look after . . ."

"What place?"

"I've bought the River Ranch, up in the hills." It would be interesting to see if money talked with the marshal.

It did.

The cold, water-pale eyes swung back to Lee and stared at him for a moment. "Well, all right . . . but I want to talk to you before you leave here."

"Now, Tod," the tall woman said, "Mr.—"

"Lee."

"Mr. Lee has just done us a favor, killing that damn

animal—Slawson was certainly a rustler—and I'm just going to take Mr. Lee backstairs out of this crowd . . ."

The marshal slowly nodded, then turned and followed one of the lumberjacks through the crowd toward Slawson's body. Everyone in the room was either gathered there or piled up at the bar celebrating. A killing like this, with no bystanders hurt, was always good for business.

"Oh dear," the tall woman said to Lee, "I should never have left the place on a Friday night . . . If you'd just follow me, Mr. Lee, I'll get you out of this."

She led the way through the crowd and around the stairwell to a narrow, green-painted door. There was a short hallway, then another door. The woman paused to dig a key out of her reticule. She was very tall for a woman, almost as tall as Lee; and she was a looker, a brunette with clear, pale skin, and light green eyes. She dressed like a lady, but wasn't one. Apparently, she owned the Arcady, or had a share in it.

And there was something familiar about her. Lee wasn't certain he'd seen her before. Maybe it had been some girl who just looked like her.

She'd gotten the door open, and Lee followed her inside. It was a heavy door; when it was shut behind them, the noise from the barroom dimmed to a dull murmur.

It was a sitting room, with another door probably leading to a bedroom. And it was furnished in fine taste, as rich as any Chicago hotel suite, with big horsehair sofas and chairs, a walnut dining table, and a rolltop desk with a big oil lamp hung over it. Everything was all fringed and gussied up. A class roost.

She sighed, taking off her net gloves. "I'll get you a drink, Mr. Lee. What's your pleasure?" She reached up to turn the oil lamp brighter.

"Straight rye will be all right."

"All right." She went across the room to a small

cabinet and took out a bottle and two glasses. "God knows, I could use one myself." She turned to look at him. "Please sit down, Mr. Lee."

Lee sat on one of the sofas, leaning back into the soft upholstery, watching her. She was a handsome woman, and maybe the marshal's sweetheart, judging from the way she'd come hurrying over to him when he'd faced Lee.

She brought the glasses of rye over to the sofa, handed one to Lee, and sat down with a rustle of silk skirts in an armchair across from him.

"Mr. Phipps and I were having dinner with some friends when we heard of the trouble."

Lee nodded. Phipps . . . Tod Phipps. Now, he had heard of that name. But where?

"Mr. Phipps had always expected trouble from Slawson. This wasn't the first time that man started something." She sipped her drink, and Lee noticed that her slim white fingers were gripping the glass hard. "Mr. Phipps could have handled the matter himself, of course, if he'd been in the place. Mr. Phipps was a deputy to Wild Bill Hickok, you know."

Tod Phipps! Christ. He'd heard that name, all right. One of Hickok's hardcases—and Hickok could pick them! It didn't mean that the man was a fine shooter, of course, but it did mean he'd killed a few. Hickok never used raw help. This fellow must have headed for greener pastures when Hickok took off for the Dakotas.

There was a soft knock at the door.

The woman started to get up, then paused for a second, giving Lee an odd glance. Then she smiled at him politely and went to the door.

It was the old Indian woman. She said something. The tall woman bent down to hear her, then answered.

"All right, tell her I'll be up in a few minutes. And tell Dolores to go get the doctor if she wants."

The woman closed the door and then came back over

to the sofa. She was still holding her drink.

"I'm sorry about that. The girl he injured is still upset . . ." She sat back down in the armchair and took a sip of her rye. "I haven't introduced myself, have I? I'm Rebecca Chase, Mr. Lee."

The name meant nothing to him.

"So you've bought the River Ranch?" She gave him that odd, quick glance again. "Well, it's certainly a beautiful property. I declare, I quite envy you, having a place like that so pretty." She leaned forward to put her drink down on a small table. "Though you certainly have gotten a rough welcome to Cree." She laughed and shook her head. "The wild West . . ."

She glanced across at him once more and suddenly stopped laughing. Her face went pale as a plaster mask.

"Oh, Jesus Christ," she said, staring at him.

"What's the matter?" Lee said. He felt his muscles tense.

"Oh, my God. You're Buckskin Frank Leslie!"

She didn't have a chance to say anything more.

Lee didn't even know how he had gotten there. Suddenly, he was standing over her, his hand clamped across her mouth. The razor-edged Arkansas toothpick was out, the bright splinter of steel lying across her throat.

He had her head forced way back across the back of the armchair. He laid the steel into the taut snow-white skin of her throat.

Everything was clear in his mind. One hard, deep slice and her head would be damn near off. Then a quick jump to the side, so the blood wouldn't spatter on his clothes, and then another jump to the door and out.

It would cost him the ranch. All that money gone. But they'd never find him. A drifter named Lee, a gunfight, and a knifing—just another of those killers the frontier threw up from time to time.

He looked down to get the cut just right—and saw her eyes.

There was nothing in them but terror. The brute, dumb terror of an animal about to be slaughtered. Nothing human left in those eyes at all. Nothing of a pretty woman living a rich life full of chance and pleasure.

The terror made her eyes ugly as an ugly doll's eyes—dirty green glass.

He started to cut. Just started. The faintest quick line of bright scarlet beaded under the blade.

Then he pulled the knife away and stood back.

For a long time she didn't move. She sat there with her head still held back, her eyes staring at him blindly.

She didn't open her mouth. She didn't make a sound.

Lee bent to slide the knife back into his boot.

"You're a very lucky woman, Rebecca."

She started, as if his voice had wakened her, and slowly sat up.

She tried to say something, but had to stop and clear her throat. "I'm sorry . . . I'm sorry, Mr. . . . Lee."

"Where the hell did you know me from?"

"From . . . from . . . Fort Grant." She tried to smile. "I just noticed. I wasn't sure at first . . . You always wore that mustache . . . and that short beard." Her color was coming back now. She knew he wasn't going to kill her. Not right now, anyway.

"Who were you with?"

She knew what he meant. "I was one of Florence Maynard's girls." She tried to laugh. "You remember old Florence . . ."

Now he remembered her. Becky Chase. She'd been a tall, thin girl. Nervous, with a stutter when she talked. They'd called her Pissy, or something like that, because she was always running out back to the jakes.

Well, Rebecca had changed a lot over the years. A heavy madame now, looking like a lady. And a businesswoman too, if she had a piece of the action in the Arcady.

"There's blood on your neck."

She gasped and put her hand up to her throat. When she looked at it, there was a drop of blood on her palm. She suddenly turned so pale, Lee thought she might faint. It had all come back to her, how close she had come to dying.

She fumbled for a handkerchief, a little scrap of lace, and walked unsteadily over to an oval mirror across the room. She stood there, dabbing at the slight cut, pressing the handkerchief to it. She was still very pale.

"And what's Phipps to you, Rebecca?" Lee asked. He settled himself back down on the sofa and watched her face reflected in the mirror.

He saw her start to lie, her eyes narrowing as she thought. Then she glanced into the mirror and saw him watching her.

"I love him," she said, pressing the little handkerchief to her throat. "I love him." She stared at Lee in the mirror, her eyes desperate.

"I have nothing against Phipps," Lee said. She looked away from him. "I have no quarrel with the man. In fact, I don't want to do a damn thing but raise horses and mind my own business . . ."

She walked back over to the armchair. She was looking better now, not so pale, and there was only a faint mark of dried blood where the blade edge had touched her throat.

She picked her drink up off the small table and drank it straight down.

"I won't tell anybody," she said, standing in front of Lee, clutching the empty glass. "I swear on my mother I won't tell anybody."

"Not a soul," Lee said. And he finished his own drink and stood up. "Because if you do, I'll finish cutting your throat for you. And I'll gun that fancy man of yours into dead meat . . ."

"I won't, I won't."

Lee walked over to the door. She turned to watch him go.

"Frank . . . *Lee*, I was sorry to hear about Rosilie . . ."

He looked back at her. She flinched.

"Don't mention her name; don't mention my name." He reached for the doorknob. "Never. And never to your loverboy, if you want to keep him."

"All right . . . all right. I never will, I swear."

He walked out and closed the door behind him.

Phipps stopped him just outside the staircase door. The crowd had calmed down now. Everybody was lined up at the bar with their drinks and their stories of how close they'd been and what they'd seen when the guns went off.

Mickey Slawson was up on a faro table. His body was covered with a canvas tarpaulin. A fat old half-breed with a straggly mustache was mopping the floor, his mop foaming pink in the pool of blood and soapy water.

The wild West.

"Lee," Phipps said in that deep voice, "from what I'm told, it was a fair-enough fight, and I don't intend to arrest you for the killing." He looked as though he was doing Lee a considerable favor. "On the other hand, I don't like killings in my town. I have enough trouble with the drunks shooting up the place just for the hell of it!"

"I'm not looking for trouble, Marshal," Lee said, looking as peaceful as he could.

Phipps didn't look quite convinced. He'd heard about Slawson's drawing first, and he must have taken a good look at the body, too, and seen the three bullet holes in the chest. He would have been able to cover all of them with the palm of his hand.

Lee wished to hell that Slawson had given him time enough for head shooting. It would have been easy enough, then, to have put that one slug into his brains and to have claimed it as just dumb luck.

But not now. And the marshal was worried about him.

"I'm a horse rancher, Mr. Phipps, not a gunman. I'm a good hand with a pistol, but I don't like to use it. And, tell you the truth, that fellow was pretty drunk."

It seemed to help. The long-haired lawman gave Lee a long, considering glance, then nodded and walked away.

Lee got the hell out of there. On the way out he turned down four offers of drinks and shrugged off five backslappers and congratulators.

He stepped out through the batwings into the sweet night air. It was dark and cool and restful, even with the cowboys still trailing up and down the sidewalks, shouting to their friends.

Lee felt the knot inside him slowly begin to ease. It seemed as though the whole damned last hour in there had just been a nightmare, a bad dream.

But it hadn't been. It had been dead real. Ask Mickey Slawson.

And now he had that damn madame onto him. How long would she keep her mouth shut? Asking about Rosilie, the bitch. When she asked about Rosilie, he'd been sorry he *hadn't* cut her throat. And he would have before, if her eyes hadn't looked so bad. It would have been like cutting a corpse's throat.

He crossed the dirt street over to Mrs. Boltwith's. As he walked, he noticed several people watching him, nudging each other.

Trouble already. He was a marked man. And only a few fucking hours in the damn town . . .

The men were gone from Mrs. Boltwith's steps. They had better things to do. There was nobody behind the small hotel desk. Lee reached back behind it, to the rack of keys, and lifted down number 223. Then he turned and started up the narrow stairs. He was in no mood to talk to Bupp or anybody else.

Upstairs, he unlocked the door to his room, stepped inside, and relocked it. He scratched a lucifer and lit the small oil lamp sitting on top of the battered dresser beside the bed. The room was tiny, but it was freshly whitewashed and clean. The bed linen and thin cotten towels looked as if they were freshly washed. It seemed that Mrs. Boltwith kept a good house.

Lee sat wearily on the edge of the bed and hauled off his boots. Then he stood and stripped off the rest of his clothes, draping them over the back of the kitchen chair by the bed. Then he slipped the Colt out of its holster, shucked the three spent shells out onto the bed, and reloaded the pistol from the rounds held in his gunbelt. He hung the holstered Colt over the chair's back, pulled the bed covers down, and slid into bed. The sheets felt cool against his skin.

For a while, Lee lay staring up at the slowly coiling pattern the oil-lamp flame threw against the ceiling. Then he raised up in bed, lifted the lamp down from the dresser, and blew out the flame.

Now only a faint light filtered through the white curtains drawn across the small room's single window. Only a little noise came through from the back alley below—a dog barking in the distance, a cowboy singing down a side street.

Lee tried to stay awake, at least until he had a chance to think it all out, to work out what the killing would mean to him. Why the hell couldn't that fool of an Irishman have kept his hands to himself? And why the hell did that little whore make such a goddamn noise about it?

And what the hell was he supposed to do about Rebecca Chase and that pretty-boy killer of hers? Wouldn't it be better now if she were dead and he already halfway out of this damn valley on the dun?

He slept.

And dreamt of Doc Holliday. Poor Doc . . . lying in a narrow white bed in a narrow white room in Denver. A sanitarium, they called it. Death house was more like it.

Holliday had been his old self—except for being so small and thin. But he had never been a big man. When Lee had walked into the room, Holliday had called out, "Draw, you son-of-a-bitch!" and had yanked a bottle of Old Overholt out from under the sheets.

They had talked for two hours. About a lot of years. Wyatt, and the brothers, and the Clanton people out in Arizona. Doc was still regretful about not having fought Johnny Ringo that day in Tombstone.

"Come out and fight me, you bony bastard!" Ringo had called. And Doc had called back, "I'm your huckle-berry!" and would have done it too, if Earp hadn't stopped him.

"I regret that, Frank," Doc had said, turning his head to cough some blood into a towel. "I regret that a lot."

They'd talked about that. In his dream, Lee seemed to be sitting in Doc's room again, watching him cough his lungs out into that towel and telling him all about having to kill the Irishman. "Slawson . . Slawson? I don't know any Slawson," Doc said in his dream. "How did he carry it, straight? Shoulder-rig? Cross-draw?"

But in Lee's dream, Doc was definite about how good it was that he hadn't killed Rebecca. "Shit she's just a twist, isn't she?" he'd said. "A judy, a nun? Hell, Frank, a man can't start killing women, or there's no hope for him, no hope at all! And a whore is the most helpless thing there is. A man can't kill a whore. Except by accident, the way Johnny Deuce killed your Rosilie . . ."

Lee awoke with a heave, fumbling for his gun. The sweat was pouring off him in the dark.

"Doc, you son-of-a-bitch," he said.

Then he remembered that Holliday was dead. Dead three weeks ago. The attendant who had told Lee he was gone had said that Doc died laughing—a rare way to go in that place—and had said only, "This is funny. . ." and then died.

"Doc, you son-of-a-bitch," Lee said into the room's darkness. "You poor son-of-a-bitch . . ."

It was a bright, sunny morning.

The sun flooded in through the single window and lit up the little whitewashed room like theater limelights.

Lee turned his head, groaning into the pillow, and tried to go back to sleep. He might have done it too, if somebody hadn't started pounding on the door.

"Mr. Lee, if you want any breakfast, you better get down to the kitchen!"

It was Mrs. Boltwith. She apparently didn't approve of people sleeping late.

"All right," Lee called out. "All right."

He rolled over onto his back and lay still a few moments remembering last night, the fight at the Arcady and Rebecca Chase.

Well, it was done. No chance of his being just another rancher come into the valley now. Not with Phipps hanging around. Still, he could let slip some of the truth to cover him. Nothing like a little truth to cover a big lie. He could let them know about Mexico, if it came to that. About the man who worked for Don Ignacio, who earned his living down below Matamoros with his gun, and who also bought Mexican horses cheap, then drove

61

them north to sell in Texas . . .

That man had already been known as Frederick Lee. It would explain where he got the money for the ranch well enough—and the gun skill, too, if it came to that. Montana was a long way from old Mexico; and after all, the story was true.

It just wasn't complete.

But Phipps should be satisfied: a below-the-border gunman makes some money horse trading and then starts fresh up in the States. Not wanted for anything either. Not in Montana.

It should do, and would do, if Rebecca kept her mouth shut. If she didn't keep her mouth shut, then that would be the end of a new life in Cree Valley. Once the word went out, every tinhorn and killer in three states would be coming to Cree to have a look at Buckskin Frank Leslie. And maybe take a shot at him, too, if they felt lucky—or got drunk enough.

That would be bad enough; it would make him a marked man, a man with no choice but to go back into the sporting life, back to the professional gambling, pimping, and killing.

But there was worse. If word got out who he was and where he was, the Texans would come looking for him. Ben Thompson for one, Wes Hardin for another. He'd killed one's brother, the other's friend. And neither Thompson nor Hardin were the forgiving kind.

Lee swung his feet out of bed and reached down for his socks. He could use a bath; he still had the trail dirt on him.

As he dressed, Lee considered the possibility that one of the Texans—or one of their friends, like Texas Jack Omahundro or Clay Allison—might show up one day. What then?

Omahundro he was sure he could take. He'd seen the man in a fight. He had been brave as a rooster—and a very poor shot. He'd tried for a man with four shots, just across a dance floor, and only hit him twice. And at that, the man had been able to get up and walk away. Nothing special there.

Allison was a different kettle of fish. Lee had seen him sober—and drunk. Sober, Allison had been a tall, handsome, courteous rancher. A prosperous rancher with a fine family. A gentleman—or as close to it as Texan ranchers got.

But that was Clay Allison sober. Drunk he was a different man. Lee had seen him drunk, just once, in Waco. Allison had looked and acted more like a devil than a man. And, as careful as Lee had been with him, it certainly would have come to shooting if Allison hadn't suddenly started to pick on someone else, a local lawyer and land agent named Bob Brice.

It had been a grim scene: Allison, staggering drunk, spitting out filthy insults about Brice and his wife, about his young daughters, all the time waiting, waiting for the poor man to try for his gun.

And Brice had had no choice in the end. It was either draw or pack up his family and get out of town. He had tried to back off, to talk his way out of it, but Allison had just laughed and said, "Crawl then, Brice, you daughter-fucker you. Crawl out of here on your hands and knees or I'll kill you where you stand . . ."

Poor Brice had gone for his gun. And made a good try at it, too. He'd actually gotten a shot off after Allison had already put two slugs in him. But Allison had put the next three into the poor man as well. He'd shot him to pieces; literally shot his guts out.

It had been simple murder. But no Waco lawman had come near the Seguaro when they'd heard who'd done the shooting. It was very simple. Even if five or six deputies had come after him, Allison, drunk, would have been happy to take them on—and would sure as hell have killed two or three before they got him.

The Waco lawmen had just passed it up as a fair

fight, and Lee and Allison, meeting the next day, had parted cordially. Allison hadn't referred to the killing—may not even have remembered doing it.

And if Clay Allison and Buckskin Frank Leslie were to face off, what then?

Lee wasn't sure. He might have Allison just a little shaded in speed. Just a little. But that difference meant next to nothing. A Jekyll-and-Hyde maniac like Allison wouldn't be stopped by a first bullet. No, he'd have to knock Allison down with the first two or three and hope the lead coming back at him wouldn't be fatal.

And Allison, for all his madness, wasn't the gun that either Thompson or Hardin were. Lee had no illusions when it came to those two. Thompson was a better show than he was, it was just that simple. And Hardin was faster. Hell, Hardin was faster than anybody. Either one of them might very well kill him cold . . .

Lee shrugged into his vest and buckled on his gunbelt. He'd have to clean the piece this morning, should have done it last night.

The hotel kitchen—also, apparently, used as the hotel diningroom—was bright with morning sunlight. Lee had met two men in the hall. He'd seen them on the hotel steps the night before, and they had brushed past him with a muttered, "Good morning," and averted eyes. He'd become the terror of the town of Cree overnight. "Good morning," he answered as sweet as pie, but they'd already hurried on their way.

"About time!" said Mrs. Boltwith; she wasn't so easily impressed. And she was even uglier in the daylight than she had been by oil lamp the night before. Nonetheless, she was done up in a fine, blue polka-dot house dress and big, starched white apron. The very figure of a respectable boarding-house keeper.

And the apron was still white, because Tim Bupp was

doing all the work. He must have already cooked breakfast for the other guests, because he was splashing and stirring at a stack of dishes in a big galvanized tub of soap and hot water. No question, Mrs. Boltwith was getting her cooking lessons paid for.

"Well, there you are!" Bupp said to Lee. "And I suppose you want me to just stop what I'm doing and fix you a breakfast—and it damn near about noon!"

"Yes, you will," said Mrs. Boltwith. "Mr. Lee is a hotel guest. You fix him some ham and eggs and biscuits and potatoes and coffee. And this time don't burn the ham; pigs don't grow on trees!"

Lee was beginning to like Mrs. Boltwith.

"And then you refill that tub so he can take a bath. He's got dirt on his butt and blood on his hands." She sniffed. "Even if poor Mickey did need killing something fierce . . ." And she bustled out of the kitchen with a rustle of skirts and apron.

Bupp sighed. "Well, dammit, just let me finish these damn dishes." He glanced sideways at Lee. "I don't know if I'd want a cooking job, if it's going to mean taking all this abuse . . ." He started hauling the platters out of the tub and cleaning them with a greasy towel. "Of course, one thing I will say," he glanced over at Lee again, "it ain't likely to be a *boring* job."

CHAPTER FIVE

The ham was burned, but just a little. The eggs were fine sunnyside up, but with the whites firm, just the way Lee liked them.

"Good eggs," he said to Bupp, through a mouthful of them.

Bupp just snorted, but seemed pleased, nonetheless.

"Tell me, Tim. What's the lay of the land in Cree? I've met Phipps, and you told me about Ashton. Do they run things? Or is there somebody else?"

Bupp grunted and hauled the tub to the kitchen door, then he swung the door open, heaved, and dumped the dishwater out into the yard. He dragged the big tub back into the kitchen, set it under the sink pump, and started working the pump handle, filling it with cold water for Lee's bath.

When the tub was half full, he stopped pumping. Then he set two big kettles on the stove to heat water for the bath.

When that was done, he pulled a chair up to the table, rolled a cigarette, and gave Lee a tutorial look.

"Listen," he said. "Phipps and Ashton do sort of run things around here, but it's not so simple." He paused for a moment, to watch Lee butter a biscuit. "What do you think about those biscuits?"

"They're kind of wet in the middle, but not bad."

"Wet in the middle, huh? I took 'em out too soon . . ."

66

"You were saying about Phipps and Ashton?"

Bupp took a deep draw on his cigarette. "It's like this: Phipps has the town, see, and Ashton runs the valley. Phipps is marshal, to start with, and beside that, he's the fastest gun around. He sure as hell is, now that Slawson's dead." He peered at Lee through a cloud of cigarette smoke. "Unless we figure you in . . ."

"Don't figure me in," said Lee.

"How's the coffee?"

"The coffee's just fine. You make good coffee, Bupp. Now, go on with what you were saying."

"Well, Phipps runs the town. He and that lady hooker of his own the Arcady and the Timber Lodge too. And Phipps has a hand in just about everything else in Cree. Has ever since he shot Matt Riboneaux. Riboneaux used to be the big cheese in Cree, but that was a couple of years ago."

"And Ashton?"

"Well now, Ashton's a horse of a different color. For one thing, he's an Englishman."

Lee wasn't surprised. The English had moved in on the cattle business in a big way in the '70s, and they had the capital to make themselves felt. Usually, though, they sent men to run the ranches for them. They seldom ran the ranches themselves.

"He own Fishhook, or just run it?"

"Hell, he owns it lock, stock, and barrel, and every acre under true deed! Ashton's rich. He's some English lord's nephew or something, and he's slicker'n grease, too."

"Ashton and Phipps get along?"

"Well now, I wouldn't say they get along. They just stay out of each other's hair, that's all." He leaned back in the kitchen chair, puffing on his cigarette, happy to be playing wiseman. "But, you know, Phipps just ain't in Ashton's class, gun or not. Ashton's rich, for one thing. And, for another, because he's rich he can hire any guns he wants. And he's got friends in Helena, too.

Big friends."

"So Phipps runs the town?"

"Yeah, but *only* the town."

"What about the town council? The mayor?"

"No mayor. They got a town council. But, hell, those shopkeepers are happy with things just as they are! Phipps don't cut a slice of their cake. He leaves them alone. And with all the lumber money coming into town this past two years, they're happy as clams!"

"A lot of lumber money, huh?"

"You bet! Hell, they're building half the mining camps in Montana out of those mountains back there! Butte and all the rest. There's a damn fortune in it, and those lumberjacks got no place to spend their bucks but Cree!"

"And that's it, Phipps and Ashton?"

Bupp pulled Lee's egg-stained breakfast plate over and stubbed his cigarette out in it. "Well," he said, "there are the farmers and small ranchers, but you pretty much took care of them last night."

"What do you mean?"

"Hell, I mean you shot Mick Slawson, is what I mean! He was a cruel bastard. And him and his boys probably did most of the cow stealing in these parts. But he was the only gun the small ranchers and farmers had. He never bothered their stock, and he wasn't scared of Phipps—or of Ashton, either."

One of the kettles started singing on the stove, and Bupp got up to pour the steaming water into the tub. When he emptied the second kettle into the bath, the tub was nearly full.

"Come on and take your bath. May as well, or we'll have that old dragon in here to throw you in it. And me, too, if I don't look out!"

Lee rode out of town two hours later.

It was past noon, and the dun was shifty, rested by a

68

night's stabling, and full of timothy and oats. Lee's saddlebags bulged with sandwiches, a side of the breakfast ham, and a dozen apples. Mrs. Boltwith didn't have much faith in a man's feeding himself all alone out on a ranch.

He was wearing new clothes, too. Denim pants and a blue flannel shirt, socks and underwear. Mrs. Boltwith had come into the kitchen while Lee was helpless in the bathtub and had taken his clothes out back to the laundry shed. Bupp had to go over to the mercantile and get him new duds, top to bottom.

It was a perfect day, with sunlight flaming down through the clear mountain air, bringing the distant peaks into glittering relief. It looked like the backdrop at a theater show, bright and light and perfect.

He thought of Rosilie for a moment. She would have loved this valley, the soft greenness of it, the towering mountains looming all around. "A fairy-tale place, Frank . . ."

That's what she would have said, if she were riding along beside him, riding on her little pinto mare, turning now to smile at him.

Lee jerked himself erect in the saddle and struck the spurs to the dun. The big horse bucked with surprise, squealed, and took off up the trail at a hard gallop, crow-hopping stumps and brush along the way. Lee had a lot to do just staying on him, and, after a half-mile run, he slowly reined the big gelding in, soothing him, patting the sweat-streaked withers, talking to him.

It was no good imagining what couldn't be. No good thinking about it.

He guided the dun up along the trail, keeping his eyes peeled. Bupp had said that the Crees still sometimes knocked a lone rider in the head if they could catch him careless. And there were Slawson's men, too. They wouldn't have taken kindly to him putting their boss under the dirt. And they might decide to do something about it.

It was early evening when he rode up into the high meadows. The shadows of the great pines stretched in broad black bars across the trail, and Lee could see flocks of birds wheeling up from the valley below into the red-gold sunset.

The dun was pacing steadily up the slopes, breaking into a trot where the high grass grew thick as prairie grass in Kansas. At the horse's hoof falls, clouds of insects came whirring up, clicking and buzzing off to disappear into the deep carpet of green again, a few yards away.

It was prime horse country. Not perfect for flat racers, maybe, might put too much muscle on the legs. But for cow work, or that new quarter-racing, or just for fine riding stock, it was prime horse country.

The sun was almost down now, dropping fast below the distant peaks to the west. Lee reined in and turned in the saddle to watch. Down in the valley, the land was filled with shadow, brimming with it like a dark green cup. As Lee watched, the darkness rose swiftly toward him as the sun sank out of sight, climbing up his backtrail like an incoming tide off the Presidio in San Francisco.

He'd be getting to the ranch in darkness.

More than an hour later, he rode over the east ridge. The ranch buildings lay below, dark and silent, barely visible by starlight. The moon was still down behind the mountains. There was a night wind breezing through the pines along the ridge. The rich smell swept over Lee as he sat the weary dun in the cool, enveloping dark.

Lee sat up there quite a while, looking over his land. His land. And, by the time the moon was up, shedding a bright silvery wash over the ranch and surrounding hills, the valley far below, he had made his decision.

He was staying. He would have to take his chances

with Rebecca Chase.

He was staying, because Rosilie would have wanted him to.

Lee sat up in the saddle, gathered the reins, and started to spur the dun down the long ridge to the ranch. Then he froze, his head cocked, listening.

"Tom Cooke," he said. "Come out here in the light."

For a long moment there was no movement, no sound but the wind in the pines. Then, from the border of the woods a few yards to Lee's left, a shadow detached itself from other shadows, and the young Indian walked silently out into the moonlight.

Lee looked down at the boy for a moment. The Blackfoot's scarred, big-nosed face was as blank as stone.

"You come to work for me?"

The boy shrugged, not answering.

"Are there deer in these hills, boy?"

Tom Cooke nodded and put his hands up beside his ears in the sign for mule deer.

Lee reached down beside his saddle and untied a thong. Then he slid the Blackfoot's old Spencer out from a keeper strap, balanced it in his hands for a moment, then lightly tossed it over into the boy's arms. Tom Cooke cradled his rifle, staring at Lee without expression, his narrow black eyes glittering in the moonlight. Then, without a word, he turned and walked away into the shadows of the pines.

Lee didn't turn to watch him go. He touched the dun with his spurs and rode off down the ridge to the ranch.

The front door to the ranch house was secured by a large, rusty padlock. Bupp had given Lee the key, but even so, it took a few minutes to work the old lock open.

Lee stepped into the house and walked carefully through the darkness to a table in the parlor. He remembered seeing an oil lamp on it from the day before. He found the lamp, scratched a lucifer on the seat of his pants, and lit the wick and turned it up full. The room bloomed into golden light.

His home.

Lee stood looking around at the rough furniture, the tanned cowhide stretched across the floor as a carpet before the big fieldstone fireplace, the heavy adze-cut timbers of the roof and walls. Then he lifted the lamp and carried it through the other rooms, which were: a bedroom almost as big as the parlor, with a double bed and firm horsehair mattress covered against dust by an old calico spread; an office for ranch business, with a shaved-pine desk and cracked-leather swivel chair; and a long kitchen that ran the width of the back of the house, complete as could be, with a pump sink and a big, grease-blackened range stacked with pots and pans. A table was there big enough to sit a dozen cowhands.

Lee walked out through the back door, carrying the lamp to light his way, and walked down the path to the outhouse.

Standing there, in the rough-sawn cedar privy, Lee sighed and took a long, relieving piss.

Home.

He went back around the front, unhitched the dun, and led it over to the corral. Then he unsaddled it and went down to the barn for feed. There were a few sacks stored up against one wall, and he put down the lantern and hauled one out. Then he lugged it out to the corral and spilled a measure into the trough for the dun and Bupp's two mares. He pumped them some fresh water, too.

He carried his saddlebags and the Henry back into the house. He didn't need the lamplight outside anymore. The moonlight was bright enough to throw his shadow along the ground before him. And he went back to the kitchen and dumped the cured ham, apples, and two left-over sandwiches on the table.

He sat eating the sandwiches in the oil lamp's yellow glow, thinking of the work to be done on the place. Sandburg would be coming in in a couple of days with the horses: the big appaloosa stud named Shokan and nine mares, pure Nez Perce appaloosa every one. And three of the mares would be trailing colts. The foundation stock for the finest mountain horses in the world.

They had cost Lee almost as much as the ranch itself, and even then, he wouldn't have been able to buy them if Bud Lowns hadn't put in a good word for him with the Nez Perce. Those Indians owed Lowns a lot, and they knew it. There were maybe three or four really honest Indian agents in the whole of the West. Lowns was one.

And there was still money to be spent: tack for the horses, tools for nailing fencing, cash for Bupp and Tom Cooke, and Sandburg and his son. And feed. And food: flour, salt, bacon, coffee, corn meal—if he could get it—and a few young beeves for beef. Beans, work-clothes, ammunition—a hell of a lot of goods. It would take most of the rest of his cash just to get set up right, and if he wasn't careful how he spent it, he might have to sell one of the colts off, or even a mare, just to pay his store bills.

And he'd have to get Bupp to put in a kitchen garden, too. Knowing Bupp, it was going to be a chore; he probably didn't know any more about gardening than he did about cooking.

Lee finished the sandwiches, put the ham and apples up in the zinc-lined foodbox, and carried the lamp into the bedroom. He'd have to buy some more lamps, too, and oil, and a good shotgun. A Greener twelve gauge might come in handy for bird-shooting or whatever . . .

No question, all that was going to take most of his money. And he was determined not to play any poker in

Cree. A professional just can't play poker with men who are amateurs at the game—not if he wants to be accepted as a friend.

Lee propped the Henry in a corner and draped his gunbelt over the bedpost. Then he pulled off his boots and undressed. He blew out the lamp, peeled back the calico spread, and slid into the big bed, stretching out on the rough mattress cover with a grunt of satisfaction.

Sheets. He would have to buy sheets, too. And blankets.

And no poker.

The square life had its disadvantages.

When Lee walked out of the ranch house at dawn, he found Tom Cooke sitting on his haunches under a larch sapling in the front yard. He was whittling on a stick with an old Barlow knife.

A young mule deer buck hung, dressed out and cooling, from the crossbeam supporting the ranch house's narrow front porch.

"Nice buck."

The young Blackfoot grunted.

"We'll have some fresh venison steaks tonight for supper. Be nice if we could hang him for another day, but all I've got is enough ham for dinner."

Lee strolled down the ranch house steps, took an apple out of his pocket, and handed it to the boy.

"Now listen, Tom," he said. "I can pay you $25 a month, at least to start—and God knows when I'll ever be able to pay you more. You'd bunk in the bunkhouse with old Tim and a couple of men I'll have coming in." He sighed. "And I guess I'll go for a pony for you to work off. You do mount the right side and ride single rein?" He suspected the boy did. Most Indians were brought up to ride that way, and it played hell with the average white-trained cowpony.

74

For the first time since the boy had took the shot at him and Bupp, Lee saw a change of expression on his face. He looked surprised, and he almost smiled. It was the pony, of course. Lee remembered the boy's old pinto going down with the Henry slug through him. That must have hit the boy as hard as the belt.

"Now, come along with me. I want to get those sheds cleared out today. And if we hump it hard enough, we can get it done."

They humped it hard enough.

The Indian boy was a hard worker and no fool. Lee never had to tell him anything twice. In fact, he had a hard time keeping up. Playing gun for old Don Ignacio had been the cause of action aplenty, but not much hard work. And even on his horse drives into Texas, he'd had two or three *vaqueros* along to help out.

But this was no romantic gun and horse work. It was just fetch and carry—and a lot of it. The sheds hadn't been touched since the old man's death, and they were piled full of every kind of scrap, busted tools, split and knotholed lumber, field mice, horn beetles, grass snakes, and coils of rusty barbed wire.

Lee and Tom Cooke stacked the lumber off to one side. It might come in handy fixing rail fences. The rest of the scrap they heaped on a bare patch beyond the corral and burned. But Lee made Tom Cooke recoil the old barbed wire. They could bury it later. Not that he had anything against it. For cows it was fine. But around fine horses, it was no use at all, just a danger.

He and Tom worked and sweated out considerable till afternoon. By that time, they had the two big sheds cleared and neat. The barn was already in fair shape, so that left them with the bunkhouse still to do.

"Tom," Lee said, "let's go eat up that cured ham."

The boy seemed surprised when Lee motioned him in through the kitchen door. It seemed that most people in the valley preferred their Indians kept out of doors.

"Pump us some water, Tom."

Lee got the ham and the last of the apples out of the foodbox and put them on the table with a couple of tin plates. He hadn't found any forks or spoons in the place, and assumed the old man had used some good family silver, and it had gone with the Chicago people's selloff. More stuff to buy, but damn sure not sterling silver!

He and Tom Cooke sat down, hauled out their jack-knives, and went at the ham like wolves. It was slice off a chunk of ham, gobble it down, take a long, cold drink of well water, and slice off another chunk of ham. Between them, they went through three pounds of meat, and then they scraped the bone.

Lee lit up one of his cigar stubs, offered another to Tom Cooke (who made a face and shook his head), and led the way out into the yard for a smoke-around walk-around before they went back to work.

A few minutes later, coming around the corner of the house, Lee saw the Indian boy crouched down in some brush out past the sheds. The damn fool was going to take a crap out there.

"Hey, damn it, Tom!" Lee yelled at him. "Get your red ass into that privy!" The boy hesitated, then pulled his pants up, and came trotting out of the brush.

"Listen, boy. You don't have to go shitting in the woods on this ranch, you understand? You go crap where everybody else does!" The locals must not like Indians in their privies, either, he thought.

Lee had never understood what people hated so much about Indians. Most of the ones he had known were pretty decent people. It was true that he'd killed a few, but that had been fair enough. They'd been trying to kill him at the time. It was true, too, that Indians sometimes treated white women and kids very cruelly. But Lee had known white men to do every bit as bad to little children, and with less excuse than the Indians had.

On the other hand, he'd never bought all that "Lo, the poor Indian" stuff that some of those church people from the East handed out. Most tribes he knew had been happily killing their Indian enemies before the whites ever showed up and had been pretty quick to enjoy the same exercise with the whites. They'd just lost, that's all. Lost for good; that was the sad part of it.

He finished his cigar stub and was just turning to call Tom back to work when he caught it. Just a flicker of movement on the ridgeline a mile away.

Lee wished to God he'd bought a good long-shooting rifle while he was in town! He'd damn sure intended to, and now he maybe was going to regret not doing it!

It was a horseman—at least one—just topping the rise of the eastern ridge. Coming right on for the ranch as bold as paint. Too far still to make out anything about him, he might be one of Slawson's friends come to call.

Lee turned his head to shout for Tom Cooke, then shut his mouth and nodded. The young Blackfoot was standing just behind him, staring at the on-coming rider. The Spencer was cradled in his arms.

A minute later, they saw that it was a woman.

She was riding sidesaddle, and they could see a feather in her hat.

Tom Cooke drifted away with his rifle, and Lee dug out another piece of cigar and set himself to wait. The woman was taking her time, keeping her horse at a steady canter. She was coming down through the ridge scrub now, the horse taking the rough ground in stride. Lee noticed the horse, too. It was a tall, rangy animal, looked well-bred, perhaps a hunter.

The woman had seen him standing there, must have noticed him some time back; but it was only now, almost in hailing distance, that she lifted her quirt with a casual wave to him. He touched the brim of his hat to reply, tossed down the cigar butt, and stood, arms crossed, waiting until she rode up to him. It was fairly certain she hadn't come as a revengeful friend of Mickey Slawson.

She rode up to him and reined the hunter in. It was a hunter, a thoroughbred by the look of it.

"Mr. Lee?"

Her voice was British, low and crisp, a lady's voice. And her looks matched it. She was a silver blond, and slim and neat as a sapling willow. She was wearing a velvet green riding dress that must have cost half a year of a working man's wages. Her eyes were a soft and guarded gray.

Lee swept off his Stetson and made her a low, graceful bow.

"Yes, ma'am. And may I be of some assistance to you?"

The girl seemed surprised. She must have expected some horny-handed rancher with a plug in his jaw, not a handsome man with experience in manners appropriate to San Francisco's opera-and-champagne-cocktail set.

"Well . . ."

"Perhaps you'd be kind enough to join me on the house porch for a few moments, to rest from your ride, and allow this handsome hunter to cool out for a bit?"

"Well . . . Yes, Mr. Lee. I believe that I will."

Lee lifted his hand to help her. She took it and slid neatly down from the sidesaddle. Her hand was slim and cool and strong.

"My name is India Ashton, Mr. Lee."

"Ma'am."

Lee led her horse into the corral, and they walked up to the house together. India Ashton was tall, only a few inches shorter than Lee.

"I understand you're my neighbor, Mrs. Ashton."

"Yes, I am. But it's *Miss* Ashton, Mr. Lee. Nigel Ashton is my brother."

There was a battered rocker on the front porch, and Lee guided her to it.

"If you'd like to rest here, ma'am, I'll fetch you a glass of cold water. I regret that's all that River Ranch can offer at the present. I haven't gotten in supplies as yet."

"Water would be very welcome, Mr. Lee," she said.

When Lee brought the cup of water out to her, he found India Ashton rocking slowly back and forth in the creaking chair, looking out over the meadows below the house and, in the distance, the soft, varied green of Cree Valley.

She smiled up at him, took the water, and sipped it slowly.

"You have a very beautiful property here, Mr. Lee."

"Yes," Lee said, leaning against the porch rail and looking down at her. "It's a very pretty place and, I hope, will be a profitable one as well."

"My brother's experience is that the cattle business is a very difficult one in which to be certain of profits . . ."

Lee smiled. "I'll be raising horses, Miss Ashton, although I'm sure that doesn't make profit any more certain."

"And I believe you have the river on your property, do you not?"

"Yes, I do." And damn well you know it, Lee thought. The lady had come on a little fishing expedition. Fishing from Fishhook. Lee wondered if her brother had put her up to it.

"The river is very beautiful, and, of course, it will give you assured water for your stock . . ."

"Yes, it does."

She sighed and put the cup down on the top of the porch rail.

"So pretty," she murmured, looking out over the meadows. "And I suppose you could dam the river up, if you chose, and even make a private lake of it . . ."

Lee repressed a smile.

79

"Miss Ashton," he said. "You may tell your brother that I have no intention of diverting Rifle River, or stopping the flow, or of keeping my neighbors from water for any reason. You may also tell him, that if he has any matters to discuss with me, he is welcome to come and do so in person."

India Ashton blushed a faint pink, and her gray eyes sparkled with anger.

"I had no intention—"

Her furious glance met Lee's smile, and her blush deepened. She stood up and shook out the skirts of her riding habit.

"Thank you for your hospitality, Mr. Lee," she said with icy courtesy. "But I don't wish to intrude on you further . . ."

Her back as straight as a soldier's, she marched down off the porch and across the yard to the corral. Lee had to stretch his legs to keep up with her.

"Oh, you're always welcome to River Ranch, Miss Ashton, but I hope next time it will be a social call, not business. It's so uncomfortable, confusing the two . . ."

It made her too angry to answer him. Those beautifully carved lips were compressed into a thin, indignant, pink line.

Lee led the tall hunter out to her. She waited in silent fury as he came around to reach down, cup her small high-buttoned boot in his hand, and toss her lightly up into the saddle.

She sat glaring down at him as if she would have liked to cut him across the face with her riding crop.

Lee reached up his hand to her with a smile.

"Friends, Miss Ashton?"

"I should prefer to say *neighbors*, Mr. Lee!"

And she wrenched the hunter's head around, spurred him sharply, and flew off at a neat hand gallop, heading east toward the ridge. She rode very well, easy in the saddle as only a lifetime rider could be. She didn't look back.

A lady, Lee thought. The genuine article, and a rare piece to boot, if you could handle her. He wondered if she had been sent by her brother to find out what he planned for the river, or if this little expedition had been her own idea.

"She ride good, don't she?"

Tom Cooke was back, without the Spencer.

"Damn good," Lee said. "Now, let's get back to work."

CHAPTER SIX

Next day, at noon, while Lee and Tom Cooke were rigging Bupp's two mares with pack saddles for a trip to Cree for supplies, they heard hoofbeats descending the west ridge.

They turned and saw a faint cloud of dust rising through the pines.

"Lot of horses . . ."

Tom Cooke was right. It took a lot of horses to raise dust in this green country.

Lee thought he knew who it was, but he strode to the dun and slid the Henry out of its scabbard just in case.

In a few moments, they could see metal sparkling in the sunlight, reflecting off neck-rein chains and bits, saddle conchos and cartridge belts. And a moment later, a small herd of horses, with two armed riders alongside, came trotting down the ridge.

Appaloosas.

There was no mistaking the odd dark and white markings, the spotted rumps. Sandburg and his boy, Jake, had made the drive up from Colorado—and right on time.

"My horses, Tom," Lee said. He was proud of those light-stepping Nez Perce beauties. The finest mountain horses in the world; only pure Arabs could beat them for staying power, and then only on the flat.

Lee saw that Sandburg's boy was lead-trailing two

remounts, both sorrels, carrying their outfits and personal goods. The River Ranch was starting to "horse up."

The herd was close enough now for Lee to make out Shokan, easily trotting well ahead of the mares, the big stud's white, black-spotted coat shining in the bright sunlight.

"A big-boss horse," Tom Cooke said, watching the stud come in.

"The best," Lee said.

All the appaloosas looked in good shape, trim and lively, the colts sprinting alongside their mothers as full of beans as if they hadn't just finished a three-hundred mile drive.

Ole Sandburg had seen Lee by the corral, and now he turned his horse's head and rode down to him, leaving his boy, Jake, to chivvy the appaloosas into the fenced meadow above the ranch buildings.

Sandburg was a tall, bald, mournful-looking man, rail-thin in his dusty Levi's and battered Stetson. His boy, Jake, was his spitting image and equally sad and silent. They were good hands with horses, though, and Lee had been lucky to hire them when the horse ranch they worked on had been sold to a local cowman for graze.

Now they were his men, and damned good men at that. They weren't interested in much else than working with horses and father and son had been working together for so many years that they had come to resemble each other.

"Mr. Lee." Sandburg leaned down from the saddle to shake his hand.

"Ole."

Sandburg's pale blue gaze flickered over to Tom Cooke, but he didn't offer to shake hands with the Indian.

"Horses look good, Ole," Lee said. "Any trouble?"

"They're in good shape," Sandburg said. "No trouble, except the stud tried to bring in a couple of wild mustang mares. We had to keep hazing them ladies off despite him."

"The colts come through the drive okay?"

"Hell, Mr. Lee, those damn colts are as full of vinegar as when they started. You want to come on over and look at 'em?"

"I'd like to, Ole, but Tom Cooke and I are heading into town for supplies, and I want to get that done. Anything you need while we're going?"

Sandburg shook his head. "Some plug tobacco is all I can think of, special."

"Okay," Lee said. "And this here's Tom Cooke; he'll be working with us on the place."

Sandburg nodded to the young Blackfoot.

"And one thing, Ole, you and Jake keep your eyes open up here. I had to shoot a man in town, I'm sorry to say, and he had some friends who weren't above a little rustling, or so I hear."

Sandburg sighed and nodded, looking over the ranchland and the solid log-and-stone buildings. "Trouble." He sighed again. "Well, Mr. Lee. I will say you have you a pretty place here; worth some trouble, I guess."

Lee mounted the dun and waved to Jake Sandburg, who was still chivvying the appaloosas up into the top pasture.

"Hey-hooo! Jake!"

Sandburg's boy waved back at Lee, and then had to spur his sorrel to turn a couple of appaloosa mares who'd decided to make for the west ridge.

"Move on in to the bunkhouse, Ole," Lee said. "We'll be back early tomorrow. And there's a side of venison hanging off the porch. Cut yourselves some of that."

Sandburg nodded, "Okay," and turned his horse to go help his son with the herd.

Lee sat his saddle a moment longer, watching the appaloosas gallop and frisk in the high pasture's lush grass. He would have been happy to spend the day up there, watching them, and maybe feeding some lump sugar to the mares. But, hell, he didn't have any sugar—or anything else, either.

"Let's go, Tom." He reined the dun down toward the distant valley and heard the hoofbeats of the pack horses behind him, as Tom Cooke led them into line.

A fine horse ranch. And fine horses on it now.

Mr. Lee was doing all right.

On his first trip down to Cree, Lee had set himself to remembering the trail, and he'd done a good job, even with all the excitement of Tom Cooke's shooting at them. Today, he didn't get lost more than twice. Once in the trees, going down, and then once more, when they were over the river.

Each time, just before he was ready to admit he was lost, Lee would hear a grunt from Tom Cooke behind him and would turn to see the boy pointing off in the direction they should be heading.

They made good time, although Lee stopped once to take a piss and rest the horses. He also picked and ate about a quart of blackberries along the banks of Rifle River. The berries were big and shiny black, tight and sweet, with juice as a young girl. Tom Cooke ate his share, too, and by the time they both were finished, the blackberry brambles had scratched them up more than a little.

Even so, it was still sun-high when they saw Cree. The town, which had been so lively at night, looked sound asleep in the late-afternoon sunlight. Only a few farm wagons rolled down main street, bringing the loads of spring fodder for the livery and stock yard to the south of town.

Lee pulled the dun up at the edge of town and reached down to check the Colt, easing it in the holster. It was possible that Rebecca Chase had spilled the beans to Phipps, had let him know who Lee was . . .

But she hadn't. Or if she had, Phipps had decided to butt out of the matter. No one troubled them as they rode in. Lee and Tom Cooke tied off the pack horses in front of a sign that read: DRY GOODS AND SUPPLY—W. KIMBLE PROP. Lee climbed up onto the high loading platform and walked into the store's cool darkness.

The big store smelled of sacks of feed, oiled leather, gun oil, hard cheese, cloth goods, pickles, and fresh-sawn lumber. It was a pleasant, rich, comforting smell. Comforting if you had money in your jeans.

A tall, dark, cadaverous man stepped out of the shadows to meet Lee. He had a long, sad face and was wearing a white apron that hung down to his ankles.

"Yes, sir? Can I help you to something?"

"Yes, you can. My name's Fred Lee. I've bought the River Ranch, and I'm in need of quite a sum of supplies."

"Oh, yes, oh, yes . . ." The bony shopkeeper nodded. "I'd heard that land had been bought. And you'd certainly need some goods. I understand those Chicago people just about cleaned that place out. You're lucky they didn't sell the ranch house for lumber!" He laughed a high-pitched, squeaky laugh.

"I've got a list," Lee said.

"Okay . . . okay!" The shopkeeper rubbed his hands. "Let's get to it!" He held out his right hand for Lee to shake. "I'm Walter Kimble, by the way."

"Fred Lee."

"Oh, yes. Now Mr. Lee, let's see that list . . ."

It was a long list, and it took a long time to pick out

the goods, stack them, and shift them out to the pack horses. Tom Cooke bundled them up and strapped the loads to the horses' backs.

"I'll tell you, Mr. Lee," Kimble said. "You're going to need a buckboard for this feed you got written down here. It's going to be too much of a load for your horses."

"I know it. Would you have a notion of a buckboard for sale in town?" It would mean unloading the horses and repacking the buckboard. It would also mean spending the night in town.

"Oh, yes indeed I would," Kimble said, his cheery voice coming oddly from that long, lugubrious face. "Matter of fact, *I've* got a buckboard I could let you have cheap enough, very cheap indeed." He shook his head. "Matter of fact, you'd be unwise to buy a new wagon, seeing that there's no proper road up to your place. Any vehicle you buy's bound to get shook to pieces getting up there and surely won't last much more than a year, if it even lasts that!"

"And what would you ask for this old second-hand buckboard, Mr. Kimble?"

Kimble laughed. "Well, she's more like third or fourth hand, Mr. Lee, but she still goes." He stood musing for a moment, his hand cupping his lantern jaw. "I suppose I'd have to ask $25.00 for her . . ."

"Throw in a set of harnesses, Mr. Kimble, and I might buy it," Lee said, enjoying bargaining with the man.

"Oh, but not *new* harnesses, Mr. Lee!"

"But serviceable, Mr. Kimble."

The tall shopkeeper sighed, stroking his chin. "Oh, very well, a set of serviceable harnesses." He gave Lee a shrewd glance. "And what about horses to draw it, Mr. Lee?" Mr. Kimble was apparently the town horse trader as well.

Lee sighed. Ranching looked to be a damned expensive operation. And he still had a good Sharps rifle to dicker for. A mountain rifle.

It was dusk when they were done.

The sagging buckboard had all it could do to stand up under the sacks of oats and hard grain, heavy tools, rolls of hemp rope and harness leather, wash tubs, and kegs of spikes and nails.

The harness horses that Lee had bought were better animals than he had expected. Kimble had, with the best will in the world, tried to foist off a pair of half-blind and all-galled old wheezers on him, but had proved pleasant and philosophical when he saw that Lee knew horses.

"Oh, I see that you're a knowing man and a considerable judge," he'd said, and laughed his high-pitched laugh and offered a fair price for two fair harness horses.

Lee'd been hungry for supper by that time, and so had Tom Cooke. So Lee'd led the way over to Mrs. Boltwith's. It was early for supper, but the usual crowd of clerks and harness drummers was gathered on Mrs. Boltwith's front steps and porch, waiting for the call to come eat.

These men glanced at Lee as he walked up the steps, but none of them said anything to him. Probably afraid of some terrible temper and a quick gunshot. Lee had felt that fear from most men for many years. He had gotten used to it, and finally had ignored it. It bothered him now, though. He didn't want that sort of feeling around him anymore.

He looked back down the steps for Tom Cooke, and saw that the Blackfoot was going the other way, heading around to the back of the house. The poor kid knew his place, no doubt about it, and it must make him mad as hell.

Lee walked through the front door and past the small registration desk—which he had not seen anybody use yet—and headed down the hall to the kitchen. He might as well see what old Bupp was fixing up for supper.

But he hesitated at the kitchen door. Tim Bupp was cooking, all right, and standing at the big kitchen range, cursing and stirring a kettle or something that smelled like Irish stew. Mrs. Boltwith was in the kitchen, too, sitting at the table, knitting at an object the color of fresh mustard greens. Lee assumed it was a muffler, or maybe a long, narrow sweater of some kind.

There was a girl sitting at the table, too.

She was a thin girl—skinny really—with dark eyes and a fairly big nose. She was dressed in light blue calico, or what looked like calico to Lee, and was really a nice-looking girl, even with that big nose. Her skin was very white.

"Well, now, come on in, Mr. Lee," Mrs. Boltwith said, and she gave him a dignified nod. "Beatrice, this here's Mr. Lee."

The thin girl turned to look up at Lee, and her eyes widened as if there was something special about him.

"Mr. Lee, this is Beatrice Morgan, a very sweet girl and a good friend of mine . . ."

"How do you do, ma'am?" Lee said.

"So there you are," said Tim Bupp. "And come to have some of this stew, I suppose—and serve you right!" Tim didn't seem pleased with his cooking.

"There's nothing the matter with that stew, Mr. Bupp," said Mrs. Boltwith. And, to Lee, "Mr. Bupp apparently never heard tell of pepper, Mr. Lee."

"Well, there's too damn much of it in this here stew, I'll tell you that!" said Bupp. "She put all that pepper in my stew without so much as a by-your-leave!"

His stew. It appeared that cooking was taking hold of Mr. Bupp.

The girl, meanwhile, had been staring at Lee without

saying a word to him. But when he hung his Stetson on the back of one of the kitchen chairs and sat down, she spoke up.

"I—I believe that I owe you a great deal of thanks, Mr. Lee . . ."

Lee looked across the table into those pretty brown eyes. She looked very sincere, but he didn't know what the hell the young lady was taking about.

"Ma'am?"

She blushed like a bride. "You . . . I understand that you are the man who . . . fought Mr. Slawson."

Now what the hell was all this about? "Yes, ma'am?" Lee asked.

"Well . . . you saved me from . . . from . . ."

Jumping Jesus Christ! It was the little whore the Irishman was dragging around the floor! He hadn't recognized her.

"Now, now," said Lee. The damn girl was so lady-like, he found himself still talking to her as if she was some decent town girl. "It was just one of those things that happens, miss, nothing for you to fret about . . ."

"Well, I do want to thank you." She held out her hand to him across the table. "It was very brave of you . . ."

Lee reached out and took her hand, feeling like a damn fool. It was a small, thin hand and very cool.

Lee shook her hand, then let it go.

"Don't think about it anymore, miss . . . uh, honey . . . It's over and done with."

"Hello, Tom Cooke," said Mrs. Boltwith. The young Blackfoot was standing at the kitchen door. "Come on in and sit down."

Tom came into the kitchen, but he didn't sit down. He went over to the range and stood leaning against the wall, watching Bupp stir the stew.

"Beatrice has been working for Rebecca Chase for almost a year," said Mrs. Boltwith. "And she don't

90

care for it more than half!''

"Oh, Rebecca's friendly . . .'' the thin girl said. She looked at Lee as she said it, her brown eyes steady, looking as if she asked him, yes, I'm a whore, and it surprised you, didn't it?

"She may be friendly enough,'' said Mrs. Boltwith. "But friendly is as friendly does, and she doesn't take care of her girls! Why, didn't she run Suzy Williams off when she was poxed up? In my day, a woman who'd run off a sick girl like that would have had a bad name for five years, and that's flat!''

So Lee'd been right. Mrs. Boltwith had been in the gay life. And more important, she knew—or felt—that Lee had been as well, or she wouldn't be talking so plain about it.

The thin girl was still looking at Lee in that odd, defiant way, as though daring him to judge her for what she was—or Mrs. Boltwith for what she'd been.

Lee had run whores himself for a couple of years in Dodge City, but he'd never made the mistake of thinking that he really knew what was on a whore's mind—or on any woman's mind, come to that.

Women would whore, same as a man would do anything, if they had to for food and shelter. But when that reason was past, the cause of a woman's whoring got very complicated. Hatred of their daddies was a big reason—hatred of themselves. And Lee had known some girls who simply loved the life—the excitement, the continual change, the free talk and the free ways that decent women could never know. And the fucking, too; no use saying that many women didn't love it as much as men.

"Do they call you Bee?'' he asked the girl, smiling.

She blushed again. A blushing little whore. "No, they call me Beatrice. My folks used to call me Bee.''

Bee. James's wife had been called Bee. Lee had met them once in New Orleans. Jesse James had been a quiet sort of man, with big farmer's hands. Nothing special about him at all. Frank James had struck Lee as the smarter brother. And Bee James had been a pretty little lady. Very dainty. They'd all had lunch at the Garvey House when the prize fight was over, and Jesse had said, "Sullivan's getting old." The Jameses were calling themselves Mr. and Mrs. Martin while they were in Louisiana. Doc Porteous had brought Lee to that lunch as a surprise. Quite a surprise — and a damn good lunch.

"Bee's a pretty name," Lee said to the girl.

"Well," Bupp said from the stove, "this over-peppered Irish stew is ready to eat. As ready as it'll ever be!"

Mrs. Boltwith had been right. There was nothing the matter with the stew; it had been peppered just enough.

Bupp had served it out to the four of them. Tom Cooke had eaten his standing against the wall—even though Mrs. Boltwith had asked him again to sit down with them—and Lee had been happy to take seconds.

Then, it had been time for the boarders to come in for their supper. "You'll want your same room, Mr. Lee?" Mrs. Boltwith had asked. Lee'd seemed to have become prime with her for some reason. Tom Cooke was invited to bunk it out back with Bupp.

So, after the stew and a piece of apple pie with their coffee, they'd cleared out for the rest of the paying customers. And Lee decided to ask Beatrice Morgan out for a walk. It was dark enough outside now, so that no one would remark that a respectable rancher, new to the valley, had taken a whore out for a stroll.

It was a moonlit night, almost light enough, Lee thought, for them to have made it back to the ranch traveling through the night. The girl knew the town better than he did, so Lee let her guide him down a narrow side street and out to the edge of town.

She didn't have much to say, so Lee did the talking. It

was pleasant enough; it had been a long time since he had gone walking in the moonlight with a girl. He was surprised how pleasant it was.

"So, you've been in Cree a year, Miss Morgan?"

"About that," she said.

"It's a pretty place, this valley, with all the green and the mountains. But I imagine it'll get sort of fierce in the winter . . ."

"It does get cold, yes."

Lee saw that she didn't know how to get on with him now, and was acting as shy as the respected town girl he was treating her like. He stopped and took hold of her slender arm and turned her toward him.

"Listen, Miss Morgan, I don't give a damn if you're whoring. It's a job like any other; better than some I've done, worse than some, too. It doesn't make you any less a nice girl as far as I'm concerned . . . or any more a nice girl, either."

She was standing, looking up at him in the moonlight, her dark eyes shadowed. He couldn't tell what she was thinking.

"So don't stay so stiff with me; I won't hurt you."

"All right . . . Lee?"

"That's right, you call me Lee . . . and I'll call you Bee."

She smiled, and when he took her hand, she let him hold it. They walked along like that for a while. Lee could hear the soft, busy sound of Rifle River passing over some rapids under the trees a little way away. A cool breeze had come up, and he thought he felt the girl tremble.

"You cold, Bee?"

She shook her head, and they walked along a little farther in silence.

"You know," she said suddenly, "Marshal Phipps beat a man up last night."

"Did he?"

"Yes." She hesitated. "It was a lumberjack. A man named Boyd. Marshal Phipps beat him badly. Sarah was downstairs then—Sarah's a friend of mine—and she saw it."

"Well," Lee said. "Keeping the peace isn't always a pretty job." He couldn't make out what was bothering her, she must have seen plenty of the rough house in the Arcady.

She glanced up at him.

"Sarah said it seemed that Marshal Phipps wanted to kill Boyd, that he was trying to force a shooting on him . . ."

"I see." And so he did. Phipps apparently felt he had some ground to make up as the town of Cree's hardcase. Bad luck for Boyd. A man like Phipps would take any ordinary working man—even a big, tough working man—apart as quick as a jeweler would a two-dollar watch.

It might mean more trouble. Trouble with Phipps if he felt his reputation injured by Lee's killing the Irishman. What nonsense it all was.

"Marshal Phipps is . . . a temperamental man," she said.

Now there was a high-falutin' word: *temperamental.* Not one your usual flat-back whore would use. Beatrice Morgan must have been raised up to be something better than she was.

"I'll bet that he is . . ." The silly little split-tail was worried for him. It made Lee feel uncomfortable. This whole damn walk in the moonlight was making him feel uncomfortable now.

It was too damn personal a thing, this worrying about him. Lee didn't like to be pushed this way, by some girl who was getting ahead of herself.

Hell, he didn't even know the little bitch.

"Let's head back," he said. And he didn't say anything more to her until they were back at Mrs. Boltwith's.

There, at the kitchen door, she held out her hand for him to shake it.

"I've got to go to work," she said awkwardly, and blushed in the moonlight. "Goodnight, Mr. Lee. And thank you very much for standing up for me the way you did . . ." She knew he had turned angry at her for some reason, but she didn't know what it was.

"Goodbye," he said and went inside.

Mrs. Boltwith and Tim Bupp were sitting at the kitchen table, smoking cigarettes. When Lee came in, Mrs. Boltwith looked up with that wise, inquiring look women have when they've been matchmaking.

"Cup of coffee, Mr. Lee?" she asked.

"No," he said shortly. "I'm going to bed." The old cow had matched him up with a big-nose whore. Some honor there!

He was up before dawn. He came downstairs with his saddlebags, while Bupp was just stoking the stove.

"Coffee'll be awhile," Bupp said. "It's a might damn early for breakfast!"

"I don't want any," Lee said. "Tom out back?"

"Yeah, he's up. Getting me some wood."

Lee went to the door. "Tim, I probably won't be in town for a while. When you get learned up on your cooking, just come on out to the ranch. I'll expect you in another week or so."

Bupp glanced at Lee's face, started to say something, then changed his mind. Instead, he sighed.

"Well, now . . . those pies. I just don't know. Stew's one thing, but those pies . . . they take a hell of a lot of learning."

"A week, Bupp," Lee said and walked out the door.

An hour later, Lee and Tom Cooke were up on the flats above the town, with the sun rising like a golden ball of fire in the east, the first of the morning's heat striking the dew-soaked grass, burning it off in streamers of mist. It was a beautiful day. Lee turned in his saddle to check the lashings on the horse packs. Behind them, he could see Tom Cooke on the buckboard. Kimble had been right. The high country would be no country for buckboards.

Tom Cooke had asked to drive the wagon, and since the boy hadn't asked Lee for anything before, he couldn't very well refuse. And it was working out all right. The Blackfoot must have driven horses before; he was doing well enough.

It would be good to get back up to the ranch. Out of that damn town. Killers and women, the pleasures of towns. Of course, he'd made a damn fool of himself with that girl. She was just trying for something more than she had at the Arcady. It wasn't her fault that Lee had another woman on his mind—and always would. And maybe it wasn't like that, anyway. Maybe she was just a soft-hearted girl.

It was surely a damn beautiful day. Lee could see the mountain peaks as clear and sharp as if they were only a mile away. They looked like a huge rip-saw blade, shining with snow and ice.

The ride went very well, until they reached the river ford. Then the buckboard jammed its right rear wheel between a couple of boulders in the shallows.

It was near to noon now and hot, so Lee didn't mind as much as he might have tying the horses to a stand of willows on the bank, taking off his boots, and wading out into the cool water to help Tom Cooke heave the wagon free. It was a real nice problem. Either they managed to hoist the loaded buckboard up high enough to free the wheel, or they'd have to unload the whole damn thing to lighten it. And if they unloaded it, they'd have to carry a lot of heavy sacks of feed, sacks that couldn't be wet without ruining them.

So they both set their backs to the wagon hard, to give it the best lift they had in them. They'd heaved a couple of times, and the wheel hadn't budged from between those big rocks. Tom Cooke straightened up and touched Lee on the arm.

"Somebody," he'd said, his head cocked, listening.

Then Lee heard it over the soft, tumbling sound of the shallow rapids.

A man was shouting.

And off to the west, Lee could see a little cloud of dust. Somebody was riding their way, coming fast through the brush and dwarf willow.

Lee and Tom Cooke left the buckboard and splashed through the shallows to the horses.

They'd just gotten their rifles out and cocked when the rider came bucketing out onto the river bank.

It was Ole Sandburg, and there was blood running down his face.

He reined in his lathered sorrel, and then started yelling.

"Mr. Lee! They stole your horses, Mr. Lee! They took 'em up to the woods! Jake's after 'em, though. My boy's after the sons-of-bitches!"

CHAPTER SEVEN

There was nothing like trouble to put juice in a man.

Lee and Tom Cooke bent and got their shoulders under the buckboard, then heaved with all their strength. The wagon lurched and slowly rose free. They shoved together, pushing it clear of the rocks. Then, Tom Cooke jumped up onto the seat and drove the team across the shallow riffle and up onto the river bank.

Lee came splashing out after him, found his boots, and sat on the bank to jam them on.

"How did it happen, Ole?"

Sandburg swung off his tired horse.

"We'd taken the herd up into those pine woods over the ridge, to loose them out on the west range there, Mr. Lee. And the bastards jumped us right there. Maybe three of them, maybe four!"

His long face flushed with anger, and he reached up to touch the bloody graze on his cheek.

"Hadn't been for this, we'd have done all right. It knocked me off my horse—out cold. And Jake thought I was killed. By the time I come too, the sons-of-bitches had their start."

"And Jake's trailing them?" Lee climbed up into the dun's saddle.

"You bet he is. And my boy'll damn sure slow 'em up, you can bet on that!"

Lee didn't feel surprised by the rustling. It seemed

inevitable that some kind of trouble had to come to the ranch.

And to him.

First Slawson. Now this. It had to be either Slawson's rustler friends, or Ashton making his first move to control the river.

Well, either way, it was going to cost them. It was going to cost them a great deal. If he had to fight to be let alone, then by God he'd fight!

"Listen to me," Lee said to Sandburg and Tom Cooke. "And do just what I tell you. Pull the buckboard back into the brush, unharness the team, and picket them out to graze. Then take the pack horses back there, unload them, and each of you pick one out and saddle it. Ole, your horse is worn out; I want both of you mounted as fresh as we can."

Sandburg opened his mouth to argue, looked at Lee, and changed his mind. Tom Cooke was already leading the wagon team off into the dwarf willows lining the river bank.

"Then, when you're mounted, follow me as fast as you can go," Lee continued. "I'll be heading up for the river falls—those rapids just down from the pass. If they're taking my stock out of the valley, that's the way they'll have to go."

Ole Sandburg didn't argue at this either, or ask Lee to wait till all three of them could ride together. He was thinking about his boy Jake up there alone.

Lee reined the dun around without another word, and spurred the big gelding into a run, heading up the steep meadow trails to the ranch. He could feel the reserves of power in the dun as the horse took the slope at an easy, floating gallop. Even so, he'd have to ease the gelding soon; it was a long climb to go.

Jake Sandburg. So much like his father, they were damn near twins. Except Jake still had his hair. Jake Sandburg was fifteen years old, and he was up on the mountain with three or four men who'd kill him quicker than spit. Up on the mountain after Lee's horses.

Lee hoped to God the boy managed to slow the rustlers down. And he hoped to God the boy didn't get killed doing it.

He reached behind the saddle to make certain the .50 caliber Sharps was secure in the scabbard. He'd known men to lose their rifles that way on a wild run. Kimble had made him a good price for that rifle and a hundred rounds to go with it. It seemed he was going to find use for them before dark.

He guided the dun up past a grove of larch and then reined him down to a canter, moving fast through deep grass across a wide pasture.

Still a long way to go.

Ole and Tom Cooke should be well on their way by now, coming up fast behind him.

There was a way Jake might hold them. At the rapids. If he could ride around the rustlers—beat them to the ford—then he might be able to keep them from crossing. Then they'd have to get over the white water under Jake's rifle—tough enough for just themselves— a whole lot tougher with a horse herd.

If Jake had thought of it.

And if he'd gotten there before them.

Lee urged the dun up into a gallop again. He had to catch up before dark, either way, or kiss the appaloosas goodbye.

He made it with perhaps half an hour to spare.

The sunset shadows were long on the mountain slope when Lee coaxed the lathered gelding out of the last stand of lodgepole pine below the falls of Rifle River.

The white water foamed past him as he rode the west bank up toward the thunder of the falls. He stood high in the stirrups, the big Sharps cradled in his arms as he searched the fields along the river in the soft, golden evening light.

Nothing.

Not a sign of them.

For a moment, Lee felt sick to his stomach. He'd been a fool. The rustlers must have doubled back down across the valley, maybe all the way to the lumber camps, deciding not to take a chance of cutting out the fast way . . .

Then he saw them.

The appaloosas first. The big stud hobbled to a birch sapling. The mares and colts shifting nervously around him as the stallion sidestepped, trying to free himself from the unfamiliar restraints. The big horse might lose his temper, might cripple himself trying to kick free . . .

Then Lee saw the men—two of them, at least. They were both belly down behind a huge birch log, each of them with Winchesters aimed out over the rapids.

Jake Sandburg had beaten them to the river.

Even as he reined the weary dun in and slid out of the saddle with the Sharps in his hand, Lee heard the crack of shots—first one, then another. The boy must be up in the rocks over there.

As the two rustlers returned the fire, resting their rifles on the big log, taking their time, Lee let go of the dun's reins and began to ease carefully through the scattered birches toward the riflemen.

The other men—one or two more at least—where the hell were they?

They had to be higher up, trying to get across to flank the boy. Trying to cross above the falls.

And they could do it. The river ran fast up there, but shallow. A steep, rocky climb. Too steep for horses. But men could do it.

Lee hoped that Jake had thought of that, too.

He was almost clear of the trees, almost out in the open. He could see the riflemen clearly now; they were laughing and joking with each other as they crouched behind the log, getting ready to fire again. They didn't look worried at all. And why should they? They probably thought they'd killed Ole when they'd seen him fall. They knew there was only one man on the other side of the river.

And sure as hell their friends had already gone across to kill him.

There wasn't time to wait for Ole and Tom Cooke.

Lee knelt beside the birch and cocked the Sharps. It would be about a three-hundred-fifty yard shot. A long shot for most rifles. Not for the Sharps.

He thumbed up the leaf-sight, notched it at 350, then settled the rifle butt into his shoulder.

He drew a low, fine bead, low center on the lower back of the man nearest to him. He was a thin man, in worn denim, laughing at something his friend had just said.

Lee took a breath, let a little of it out, and squeezed the trigger.

The rifle butt slammed back into his shoulder at the blast of the shot. It hurt like a hard punch in a saloon fight. Lee rolled out to the right to clear the smoke, opened the action and reloaded, and came up on his elbow to shoot again.

The thin man was lying still beside the log; the other man was shooting back. Lee saw the quick bright flash from the Winchester muzzle. Then another. The man was fast with that piece. Then, just as Lee set himself to fire, the rustler jumped to his feet and dove over the huge log to cover on the other side. Lee almost chanced a snap-shot, then didn't.

A moment later the man's pale face was over the edge of the fallen birch, and the Winchester with him. He fired twice, taking his time. Lee heard the slugs humming into the woods a yard or two to the left. Too much range for the carbine.

102

Lee steadied the long barrel of the Sharps, lining the fine sights on that distant little patch of white face that just showed over the log's rough-barked bulk.

This time he was ready for the big rifle's recoil.

When the smoke cleared, the man was gone. No face and no Winchester appeared over the top of the log.

It could have been a near miss; the man could have ducked down. He could be waiting for Lee to step out into the open.

Lee didn't have the time to play it careful.

He reloaded the Sharps, got to his feet, and started walking through the high grass toward the log. It looked like a long 350 yards.

He kept his eye on the log as he walked, ready to snapshoot and hit the ground if the man came up shooting. Lee was damn glad he'd been too young for the war; this was the sort of thing the soldiers must have had to do: walk across a wide field not knowing whether or not a gun was waiting on the other side.

By the time he got across the field, Lee was sweating. The first man he had shot was dead. The .50-caliber slug had smashed his spine.

There was no sound, no movement behind the log.

Lee took up the slack on the Sharp's trigger and stepped around the end of the log.

The man was as dead as his friend. The bullet had struck him in the forehead and torn the top of his head off. The skull was like a fresh-emptied can of red paint; the brains had been blown out of it.

It was a bad sight to see.

Lee had always hated fighting with rifles. He wasn't that good with them to start with, and even when you won, it didn't seem right; it seemed cowardly to stand off and kill a man the way you would a buffalo or deer, without even looking in his eyes.

Then he heard something.

Like a hawk hunting, some cry like that.

A scream.

He reloaded the Sharps on the run, making for the river bank as fast as he could go, jumping the fallen timber, bulling straight through the tangled brush, leaving his hat behind in the scrub. Just as he made the river bank, he heard the scream again.

It was Jake Sandburg.

Lee charged out into the rapids of the ford, stepping high over the foaming riffles, splashing through, sliding, slipping, jumping from rock to rock.

The first shot came at him when he was more than half way across. Pistol shot. And a miss.

He kept running, ducking, plowing through the shallow water. A second shot came closer; he heard the deep hum as the bullet went past his head. Close enough.

He made the bank and scrambled up it, hanging onto the Sharps with one hand, grabbing at reeds and willow branches with the other.

The third shot clipped some bark from a sapling just beside his face. Good pistol shooting.

But not good enough.

Lee felt the calm coming over him, the odd feeling that he usually had in a fight; the feeling that he was moving very slowly, and other people moving even slower. Everything looked clear and bright when he felt like that. It was as if he could see everything that happened for miles. And everything happened very slowly.

He lunged up through the thickets, found the first of the big, rough boulders that edged the river over there, and began to climb.

There were shouts from back across the river. Lee could hear them faintly over the seething shuttle of the rapids. Sandburg and Tom Cooke had come up. It was all right. He wouldn't need them.

Lee reached a wide ledge, climbed up onto it, and

found that there was a clear way up into the top of the rock formation. The jumble of brush-grown boulders here was like the ruins of some ancient city. Close and dark-shadowed.

He bent and put the Sharps down. No 300 yard shots up here.

He didn't trouble to draw his Colt. It wasn't necessary. He walked up the rough ledge path into the shadow of the rocks.

Nothing for a moment. Lee stopped to listen. Nothing but the rush of the river far below. Some little sounds of squirrels or chipmunks.

Then he heard a boot heel grate on the stone some distance above him.

A swift shadow stretched across the rocks further up the ledge. A tall man in a stovepipe hat and long white duster stepped out into the open. He was smiling down at Lee, as if he was pleased to see him. He had a Russian model Smith and Wesson in his hand.

"You're an uninvited guest . . ." the man called down to Lee, smiling. He was a good-looking man, with a big cavalry mustache. "I'm afraid that—"

Lee drew and shot the man twice, just above his belt.

It was painful to see the man's face. To see the shock and the humiliation as he realized he had been killed so quickly, from such a distance, while he still had something to say. Before he even had a chance to fight. He looked as though it was all a mistake, as though it should be done over again in order to get it right.

The bullets—coming one, two—had shoved him back hard, like a bully's push, and the man couldn't recover his balance. He fell into the side of a boulder and gripped the rock with one hand to hold himself up. With the other hand, he raised the Smith and Wesson and tried to aim it at Lee.

It was all too late. Too late and too slow.

Lee shot him once more, through the upper chest,

hitting him in the heart as the man stood turned to the side. The man's stovepipe hat flew off, and he fell back onto the stones of the ledge, struggling and kicking as if he were trying to swim his way up from death.

Lee went by him at a run, ducked through a kind of broken arch of stone, and found Jake Sandburg lying in the sunshine.

His throat was cut.

A man was lying stretched out along the sloping top of a boulder to Lee's left, facing away, peering down over the edge.

"Hey, Tom," the man called. "Did—"

He heard Lee's step and jerked his head around to stare at him, eyes wide in surprise. He had a long-barreled .45 in his right hand. But it was a long way to turn and bring it around to bear on Lee. Too long a way.

The man was a cowboy, and pretty old—in his forties, anyway—with a little potbelly and short, bowed legs.

"Oh, my God," he said. "Please don't kill me, mister."

He loosened his grip on the .45, and it clattered onto the stone. The man was staring into Lee's eyes, frozen, as if, if he didn't blink, Lee wouldn't shoot him. "Oh, please, oh, please, oh, please," he said. "Don't do this . . . don't *do* it!" When he'd said that, he didn't say anything more.

After a few moments, Lee heard bootsteps on the rocks below, and right after that Tom Cooke and Ole Sandburg came ducking through the stone archway with rifles in their hands.

When Sandburg saw his boy lying dead there in a bright puddle of blood, it was a bad time.

They hanged the potbellied cowboy from a willow tree down beside the river.

"Oh, you won't get away with this," he said, when

106

Tom Cooke had gone across the river and come back with a lasso to hang the cowboy with.

"Oh, you won't get away with this," he said. His face was red, and he was weeping. "Mr. Ashton will make you sorry for this . . . if you do this to me . . ."

"You Mickey Slawson's friend," Tom Cooke said to him.

"Well I'm working for Mr. Ashton now, you dirty red nigger!" He was staring at the loop of rope in Tom Cooke's hand. "Don't you put that thing on me," he said. His nose was running like a crying child's. He looked around for a moment as if he'd forgotten what was going to happen to him.

"I wouldn't be in your boots, mister," he said to Lee. "I wouldn't be in your boots for any money in the world. That was Tom Small you shot back there. And God help you when his brother finds out."

Lee wasn't too surprised. The man in the stovepipe hat hadn't seemed like a cowpoker. So he'd been George Small's brother. That was who the cowboy must be talking about. More trouble.

"God help you, that's all I've got to say," the cowboy said.

Tom Cooke had finished making the knot.

"I didn't kill that boy," the cowboy said. "I never killed anybody. Not in my whole life long."

Lee took the rope, threw the bitter end of it up across a thick willow branch, and went up to the cowboy to fit the loop around his neck.

"I never hurt those horses either," the cowboy said. "Those are some of the finest stock I ever saw. Real pretty horses. I'd never hurt a horse like that. I drove 'em as careful as you would yourself . . ."

Lee stepped back from him, took up the slack in the lasso, got a grip on the rope, and doubled it over his fist.

"You aren't going to do this," the cowboy said. He'd stopped crying. He looked Lee straight in the eye, a man looking at another man. "I'll be all right. You're not going to do this."

Lee planted his bootheels in the soft dirt of the river bank, set himself, and hauled back on the rope as hard as he could.

Sandburg yelled something and grabbed hold too, pulling with all his strength. And Tom Cooke picked up the bitter end, put it over his shoulder, and pulled along with them.

The cowboy rose up off the ground in a slow swinging surge, staring as he went up into the air. It was as if so far he thought everything was all right, just a surprise to be swung up into the air like that. He was only a few feet off the ground.

Then he tried to breathe and couldn't. His face got very red, dark red, and he kicked and heaved himself and spun in slow circles at the end of the rope. After the first few times he kicked, he stopped moving and just hung there staring up into the willow. His eyes were red with blood where the little vessels in them had broken.

Tom Cooke had tied the rope end off on a sapling larch. The three of them had nothing to do but watch.

The cowboy hung still like that for a few moments, then he started to kick again, but more slowly, pulling his knees up high, almost to his chest, and then kicking down, first with one foot, then the other. Very slowly, spinning a little from the twist of the rope.

Then the hanged man stopped doing that, and Lee could smell the odor of shit coming from him. There was a black stain growing on the seat of his pants.

"That's it, that's the finish of the son-of-a-bitch!" Sandburg said. "You smell what he did in his pants?"

"All right," Lee said. He felt tired of the whole thing. "Let's go bury your boy, Ole . . ."

None of them had much to say when they had Jake

Sandburg's hole dug beside Rifle River. They'd dug it with their sheath knives and a split stick across on the west bank, away from the hanged man, and they'd wrapped the boy in a blanket.

Ole picked him up and put him in the grave without wanting any help from Lee or the Blackfoot. Then he took his saddle canteen and filled it at the river, and put that in with the boy.

Lee didn't know if that was something religious, maybe Lutheran, or whether Ole had slipped with grief. Tom Cooke seemed to think it was natural enough, though.

"Oh, my God . . ." Sandburg said. "Oh, my God." Then he couldn't seem to think of anything more to say. He stood looking down at young Jake lying there wrapped in the blanket without saying anything else.

"All right, Ole," Lee said. "You go and catch up the horses. We'll take care of things here." He took Sandburg by the arm and gave him a little push. "Go on, I said . . ."

And Sandburg turned and walked away with his head down, like a man thinking hard.

And that I'd bet you are, Lee thought, watching him go. You poor son-of-a-bitch . . . was thinking just what Lee had thought after Rosilie was killed, and what Tom Cooke after his mama died. They were alone, all alone now.

Lee and Tom Cooke kicked the dirt back in the grave and then got stones from the river bank to cover it with, to keep the coyotes and wolves from digging the boy up. They heaped up quite a number of them.

"And them?" said Tom Cooke when they'd finished, gesturing with his head across the river.

"Let them lie and hang and rot on both sides of the river," Lee said. And he turned and walked away to the meadow, where Ole Sandburg was standing with the saddle horses. He'd unhobbled the stud, and Shokan was pacing and trotting around the grassy field, nickering and nipping at his mares, the big appaloosa's spotted white hide rippling over his muscles as he moved.

There's a handsome sight, Lee thought. There's a creature on this mountain that isn't unhappy at all . . .

"Let's mount and move," he said. "I want to be home by dark."

It looked to be a pretty evening.

Lee rode a little ahead, and Tom Cooke and Sandburg rode back with the cavvy, keeping the stud and the mares moving down the mountain.

Lee looked back to make sure the colts weren't tiring. The rustlers must have pushed the horse herd hard. But they were lively as June bugs, racing each other around the herd, prancing up to the mares to nuzzle at their teats and then tossing their heads and trotting away to play again.

He saw a little filly, racing after a colt a month older than she was—and catching him. Fast, and so pretty. Lee thought he might call her Lightning Bug.

When they got down to the east ridge, it was nearly dark. Sandburg and Tom Cooke eased away from the appaloosas and let the herd spread out into the fields above the ranch buildings.

Sandburg rode on down to the ranch without saying anything, but Tom Cooke came up to Lee for orders.

"Nothing more tonight," Lee said. "Go on down and get something to eat. And try and see if Sandburg will have something."

Tom Cooke nodded and started to turn away, but Lee called after him, "Do you know what that old cowboy's name was?"

"His name Charley."

110

"Charley what?"

The young Blackfoot shrugged and turned his horse away.

"Well," Lee said angrily to the empty air. "Well, I'll kill any man who tries to take what's mine . . ."

CHAPTER EIGHT

The next week they worked at putting up the long rough-plank fences for the horse pastures. It was dawn-to-dark work, and it sweated some of the badness of Jake's death out of them.

Ole Sandburg had started the week with nothing to say, either to Lee or to Tom Cooke, but splitting the planks out of raw timber, dragging them down to the pastures, setting the posts, and finally nailing the horizontals straight and true, gradually worked the sorrow and the silence out of him. By the end of the week, Ole could talk about Jake, and was telling Lee about what a brave little boy he'd been, up on a horse when he was only five, and running stock into a corral like a Mex *vaquero*.

The week had done them all good. And no trouble about the supplies. Tom Cooke had ridden down the morning after the fight to bring the wagon up and had found it undisturbed, the pack horses safe, but restless, tugging at their tethers to reach fresh grass. So the supplies all came up, but even so, they ran short of nails. Lee sent Ole down to town for them at the end of the week and wrote a note for him to take to the marshal when he got there.

Lee wrote Phipps only a few lines telling him what had happened. He mentioned the names of two of the rustlers, the only ones that Lee knew: Charley and Tom Small.

Lee'd been thinking about George Small during the week. Tom's older brother, the cowboy had said. Well, he had to be pretty old by now. From what Lee remembered hearing, George Small had been a bad man on the Missouri border before the war. That would make the man at least fifty by now, maybe older. A ring-tail terror in his day, he must be a little slower by now, though. A little smarter, too, it could be.

And it could be that he wouldn't give a good damn what had happened to his little brother, that cutthroat son-of-a-bitch.

And it could be that he would.

And Ashton would be certain to let him know his brother was dead, when Phipps told him what had happened to his men.

The afternoon of the day he'd sent Ole Sandburg to town, Lee rode out over the east ridge to have a look at his borderline with Fishhook. If Ashton was hunting trouble that hard that he'd send rustlers and a killer out to take Lee's stock, then it was just as well that Lee saw how the land lay between them.

He'd taken a hunk of deer meat and a pocket full of store crackers with him when he rode. They'd have to get some steers on the place soon for beef. Once he'd ridden over the ridge, and down through the trees, he drew the dun up under a clump of beech trees, swung out of the saddle, tied the big gelding off, and sat with his back against a tree trunk, his canteen in his lap, for a little country lunch.

The venison was tough and chewy, but it had the sweetness of wild meat, the tang and sharpness to it. Lee wished he'd brought some salt with him, just a pinch, but there was salt on the crackers, and he made do. Some cheese would have been nice, too. He reminded himself to buy some store cheese when next he went down to Cree. Hell, no reason he shouldn't buy a full ten-pound round of that sharp yellow cheese that stuck to the roof of your mouth first, then stuck to your ribs.

He was chewing a mouthful of crackers and looking out over the rolling, broken, open land that lay beneath him, when he saw the horseman.

A man in a plaid shirt, riding what looked like a good little chestnut mare. Cutting back and forth through the brush in the low places down there, coming Lee's way. No way to tell who it was from this distance, even if Lee had known any of the people around there . . .

The rider was heading on for River Ranch land.

And he was coming careful.

Lee took a long drink out of his canteen, and then stood up, brushing the cracker crumbs off his pants. The horseman was out of sight for a moment now, riding along the bottom of a scrub-larch draw.

Lee loosed the dun and swung up into the saddle, leaning back to check that the Sharps was riding safe in its scabbard. He spurred the dun off to the right, to cut the horseman's path at the edge of the mountain woods.

He held the gelding down to an easy canter; the stranger still had a good way to go. The thought of George Small crossed his mind, but this man was younger. He rode like a young man, limber and light in the saddle.

Lee rode along, just below the ridgeline. He didn't think the man could have seen him before, and he didn't intend for the man to see him now. And if he hadn't been on the ridge this afternoon? Then the horseman would have come down on them, down the ridge to the ranch buildings, and they wouldn't have known it until he started shooting. It was a disadvantage, that way, trying to run a ranch with three men hired—two men, now that Jake was dead, and not counting Tim Bupp. There weren't enough men to circuit ride the land.

Lee was into the woods now, and he bent forward on the dun's withers to keep the beech limbs from knocking him out of the saddle. He broke out into a small clearing, then spurred the gelding on into the woods again. The trees were more scattered here, and Lee lifted the dun into a lope. The wind was blowing from the east, and the trespasser hopefully wouldn't be able to hear the hoofbeats.

When he broke out of the woods a second time, Lee found himself on a small rise overlooking the steep reverse slope of the ridge. He reined the gelding in and scanned the country below.

Nothing.

He was just turning the dun's head to ride further down the ridge when he caught a flicker of movement off to the left. The rider's mare just stepping down into a wooden draw. Lee glimpsed just the touch of blue from the man's shirt, the look of a broad-brimmed straw hat—and he was gone.

It was working out just fine. That nice steep draw would bring the horseman up onto the slope into deep brush; he wouldn't see shit for a hundred yards.

It was a chance for Lee to take the man alive. No dead rustler to write to Phipps about, no cowboy to have to hang, but a *live* man to take to Butte or Helena to testify. And to put some hot spurs to Ashton. This was far enough north for Lee to take the chance on being recognized. There wouldn't be many Rebecca Chases waiting around the federal judge's courtroom up there . . .

Lee spurred the dun on, driving the big horse deep into the brush, bending low over the saddle so that his Stetson took most of the whipping from the limber branches.

When the gelding's hoofs clattered on the rocky shelving of the draw, Lee reined him in and leaned forward over the horse's neck to gently grip his soft nose and quiet him. He didn't want any nickering to warn the on-coming rider.

The dun sidled restlessly for a moment and then eased, only shaking his head a little under Lee's

115

restraining hand.

For a few minutes, there was almost no sound at all in the woods, except for the chatter and scurry of a pair of red squirrels running through the tangle of larch and mountain willow. When the squirrels were gone, there was only the murmur of the wind gently combing through the brush.

Then Lee heard the horse coming, the slight crush and snap of scrub twigs under its hoofs. Yes, a mare for sure, to be moving so lightly.

The horse and rider were still off to his left and a little below him. Still climbing up through the draw.

Lee closed his eyes for a moment, trying to remember exactly what the horseman had looked like when he'd had that long look at him, riding far in the distance. Young. And slight. A revolver worn high up on his right hip. Maybe a .38. And a Winchester, likely a Winchester, in a front saddleboot.

The mare was closer now.

Lee'd known a man once who'd carried his pistol high on the right like that. But that sure as hell wasn't this man. Pace had been a big man, bony as Abe Lincoln. And still was, as far as Lee knew; he hadn't heard of the Texas gunman being shot in the back yet. Which was about the only way anybody was going to kill Frank Pace.

No, this was a much smaller man, and Lee didn't know him. But he rode in a way that seemed familiar . . .

The horseman was up out of the draw. The dun shifted nervously under Lee as the other horse came on—no more than forty feet away now.

Thirty.

Twenty. The rider would be passing only a dozen feet in front of Lee, unseen in the thick greenery.

Lee let him get just abreast. Then he kicked spurs to the dun.

The big horse erupted out of the foliage like a bat out of hell. As they smashed free of the brush, Lee was already shaking his boots free of the stirrups. As the dun thundered down on the rearing, terrified chestnut mare, Lee left the saddle in a long, driving dive to pile into the rider.

He struck the man hard enough to knock him clear out of the saddle. They fell together in a tangled heap into the scrub. Lee held the man away with his left hand—must be only a boy, not very strong—and went for his boot knife with the other. But, boy or not, the man was kicking hard, trying to get free of Lee's grip. Lee remembered that .38 and lunged again as the knife came free into his hand, piling on top of the man, driving him back down into the brush, staying on top of him, trying to pin him with his knees.

Then he was on him. He had his knees biting into the man's arms, pinning him good. And he had his fingers in the man's hair, yanking his head back to set the knife blade at his throat.

"Now, you little son—"

India Ashton lay beneath him, pale as death, her blue eyes wide with terror.

For a moment, Lee stayed crouched over her, frozen, the knife blade still held to her throat. Then he cursed and rolled away, got to his feet, slid the knife back into his boot, staring down at her.

India Ashton lay in the crushed foilage looking up at him, still pale with shock. The straw hat had been torn from her head, and the long, golden-white hair had fallen loose, swirling in the greenery around her shoulders, bright as sunlight. Her man's plaid shirt had been ripped leaving a slim, ivory-pale shoulder bare to the world.

Suddenly, recovering, the girl struggled to sit up, glaring at Lee.

"How—how *dare* you. You tried to kill me!"

Lee reached down a hand to help her up, but she slapped it aside and clambered to her feet without his help.

"I'm very sorry, Miss Ashton. I didn't recognize you."

"And do you go around the country attacking people you don't recognize, Mr. Lee?" The lovely, aristocratic face was pink with rage. Her hands trembled as she tried to pat her hair back into some kind of order, then brushed futilely at the twigs and leaves covering her denim pants. She tugged the torn shirt over her bare shoulder.

"Strange men who come onto my land through the woods, I do," Lee said. He knew his own face was red; he'd made a prime fool of himself, and there were no two ways about it. His quarrel with Ashton now looked like it might become a personal matter, with the man's sister being handled this way. For an instant, Lee's blood chilled at the thought that he might have used his gun and not been close enough to see what he'd done until it was too late. The thought made him feel a little sick.

"Well . . . I think that you are a rough, loutish fool, Mr. Lee!" She was looking around for her mare. "And you have frightened off Sally—and maybe hurt her!"

"I'll go catch up with your mare." India Ashton was a beauty, no doubt about it, and she had her share of guts, too. Most well-bred women would be in a faint or hysterics at being handled so roughly.

"I'll find her, *I'll* find her, Mr. Lee. I don't want your help . . ."

Lee tried to calm her down. "Now, please listen, Miss Ashton, we've—we've had some trouble up here . . ."

She turned as cold as ice and bent down to pick up her hat. "I'm sure I'm not interested in your difficulties at River Ranch, Mr. Lee. Now, if you will just catch my mare, I can be on my way. I can tell you, though, that

118

the men of this country don't approve of bullies attacking women who are riding alone and minding their own business."

"And what was your business up here, Miss Ashton?" Lee said. "This ridge is a roundabout way of getting to the ranch house, if you were coming visiting."

"I was not 'coming visiting,' " she said, with a toss of her head. "I—I was out looking for a friend." She bit her lip and looked around through the brush, searching for her mare.

"Come on," Lee said and took her arm. "We'll find the mare. I don't think she was hurt."

She looked down with a grimace of distaste, then pulled her arm away from his hand. "I'd prefer that you kept your hands to yourself, Mr. Lee."

"All right." Lee gritted his teeth to keep his temper. After all, it had been his damn stupid mistake. He was lucky he hadn't hurt her. "Follow me, then. Chances are she's with my dun, and he's not much of a strayer."

Lee led the way out of the thickets into a small clearing and stood looking for the horses as the girl kicked her way out of the brush behind him.

"They're probably further down."

When she said nothing, Lee started off into the woods, heading downslope of the ridge. The dun would likely be grazing in the first lush patch of bear grass it came to. It was rough going for a man on foot, the land being tangled with scrub and broken and scarred by run-off water and lightning fires. Lee went on his way and didn't offer to help the girl when she stumbled into thorn patches or over fallen timber.

It was the damnedest thing. To have been so foolish as to take her for a boy, anyway. And after seeing her twice, even at a distance, he sure as hell should have known better. And he'd even recognized the way she rode. He remembered thinking that just before he'd jumped her.

"Would you mind not going so fast?"

She still sounded mad as hell. Probably ashamed of having been so frightened when he'd knocked her off her horse. She must have thought him stark crazy . . .

He stepped over a fallen larch log and stood waiting for her to catch up. She didn't look quite the perfect lady now, tugging her way through a patch of wild blackberry. Lee had seen whores wearing pants, of course, and some tough old ranch wives wore them too in order to do their chores. But this was the first time he'd seen a pair on a lady. Maybe getting wrestled off her horse would teach her to stick to dresses and side-saddles.

When she climbed over the log to join him, she was panting from her effort and had to stand for a moment to catch her breath.

"You said you were out looking for a friend?"

She gave Lee an odd sidewise glance. "Yes . . . yes, I was. A—a guest at Fishhook. He rode out with some of our men some days ago to gather stock. But they should all have been back by now."

"A man?"

She flushed. "Yes. A friend of my brother. A business acquaintance—if it is any affair of yours!" She was getting angry again.

Lee started to turn away. There hadn't been any stray dude wandering the range that he'd seen. Suddenly, he stopped. There was no reason for it, no reason to be so sure. But he *knew*.

"What was this man's name?"

He could see she was puzzled by his tone, the look in his face. She flushed again.

"The gentleman's name is Thomas Small," she said.

She had started to walk on down the slope when Lee reached out and gripped her arm.

"Oh, how dare—"

Lee had her by both arms now.

"You said Tom Small?"

120

"Yes, I did . . ." She stared up at him, frightened, puzzled by the look on his face.

"He meant something to you, Miss Ashton?"

"He . . ." Her face reddened. "Mr. Small is a . . . a friend."

Of course. Lee remembered the tall man, the handsome, smiling face with the dashing cavalry mustache. Smiling. "You're an uninvited guest," the man had called to him just before Lee'd killed him.

"Now, will you take your hands off—"

"He's dead," Lee said.

For a moment, she didn't seem to understand, didn't seem to hear. "Let me loose, damn you! What did you say?" Her eyes widened. Her voice was shaking.

"I said, your friend is dead." And if she'd loved the cutthroat son-of-a-bitch, so much the worse for her.

India Ashton sagged suddenly in his hands, almost falling to her knees. "No, no, no," she said, rapidly, over and over. "You're mistaken . . . you're mistaken."

She straightened suddenly and pulled away from him.

"What are you saying?" Tears were in her eyes now, tears of rage. "You fool! You don't know what you're talking about! You don't even know him!"

And what the hell could he say to that? The news hadn't reached Fishhook yet.

"He was shot . . ." Lee said.

"Shot? Shot? What are you talking about?" She looked wildly around, as if she were trapped in a nightmare. "Nobody would shoot Tom . . ."

Lee cursed Ashton for keeping a handsome killer in his house for his own sister to stumble over.

"He and the men with him . . . they stole some of my horses . . ."

The girl looked up at him as if he'd gone crazy, as if he were speaking some foreign language she couldn't understand.

"They stole my horses and they killed a boy." No

121

need to tell her it was handsome Tom who'd cut poor Jake Sandburg's throat.

"You—oh, you dirty, dirty liar!" she screamed at Lee. She backed away from him, shaking her head.

Lee held out his hand to her and spoke softly, trying to calm her. "Small was a gunman, Miss Ashton, a killer. I'm sorry."

"Shot?" she said, staring at him. Now she believed it.

"I'm afraid so." Lee hoped to God she'd calmed down. She must have been head over heels in love with that bastard.

"How was he killed?" she said. "How was he shot?"

"He and those cowboys came up here and drove off my stock . . ."

She was staring at him, her eyes as wide as a child's.

"A man of mine—a kid named Jake Sandburg—followed them over to the river. He held them at the ford."

She didn't say anything. Just stood there, watching Lee talk.

"They killed the boy. Then, when we came up, there was a fight. That's when Small was killed." How the hell could he make something like this easier? "I sent word down to the marshal and, well, I'm sorry."

"You killed him, didn't you?" she said, in an odd, dead voice. "You killed him, didn't you, Mr. Lee?"

Christ.

"He . . . he came at me with a gun in his hand, Miss Ash—"

He saw her move, but he couldn't believe it. With a quick, awkward clawing of her hand, she had reached down to her hip to draw her .38 pistol on him.

He had just time to see how funny it all was: Buckskin Frank Leslie drawn on and shot dead by a pretty English lady. In the next instant, he moved. There was no drawing against her; better to be killed than do that. He would have to get his hands on that gun before she had time for a shot.

The .38 was out now and starting to level; she'd have time for a first shot before he reached her.

The gun went off in his face. He felt a blaze of pain along his ribs, and he had her, had his hand on the gun, twisting, tearing it out of her grasp. He got it, and he turned, still holding her by the wrist as she spat and struck at him. He threw the revolver away into the brush.

Then he glanced down at his side. The bullet had drilled through the material of his shirt and burned across his ribs. A slow, slight stain of blood was marking the faded cotton.

Suddenly, Lee felt a rush of fury. The stupid bitch had almost killed him. If she'd had time for another shot, she probably would have! And all for a cutthroat killer, a child killer.

He swung his other hand hard into the girl's raging, contorted face. The blow sent her staggering, and he deliberately hit her again. She fell, and they went down together into the thick meadow grass, she scratching at him, trying to bite his forearm as he held her pinned down.

Lee raised his open hand again.

"Stop it! Stop it, God damn you, or I'll beat the hell out of you."

She subsided, panting, glaring up at him like a trapped animal.

"Now, you listen to me," Lee ground out, "you spoiled bitch! That grinning bastard Small was the one that killed my man. He cut the throat of a boy fifteen years old! And then the bastard came at me with a gun in his hand. Did I kill him? Hell, lady, I shot the living shit out of him!"

"You're lying." She was starting to weep, struggling to get out from under him.

He never knew why he did it. Why he started. Maybe it was her crying like that. Maybe the feeling of her held so close.

He bent down and kissed her mouth.

She convulsed under him desperately. Lee found himself gripping her hard, bearing her down into the grass, kissing her soft mouth with a kind of murderous hunger.

She tried to twist away, to bite at his lips; but he paid no attention, though she bit him till his lips bled. He clamped his mouth to hers as if his life depended on it, kissing, sucking, loving her.

And his hands were on her now, pulling, tearing at her plaid shirt, ripping it open, yanking down the soft cloth of her undershirt to expose her small breasts. And his hands were on them, gripping the delicate white flesh.

She screamed, pushing at him, trying to shove him away, but Lee bent lower to suckle at the soft, pouting pink nipples, biting at them, licking them.

She groaned as he turned and held her to him as he unbuckled her pants belt and reached down to pull the material down over her hips. She tried to kick out at him, but the cloth was down at her ankles now, binding her, leaving her thrashing helplessly under him as he slid his hand to her groin.

She screamed again. "Oh, please don't . . . oh, please!" He touched her, gently cupping her in his hand, the downy chevron of her sex, white blond against the snow-white of her skin.

Lee forced his fingers into her, thrusting into her roughly, feeling the warm moistness close around them. He drove his hand against her hard, the damp, soft petals of her sex against his palm.

She gasped and suddenly lay still, not struggling against him anymore.

Lee thought she had finished, but she hadn't. She lay looking up at him, her face blank, pale with shock. Lee tried to make himself stop. He knew he should. He knew he'd already done enough, more than enough to deserve hanging . . . like that poor old bastard of a cowboy. Poor Charley. And he was no goddamned better!

But he couldn't. He couldn't stop himself. She was there. And he was there. And now, she was naked against him . . .

He reached down and unbuckled his trousers, kicked them down. He was hard as iron; so hard that it hurt him.

"Ah, Christ," he said, and lifted up, placed the swollen head of his cock against her softness, her dampness.

"Ah, Christ." He thrust into her. Pushing, pushing at first, against the soft fur, her small cleft. Then into her, in a steady, hot slippery thrust. In. In all the way.

She was tight in there. Wet, and hot, and tight. It felt as though a whore was sucking on him, sucking hard on the whole length of him.

The girl was no virgin. He remembered the smiling killer standing high on the ledge above him. "Uninvited guest . . ." the words echoed in his mind.

Then Lee thought of nothing.

He began driving into her. Driving into her so hard that he felt her slight body shaking from the thrusts. She was grunting a little as he fucked her, grunting each time he sank deep into her.

Lee groaned with pleasure. It was sweet. Sweet . . .

She gasped when he went into her harder and deeper. He ground his cock into her, twisting his body, driving into her as if he were trying to nail her to the ground.

She cried out and reached up to twist her fingers in his hair, to tug, to push his head away; he felt her slim bare legs writhe against his naked thighs. And he kept at her—in and out, in and out. He could feel her warm breath panting against his throat. There were wet sounds coming from between them now. He could smell the delicate salt smell of her sex as it began to run with wet.

Suddenly, she let go of his hair, stopped trying to

push him away. Lee felt her hands clutching at his shoulders. She made a hoarse groaning sound, and he felt her legs thrash and kick against him.

"Oh, Tom!" she screamed. And he looked down and saw her weeping wildly, her head turning from side to side as he thrust into her. "Oh, ohhh . . . Tommy . . . Tommy!"

An uninvited guest.

She bucked under him, the long, slender white legs thrust high in the air, straining up, her feet arched in an agony of pleasure. She was soaking now, her cunt made a sucking sound as he fucked into her.

Then it came. It came for him first. It seemed to come pouring out of him in a flood, as if his back was breaking from the pleasure of it. He called out and shot into her, spurt after spurt. It never seemed to stop.

And she writhed and heaved against him with astonishing strength, and drew up her knees and moaned as if she were giving birth, her face and small white breasts flushing deep pink as she came. She stared blindly up into Lee's eyes, groaning softly in ecstasy.

"I'm sorry," Lee said, as she sat silent in the grass, trying to button her torn shirt around her. "There's no forgiving what I did . . .

He walked down into the meadow, searching.

After a few minutes, he came back to her. He had her .38 in his hand. She was standing now, brushing the grass from her trousers.

"Here." He handed the weapon to her. "Go ahead and use it, if you want."

He stood there, waiting.

But the girl just put the gun back in its holster. Then she looked at him, and it was a grim look.

"Not for me," she said, and shook her head. "For Tom. It's for Tom Small that I'm going to see you dead."

And she walked past him, down the meadow slope, to find her mare.

CHAPTER NINE

For the next three days, Lee tried to get it out of his mind, tried to forget what he'd done. It wasn't easy. He'd never thought of himself as a hardcase, as the kind of man who'd do any damn thing he pleased.

He'd thought—he'd hoped—that he was a better man than that. A man, not a dog. Well, now it looked like maybe that wasn't so. It seemed that there was still a lot of Frank Leslie left in Mr. Lee, and a badness, a cruelty, that had nothing to do with being forced into a fight or having to fight or hurt someone to save himself. No excuse for this last thing. No excuse.

And now, if India told her brother what he'd done, it would be a killing matter sure—and a killing with dirt on it. Forgetting the rustling, young Jake's death, he'd be shooting Ashton down for defending his sister, for going up against the man who'd raped her. A dirty killing.

Lee found himself hoping the girl would be too ashamed, after all, to tell Ashton what had happened between them. And that very hope was cowardly.

For the first time since Rosilie had died, Lee felt glad that there was something about him that she would never know. That was the worst feeling of all. It was as if he had spoiled her memory, spoiled it in a way that all the casual girls he had taken since her death couldn't. Rosilie would never have grudged him any kind of love;

128

but what he'd done to that grief-crazed girl had nothing to do with that. Nothing to do with love at all.

He threw himself into his ranch work, driving himself from first light to pitch dark; fencing, cutting timber and firewood, mucking out the old stables clear down to fresh mountain clay—and working with the horses.

Those were the best times, the times that gave him peace, that helped him best to forget that afternoon in the bear grass with India Ashton.

They were working out the colts, starting to halter train them, get them used to being led, to being held gently on a long rope. It was delicate work. The same intelligence and spirit that made the appaloosas so valuable as mounts in rough, dangerous country made them very tender to train. A beating, even a quick cut with a rope's end—even a harsh word at the wrong time—and the lively, lean-limbed little colts would balk and shy, losing their trust in the noisy, tobacco-smelling men who held them prisoners at the end of thirty feet of hemp.

In a way, treating the little soft-eyed colts with gentleness, coaxing them, stroking them into obedience, seemed to make up, somehow, for the cruel way he'd manhandled the girl on that damned afternoon.

So Lee worked himself into exhaustion, and he trained the little horses. And he waited for the hour when Nigel Ashton would come riding over the ridge, coming to kill the man who'd raped his sister.

Three days went by, and no horsemen came riding over the ridge—none but Sandburg and Tim Bupp, coming back from town.

Lee was glad to see the old man; it was good to have him back on the place. Bupp, although full of complaints about Mrs. Boltwith's tyranny and foolishness, was now almighty proud of his cooking, and indeed could make a fair steak, a good stew (though a little short of pepper), and a reasonable, if somewhat watery, dried-apple pie. He was still pretty weak on eggs; it seemed hard for him to keep his mind on them early in the morning, and they were usually tough enough to need some knife work to really subdue them.

Still, it was good to have the old man on the place. He got on well with Sandburg. One day, out of the blue, he said to the Swede, "I sure am damn sorry, Ole, I never got to meet that boy of yours. I hear that boy was something prime!"

Lee was working on a fenceline nearby, and when he heard what Bupp said, he paused, expecting trouble. But all that Sandburg did was sigh sadly and nod.

"He was the best boy ever in the world," he said.

And that was that.

For four more days, Lee and the others worked the main range. Then it was time to ride circuit. Lee felt like doing it himself; it would mean another week, maybe two, out in the rough, far from meeting any other people for any reason. It was a hard temptation for him. Too much of a temptation. He decided to send Sandburg and Tom Cooke out; Bupp could handle the home chores while they rode the circuit. And Lee would go into town.

There was no use ducking it. After almost two weeks, Ashton had not come riding to revenge the deaths of his paid rustlers or his sister's rape. If Lee met the man in town, then he met him—and the devil take the hindmost.

Dawn on a Thursday morning, Lee had a long talk with Tom Cooke, Sandburg and Bupp. He trusted them now; any one of the three was as good a hand, as good a friend, as a man might find or make in a few weeks in a strange country.

They were to ride careful and well armed. Lee knew that Ashton, who must have his own reasons for not bucking Lee directly, would not have forgotten or for-given the deaths of his men. Lee was now certain that India hadn't told her brother what had happened to her.

Tom Cooke and Sandburg were to ride together, even if that cost them time in covering the ground. And if they found Fishhook stock on River range, they were to just drift it back over the line. Lee had no patience with killing animals for people's quarrels.

"And, Tim," he said to Bupp, "you keep a carbine handy while you work around the place. One way or another, sooner or later, there'll be trouble coming."

"Now, that's nice stuff to hear," Bupp said. "I suppose I'm supposed to sleep real good after hearing that stuff!"

"Just sleep light," Lee said.

Lee swung up on the gelding and left the three of them standing in the ranch house yard looking after him. It made him feel peculiar to know they were so dependent on him. It made him uncomfortable. It was one of the uncomfortable things about bossing a property: having men bound to you. It meant he had to think about them all the time, in whatever he did. Just as he was thinking now about what might happen if Ashton sent some more people onto the land to rustle.

If that happened, he was sure to lose a man whichever way it went. Tom Cooke? Sandburg? Old Bupp? And if he did, what the hell would that man be dying for? Some big-name gunman's second chance? Frank Leslie's new life? Why should one of those good men die for that?

It made Lee uncomfortable just thinking about it. He tried to put it out of his mind, but it went hard. There would have been just about time for a telegram to get to Missouri, or wherever Tom Small's big brother was holed up, to tell him to come gunning. Ashton must have sent that wire; he'd have been a damn fool not to. And if he had, and George Small came riding up to the ranch in the next two or three days, Lee wouldn't be there. No sirree. The new owner of the River Ranch would be sitting on his ass in Cree, waiting for a crate of horse medicine and a bank draft from Nogales, Old Mexico.

The Don's last payment, overdue but welcome. And damned well earned, too, since Lee had taken a .44-.40 slug in the muscle of his leg keeping the old bandit alive.

If Small came to the ranch while Lee was gone, he'd kill all three of those men. Cooke and Sandburg had guts enough, and probably so did old Bupp. But that wouldn't help them against a man like Small, even if he was past his prime. A normal man, even a brave one who might have killed a man or two, just couldn't stand against a shootist like George Small, even if he was getting old. Small must have done—a hundred men in his day, and maybe half of those in face-to-face fights.

An ordinary man would have no chance against him. No chance against someone who'd done a hundred killings and remembered how each one had gone. A man so familiar with killing, with death, that the most desperate fight was like an old friend—that familiar and comfortable.

No. If George Small came to Cree Valley, God send him to town and not out to River Ranch.

The dun was a little overworked from day after day of hard labor, though Lee had tried to spare him and used the remuda horses when he could. Truth was, they could use another few good cutters on the place. And he hadn't yet done what he promised and got a nice pinto for Tom Cooke to keep. That had to be done, too. But one thing: they sure as hell weren't going to work the appaloosas until they were ready for it, and that wouldn't be for a few months, anyway. The mares could do with a little riding, maybe. Tom Cooke was too rough, but old Bupp had good hands.

Cree looked empty in daylight when Lee drew the dun

up in the rise outside of town. It would be another day and night befor the wagons full of lumberjacks came rumbling in from the northern mountains. The Fishhook and Bent Iron men rode in from the valley.

Lee cantered the dun down through the town, across the alley behind the general store, and out into main street. There was nothing there that afternoon but a dusty line of buggies at the store and a couple more rigs tethered up by Martin's Yarn, Dress & Knits store. Lee wondered how it was that Kimble hadn't been able to get his hands on that store; he owned just about every other mercantile in town. Martin—male or female—must be a pretty tough customer, commercially speaking.

As Lee rode by, he bent in the saddle to look into the display window. There were three or four women in the place, shopping, and a squat, frog-looking man with a measuring tape across his shoulders was waiting on them. Mr. Martin. And he looked tough enough to give old Kimble a hard time.

It made Lee feel good to think of Cree as his home town now, with all the storekeepers and businessmen, saloon people and whores, ostlers and stablemen, drummers, lawyers, lumbermen—all of them his neighbors in a way. All of them people he might know for years now. Maybe for the rest of his life.

It was what people meant by the word home. A home town.

If Ashton let him alone. If Rebecca Chase kept her mouth shut. If . . .

A farm family came rumbling down the graveled street in a big overloaded wagon. A tall, rawboned man with a worn, lined face. His small, work-worn wife. Three kids—no, four kids; one had just been rooting around down in the wagonload of vegetables. There was a hard life. Lee didn't see how a man, a family, could bear it, farming up so high in the mountain country.

133

What the hell could they grow so high, with the winters as cold and long as they must be? Cabbages, it looked like from the wagonload. Cabbages and cauliflowers. To work your heart out to raise cabbages and cauliflowers! It struck him that farming was the strangest way of life of them all.

He reined the dun over to the front of Mrs. Boltwith's hotel, swung out of the saddle with a grunt of fatigue, and tied off the reins at the hitching post.

For a change, the steps were clear; the ostlers must be at the stables, the harness drummers and whiskey drummers out on their rounds. Nobody to stare at the man who'd killed Mickey Slawson.

The man who'd raped India Ashton . . .

Mrs. Boltwith was seated at the little hotel desk just under the foot of the stairs. Her bulk made the desk look even smaller. Mrs. Boltwith was in yellow print today, looking like a lady schoolteacher with her spectacles. She looked up when Lee came through the front door and gave him a cool greeting nod.

"Mr. Lee."

"Any room in the inn, Mrs. Boltwith?"

She nodded again.

Mrs. Boltwith was definitely angry about something, and it couldn't be losing Bupp's help in her kitchen.

She led the way up the narrow stairs.

"How long are you going to be staying, Mr. Lee?"

"Probably three days. I'm waiting for a bank draft."

She stopped at the end of the first-floor hallway, at the door to the small room Lee had slept in before, and silently handed him the key.

Might as well meet it head on.

"Is anything troubling you, Mrs. Boltwith?"

She gave Lee a hard look. "Now that you ask, Mr. Lee, yes, there is something troubling me." She hesitated for a moment, then cleared her throat. "I just don't think . . . I just don't think much of a grown man

134

that will mistreat a woman."

Lee felt sick to his stomach. He had thought—hell, he had hoped—that India Ashton hadn't told anybody about what had happened. And it looked as though a hope was all that it was.

"When I introduce a friend of mine," Mrs. Boltwith continued, "to a person I consider a gentleman, I expect that person to *act* like a gentleman and not be discourteous and rude to as nice a young girl as ever drew breath."

For a moment Lee didn't know what the hell she was talking about. Then, with a rush of relief, he realized the old dragon wasn't meaning India Ashton at all; she was talking about that little whore, Beatrice. He'd been pretty short with her, he remembered. And that's what had the old hen's tail feathers in a fluff.

"Beatrice Morgan," Mrs. Boltwith continued, "is a nice girl."

"I'm sure you're right, ma'am," Lee said. "I guess I was a little short with her, a little rude . . ."

"Yes, you were. And Beatrice assumed it was because of her trade . . ."

"Now, Mrs. Boltwith, you know it was no such thing," Lee said. "I've been around enough to know better than that." He turned to unlock his door. "But if I upset her, I'll be glad to apologize."

Mrs. Boltwith appeared satisfied with that and gave Lee a pleasant horse-faced smile as he stepped into his room.

Lee tossed his saddlebags down on the bed and went to the washstand, splashed some water from the big china pitcher into the bowl, and washed his hands and face, wetting his hair and combing it back with his fingers. He looked up into the mirror over the stand. No San Francisco dandy there; no gunman or pimp, either. This man looked like a worried, weather-worn, money-short horse rancher. And, by God, that was no lie.

He brushed some of the trail dust from his buckskin jacket, eased his gunbelt on his hips, gave his dusty boots a quick wipe with his bandanna—no dandy, now, for sure!—and left the room, locking the door behind him.

Mrs. Boltwith wasn't behind the desk at the bottom of the stairs, and the front steps were still clear of stable hands and drummers. Lee went down the steps, out across the high boardwalk, and down to the dusty street. The gravel they laid on the road kept a lot of the dust down, but not all of it.

He walked diagonally across the street toward the Arcady. A cold beer would go down very well. They should have their beer on ice, this close to the mountains. And while he was at it, he'd give Rebecca Chase a little look-in, just to remind her to keep her mouth shut concerning that vanished gunman, Buckskin Frank Leslie. A reminder never hurt.

As he went up the steps to the Arcady's swinging doors, Lee noticed a row of cow ponies tied along the rail outside. There was a very nice roan gelding among them. Damn near a thoroughbred, by the look of him.

It registered on him just too late who the hell that thoroughbred belonged to.

Too late. He was already through the doors.

The big bar room was almost empty. It looked as though Cree was a serious working town not heavy on afternoon drinking, at all.

Almost empty.

Not quite.

Six cowboys were lined up along the far end of the bar. A relief barman was serving them beers in ice-frosted mugs.

Standing at the head of the line was another man. Not a cowboy. Not by a long shot. He was bigger than the other men, for one thing—damn near six and a half feet, Lee thought—and he was burly as a bear. But there

136

was more to him than that. The man was a foreigner for sure. His hair was carrot red, and he wore a broad, curling beard the same bright ginger shade. He was wearing a moleskin jacket and a white, stiff-collar shirt, a curl-brim derby, and a pair of riding breeches and long-top English boots.

There was only one man it could be, and Lee was mortified to feel himself ashamed to face him. It was India's brother, Nigel Ashton.

Then Lee remembered Jake Sandburg lying dead with a cut throat—by this man's allowance for sure, if not his direct orders—and he felt less ashamed. This foreign son-of-a-bitch was no better than any other man, and worse than most.

The cowboys had looked up when Lee came in, and the big, red-headed Englishman had looked up too. He had small, bright blue eyes. Then they went back to their beers. They hadn't recognized him. No reason they should; they hadn't seen him before.

Lee was just starting to think he might have his beer and get out of the Arcady without trouble, when he saw the relief barmen lean over and say something, softly, to one of the cowboys at the far end of the bar. The cowboy looked quickly back over at Lee then, and he knew the jig was up on that. He'd have to remember to have a word with the barman about that loose tongue of his.

He saw the news being quietly passed down the line of cowpokers to the boss. When the Englishman got the word, he stood still for a moment, then he slowly put his beer down an the bar and turned his head to stare at Lee.

The Englishman looked down the bar at Lee, as if Lee were a mongrel dog taking a shit right there on the barroom floor. It was a long, cold, contemptuous look, perfected, Lee supposed, on generations of serfs and commoners.

Lee gave the big man a friendly smile, nodded in the

nicest way, as if they were old pals from way back, and tapped on the bar for service.

The barman came drifting down to him, looking a little concerned.

"A tall beer—cold," Lee said.

He kept his eyes on the barman while he drew the beer, and, at the same time, kept his eyes on the Englishman and his men in the mirror behind the bar. The Englishman wasn't armed, unless he kept a Derringer in a back pocket, and none of the cowboys looked to be a fast gun. It was true that sometimes a cowpoker got very sudden with his Colts, but that was rare. Practicing took too much cash for ammunition when a man only earned forty dollars a month.

That didn't mean, of course, that the six cow punchers couldn't shoot him to rags, if they all set in to do it together. He would be able to kill two or three, but he'd still go down for sure.

It didn't worry him. Not many had the nerve for that kind of slaughter.

The barman brought his beer and set it down carefully on the bar in front of him. He started to turn away, when Lee reached out and gently took his arm, to hold him.

"You know," Lee said to the man with a pleasant smile, "you have a very big mouth, friend."

The barman, a tall man with a cast to his right eye, seemed about to say something rough in return. Then he looked at Lee's face and changed his mind.

"I—I guess I was out of line, pointing you out, Mr. Lee." There was a line of sweatbeads across his forehead. "I sure am sorry about it . . ."

Lee let him stand there for a moment, sweating. It gave him no pleasure to frighten a man who was so plainly not a fighting man. But sometimes it was the only way for people to learn.

"Don't do anything like that again," Lee said. "I'm

138

surprised a good bartender would quack like that, to any damn fool across your bar . . ."

The barman wiped his forehead with his bar rag. "Well, I sure won't do it again."

Lee nodded, and the barman eased away back down the bar. Lee saw one of the cowboys lean over to speak to him as the bartender went by, but the man just ducked his head and kept going. He went all the way around the end of the bar and through a door there. The supply room, Lee thought. He marked the door in his mind, just in case of trouble. He'd known shy men before, insulted or angry for some reason, wait until other men started trouble and then suddenly decide to join in. So Lee kept the barman in mind.

He raised his beer mug and took a long, slow swallow. It was damn good beer, home brewed, he supposed, or maybe freighted in from Butte, though it seemed a hell of a long haul. Damned good and ice cold. He took another long pull, feeling the smooth, cold, burning pleasure of the beer in his throat. When he finished this one, by God, he'd have a couple more, if that shy bartender ever came back behind the bar.

"Looks like this fella has scared off old Bill."

True enough. It was the opening note of the waltz. A dance Lee had heard many times before. He threw his head back to finish the beer and took a good look in the bar mirror as he did. None of them had moved up there; the Englishman was closest, maybe twenty feet to Lee's left. The cowboys were still lined up on the other side of their boss. None of them had cleared room for drawing and shooting.

So it was to be just talk for a while yet.

"I'd say this citizen must be real rough." Another cowboy. "Ain't he the one killed that Irishman while he was drunk?"

"Must have been. I'd say bartenders are more in this pilgrim's line."

Any time now one of them would step away from the bar and stroll down to Lee's end to chivvy him close up. It was a problem. If he stood it and just put down his two bits and left the place, it would only mean postponing trouble. On the other hand, to flat out kill the cowboy, and maybe a friend of his, too, would be bound to set Lee as a quick gunman in the mind of every man in Cree. It was something he didn't want. He didn't want that ever 'again.

A problem.

The Englishman solved that problem for him.

"That's enough," he said to his men. He had a high, tenor voice, with that fancy Oxford accent most rich Englishmen had—at least most of the rich ones that came out West talked like that. It was a high-pitched, funny kind of voice, and a funny way of talking, but there was a cold toughness to it. Those generations of serfs and poor people must have jumped pretty quick when they heard it.

It shut the cowboys up, for sure. Nobody argued with him; there wasn't a peep out of them. Mr. Nigel Ashton ran what sea captains called a tight ship: it was useful to know.

Lee put his beer mug down and turned to go. What the hell, he'd have his seconds and thirds of beer another time. Leave well enough alone.

"Just a second, sir."

Lee didn't have to glance back to know who was talking—and who to.

He turned to see the Englishman standing away from the bar, his legs set wide apart, his small blue eyes drilling into Lee's.

"Yes?"

"I have a bone to pick with you, Mr. Lee. That is your name?"

"It's my name."

"Then I say I have a bone to pick with you concerning the murder of four of my men."

Lee felt the same rush of relief he'd known at Mrs. Boltwith's. India Ashton hadn't told her brother what he'd done.

Maybe it was that feeling that helped Lee keep his temper.

"Murder? And what does the local law have to say about that, Ashton?" No "Mister" for this arrogant son-of-a-bitch.

The big man's face reddened over the carroty ruff of his beard. "Whatever Mr. Phipp's opinion, *Lee*, my opinion is that you and your people committed murder."

Lee took a deep breath.

"Now, you listen to me," he said. "Your four men, and one of them a well-known killer"—the big Englishman's eyes narrowed at that—"came riding onto my place, onto my land, and drove off all of my appaloosas! They ran them clear up to the river, and they would have crossed them too, but for a boy that worked for me catching up to them and stopping them getting the herd across."

Ashton started to say something, but Lee talked right over him.

"And that fine killer of yours, that Tom Small, he killed that boy. Fifteen years old! And that man cut his throat." Lee got angrier and angrier as he spoke about it; it seemed to make the whole thing fresh in his mind. "And did I kill those men? Why, you can just bet your English ass I killed them! I shot 'em and hung 'em, and was damn glad to do it!"

The big man's face was red as fire now. It nearly matched his beard.

"And I say," retorted Ashton," *I* say, that you, sir, are a damned liar! And that my men, if they had anything to do with your horses at all, were simply checking their brands to find whether they weren't Mr.

141

Allenson's stock! His ranch is only thirty miles from the valley, and he also runs a few of those Indian ponies."

Now, Lee wasn't angry at all. The time for that was past.

"Ashton, you're the liar. And a coward to boot! You sent those men to run off my stock and steal it; you didn't have the sand to come yourself. You're a liar, a coward, and a thief."

And by God, that should tear it.

And it did.

Ashton stood frozen, his face gone as white as it had been red. Lee doubted that he had been spoken to so hard in his life—and he didn't look likely to bear it.

"All right, you mouthy son-of-a-bitch!" A young cowboy had stepped away from the bar, his hand hovering over his pistol butt. He was just a kid, with a thin work-worn face framed by wispy blond sideburns.

Lee didn't want to have to kill him.

"No, Franklin," Ashton said, without turning around. "I'll handle this." He stared Lee up and down a moment more. "I wonder," he said. "I wonder if you're any sort of a man without that revolver strapped to your side?"

It suited Lee. Right down to the ground. Better a fist fight than a killing.

"Man enough to knock you on your ass, Englishman."

"That, by God, we shall soon see," Ashton said. And he strode over to a nearby table, shrugged out of his riding jacket, stripped off his stiff shirt collar, and began rolling up his shirt sleeves. He seemed pleased the way things had worked out.

"We'll fight out back," he said to Lee, curtly. His sleeves were up now, his arms bare. They were massively muscled, red furred—the arms of a blacksmith. Lee had heard that some English gentlemen fancied themselves fist fighters, even trained with professionals. It was possible Ashton was that kind; he had the muscles for it.

"Hold your gun, Lee?"

The voice had come from behind him. Lee turned and saw Tod Phipps standing by the swinging doors, smiling at him. He'd come in very quietly; the doors hadn't squeaked at all. Still, Lee cursed himself for his carelessness in standing with his back to the door. If there had been gun play with Ashton's cowboys, Phipps would have had him cold.

Phipps held out his hand, grinning. It seemed that everyone was happy about this coming fight. And it was natural that Phipps would be. Either way it came out, he couldn't lose. Either the high and mighty Nigel Ashton got a beating or the new fast gun in town got thrashed. Either way, good for Tod Phipps.

Lee unbuckled his gunbelt and handed it to the marshal.

"The knife, too?" A big smile then.

Lee reached down, slid the toothpick out of his boot, and handed it over.

"Don't worry," Phipps said. "I'll see fair play."

Lee wasn't so sure that he would, and he wasn't so sure now that this fist fighting was such a good idea. Not that he couldn't beat Ashton. That wasn't the trouble. He'd beaten and kicked stronger and harder men than Ashton down. The trouble was that he was unarmed. Unarmed against Ashton and his men, and unarmed before Phipps, which might be worse.

Well, he'd made his choice when he'd taken the big Englishman up on his challange. The hand was full dealt now, and he'd have to play it out.

Lee walked out through the Arcady's back hall, along with Ashton's men, following the Englishman's broad back. A big man, and no mistake. He'd have to hit him fast and hard and get the boot into him the instant he was down. Kick a kneecap off him to start, maybe . . .

The cowboys seemed almost friendly to Lee now,

winking at him and nudging each other as they crowded out through the back door into a broad, sunny alley. Their sharp-toed boots kicked up little dust devils as they trotted out into the sunlight, making a wide circle. They were mostly young boys, with a few busted-up old rannies among them. They were all grinning and shifting nervously, waiting for the fight to start. It wasn't so often that a couple of ranch owners, rich men as far as the cowboys were concerned, would square off for a knock down and drag out. It made a kind of holiday.

"Go it, Mr. Ashton!" "Git—git—git on him!"

Lee shucked his buckskin jacket and draped it over the Arcady's back hitching rail. Then he rolled his shirt sleeves up. Ashton had already walked to the center of the circle of men and stood waiting. Lee noticed he was standing so the sun would be slanting into Lee's eyes.

"Good luck," Phipps said to him. He didn't seem to mean it.

As Lee stepped into the circle, he heard women talking just above him. Looking up, he saw that some of the whores had come out onto a little second-story balcony to watch. They were giggling nervously, staring down at the men crowded into the alley, at Ashton and Lee standing, facing each other in the afternoon sunlight.

"You do know the Marquess of Queensbury's rules, Lee?" Ashton said.

Bad news. And Lee should have figured it. Of course Ashton would fight by gentlemen's rules. And that meant no kicking, no gouging.

It meant trouble. Lee would either have to speak up, now, for fighting like a gutter rat, or he'd have to box like a gent, and very likely get his head knocked off. He didn't have to glance around to know that Phipps was grinning at him.

The hand was dealt. He'd wanted land and respect-

144

Join the Western Book Club
and GET 4 FREE* BOOKS NOW!
— A $19.96 VALUE! —

— Yes! I want to subscribe —
to the Western Book Club.

Please send me my **4 FREE* BOOKS**. I have enclosed $2.00 for shipping/handling. Each month I'll receive the four newest Leisure Western selections to preview for 10 days. If I decide to keep them, I will pay the Special Members Only discounted price of just $3.36 each, a total of $13.44, plus $2.00 shipping/handling ($19.50 US in Canada). This is a **SAVINGS OF AT LEAST $6.00** off the bookstore price. There is no minimum number of books I must buy, and I may cancel the program at any time. In any case, the **4 FREE* BOOKS** are mine to keep.

*In Canada, add $5.00 shipping/handling per order
for the first shipment. For all future shipments to
Canada, the cost of membership is $16.25 US,
which includes shipping and handling.
(All payments must be made in US dollars.)

NAME: _____

ADDRESS: _____

CITY: _____ **STATE:** _____

COUNTRY: _____ **ZIP:** _____

TELEPHONE: _____

E-MAIL: _____

SIGNATURE: _____

ability; now he'd have to earn it.

Lee nodded. "We'll fight Queensbury's rules."

And no sooner had he said it than he heard Phipps's voice call out, "Time!" and Ashton was on him with a fast straight jab and a right cross to follow. For a big man, he was very quick.

The right caught Lee in the mouth and knocked him flat.

CHAPTER TEN

He wasn't hurt, but he was sure as hell down. Lee didn't try to jump up, to show that Ashton hadn't hurt him. Instead, he got up slow, shaking his head. The cowboys were yelling like Indians, stomping up and down in the dust.

"You put that pilgrim away!" "Hand it to him, Mr. Ashton!" they yelled.

Lee saw Ashton peering at him closely as he straightened up, measuring how he'd weathered the blow. The whores on the balcony above were murmuring like doves in a dovecote.

Lee pretended to lose his temper and rushed in at the Englishman, throwing his punches wild and pulling them, too. The big man blocked them fast, brushing them aside, moving and ducking. It was like striking at a moving tree. Even when one of his punches landed, Lee saw that the Englishman didn't even blink.

And out of that flurry, the big man struck a right upper cut into Lee's gut that would have doubled him up and out of the fight if it had hit him square.

Lee backed off, still playing weak and flustered.

The Englishman seemed satisfied. He smiled a little to himself and began to move after Lee as steady and certain as a rockslide. Lee kept on backing around the circle of yelling ranch hands, letting the red-bearded rancher come on.

And come on he did. The Englishman was an easy mover, moving to one side or the other, but he was fastest coming at you. Lee backed and backed, playing a little shy and watching the big man's style. No question but he'd learned from a professional. It wasn't that he hit hard; plenty of men who never studied boxing hit hard as a mule kicked. It was the way he covered up, moving with his chin tucked down into his shoulder, his left well up.

The cowboys were calling for Lee to show some sand. They had him figured for scared from that fast knock-down. Lee hoped that Ashton believed the same.

Lee pulled back one more time, backpedaling across the circle, looking as sorry as he could. He caught a glimpse of Tod Phipps out of the corner of his eye. Phipps looked pleased enough with the way the fight was going.

Just as Lee reached the circle of cowboys, Ashton suddenly strode out after him, lunging across the dusty ring to swing hard with a wide right hand. He swung at Lee's head hard enough so that Lee heard the fist whiffle past his ear like an Indian arrow.

Lee stepped in under the blow, twisted his body as if he were throwing a baseball pitch, and hit Ashton flush on the nose with his left fist as hard as he could hit.

It hurt him.

The big man's head snapped back and the small blue eyes widened as the pain of the blow struck him. The cowboys yelped with surprise. But whoever the English fighter had been who'd taught Ashton, he'd taught him well. He'd taught him what to do when a punch hurt him.

Ashton didn't move back and he didn't rush. He stayed where he was, set himself, and punched. He went for Lee's body again, going to double him up, striking with an uppercut and a hard hook up into the ribs without a pause between them.

Lee slid away, shifted back to stand square, and hit Ashton in the left eye twice. He came within an ace of putting the thumb in then, but remembered just in time and kept the blow clean.

There must have been a little hesitation there, though, just for a fraction of a second. It was enough for Ashton to club him across the temple with a quick swinging blow that made his ears hum.

Lee slid away. Another like that might have put him down.

And he was moving across the circle again, thinking hard as he could what he might do to put the big man away. He surprised him, and he stung him. But he hadn't put him down.

Ashton was coming after him again. A bright line of blood was running from his nose, his eyes clear and eager—except for the left, which was swelling across the lid.

He tried for Lee with a long jab. It looked rather slow coming in. The jab tagged Lee on the point of his shoulder, and it hurt as if someone had rapped him with a heavy stick.

Lee hit the big man with his right. Digging deep into the man's gut, it was like striking into a feed sack. Ashton just grunted and kept coming.

Then Tod Phipps called time.

A fat young cowboy, couldn't have been more than sixteen, made a knee for Lee to sit on to catch his breath.

"Mister," the boy said, "you're doing good just to be alive."

Lee couldn't much disagree with him. He sat, a little bent over, taking in as much air as he could manage. He saw Tod Phipps standing across the circle talking to Ashton and laughing. Phipps had picked the winner.

As the seconds of rest ticked away, Lee glanced up at the Arcady's balcony to see how the soiled doves were enjoying the fight and looked straight into the eyes of Beatrice Morgan. The thin girl was all done up as a right good whore, but her face was pale under the rouge and mascara. She'd looked upset just as Lee glanced up, but when their eyes met, the girl forced a bright smile and held her small fist up with a rakish, encouraging air, as if he were whipping the pudding out of that poor Englishman.

It gave Lee an odd feeling for her to do that.

And Tod Phipps called, "Time."

He sounded like a happy man.

Lee got up off the cowboy's knee, went out to Ashton, and hit him fairly on the jaw. Ashton punched straight out in return, caught Lee in the neck, and forced him back into the screeching cowboys, bulling him, punching into him up close.

Lee resisted a damnable urge to knee the big man in the nuts, and then just managed to twist and fight his way back out into the circle. But it cost him: Ashton had gotten in a hard punch to Lee's ribs. It felt as though one was cracked, judging from the pain when Lee took a deep breath.

And the Englishman was still coming.

Lee ducked a short punch to his face and rode out another one that thumped into the side of his head.

It was simple: Lee hadn't yet seen a way to hurt Ashton, but Ashton was making considerable progress in hurting Lee. Much more of this and the big man was bound to get a flush punch home and put Lee down hard. After that, it would just be a beating for as long as Lee could stand up under it.

Get doing or go under. It was as simple as that.

The next time Ashton moved in punching, Lee hit him in the left eye again. Hit him twice, then struck him in the gut. But the body punch was just to keep Ashton from realizing what Lee was after.

Lee was going to blind him.

If he could. If he stayed lucky—and on his feet.

He almost made it.

He hit Ashton in the eye once more, a good hard punch that hurt the big man. He hit the man alongside the head as well.

Then, as he was backing across the circle, measuring the Englishman for more punishment to that left eye, something happened.

Lee never knew what punch the big man caught him with.

Suddenly, without knowing how he got there, Lee was on his hands and knees in the dust.

The cowboys were jumping around screeching, and Lee could hear the women yelling high up over his head.

He hoped Beatrice Morgan hadn't stayed to watch this.

Lee didn't know if he was on his hands and knees on the way to getting up or on his way down into the dirt. There was only one way to find out. He got a foot under him, then two, and tried to stand up. He was feeling a little sick to his stomach.

Then, while he was still trying to stand up, he heard Phipps counting.

"Six . . . seven . . ."

Lee got to his feet. His face was numb. All the faces around the circle were drifting slowly to the side wherever he looked at them. Ashton had knocked him silly.

And the Englishman was coming to finish the job.

Lee sensed rather than saw the bulk of the man moving over the trampled circle towards him. He forced himself to move, to move away until he could think clearly again.

Ashton tagged him a hard punch to the side, anyway. It was the side with the hurt rib, and the sharp pain seemed to help wake him up.

Lee caught his breath and felt his legs well under him

150

again. He began to fight back.

He stood up to the Englishman when he came in again, took a hard punch to the chest, and hit the big rancher in the right eye.

Ashton swung back, but Lee managed to duck the blow and hit the Englishman again. Again in the right eye.

Ashton now knew what he was about, and Lee saw him raise his guard to protect his face from those punches. But Lee didn't care. He struck at the big man's face anyway, once, and twice, then again. The last punch went through Ashton's guard and hit his left eye. The swollen lid began to bleed.

Ashton stepped back to collect himself, to get his left well up. It was the first step back he had taken in the fight.

Lee jumped after him and struck out left and right as fast as he could. The big man brushed most of the punches off, but one struck his right eye. He shook his head like a bull toubled with flies, jabbed Lee sharply, and swung a roundhouse right at him that just missed.

Tom Phipps called time.

"Well, you're doing the smart thing out there, but you started too late," the fat young cowboy said as Lee sat gasping on his knee. Right then Lee would have given a good deal to see the fat cowboy out there in that circle.

"I guess you want me to shut up," the fat young cowboy said, and Lee nodded and took a deep breath, trying to set that cracked rib somehow so it wouldn't hurt him so bad.

He glanced up at the balcony. Beatrice Morgan was looking at him. He didn't know why he did it, but he smiled and raised his fist to her the way she had done to him. Everyone there must have seen him do it, making up to an Arcady whore.

"Time!" called Tod Phipps.

"Well, pardon me," Lee said to the fat cowboy. "I have to get to work." He stood up and went out to meet Nigel Ashton.

Ashton's eyes looked better. One of his men had been washing them with cold beer. The big man was as fresh and strong as ever. He struck out at Lee like a grizzly bear and hit him on the shoulder and high on the cheekbone. The last one was a jolting punch, and Lee moved back and around the circle, waiting for his head to clear from it.

Then he moved to meet Ashton again and hit him a very hard punch on the left eye. Ashton made a quick face from the pain, and the eye started to look bad right away. Some cowboy in the crowd said, "Uh-ohhh."

Ashton rushed Lee then, and Lee hit out at the Englishman's face as hard as he could, punching short, sharp punches at the big man's eyes.

Ashton hit Lee an uppercut into the belly that took his breath away. And Lee just let his breath go, figuring it would come back sometime, and took the chance to reach out and hit the big man in the right eye. It was looking almost as bad as the left one, and the Englishman was squinting to see through it.

Lee felt better and better. He hurt like hell, and Ashton was still likely to knock him cold, but he found himself enjoying the fight. Everything looked nice and clear now, and moved slowly and clearly, the way it did when he fought with a gun. It was a pleasant feeling.

Lee smiled at Ashton, and the Englishman came in and knocked him into the ring of cowboys watching the fight. Lee spun away from them and hit the big man in the side as he rushed in, hitting him in the short ribs as if he were chopping wood. Then he jumped back into the center of the ring and waited for the Englishman to come back.

When Ashton came back, Lee jabbed at his eyes. When the big rancher brought up his guard, Lee made a feint to the man's belly, then swung overhand and caught him in the eye as the Englishman's guard came down.

Ashton grunted and swung a right. Lee hit him in the left eye and blood spattered from it.

"Uh-ohhh." It was the same cowboy as before.

Ashton was beginning to make panting sounds, as if being hit in the eyes and hurt that particular way was making him tired.

Some cowboys had stopped yelling. It was now quiet enough so that Lee could hear his feet and Ashton's as they scuffled through the alley dust.

He feinted another punch at Ashton's eyes and saw the Englishman wince a little.

Lee was feeling better and better.

Ashton came on the same as ever, trying not to hold his guard up too high to only protect his eyes. The big man had some sand, and the man who'd taught him had known his business.

Lee hit the Englishman in the jaw. Ashton didn't heed it.

Lee hit him in the jaw again, laying the punch with all his strength.

Ashton's guard came down to cover—had to come down to cover—and Lee hit him in the eye. Blood spattered across his face.

No sound came from the cowboys now, not even when the big man hit Lee in the chest hard and hurt him. He struck at Lee again with a clever left hook and sent him staggering sideways. But Lee came back straight away and jabbed Ashton in the right eye. That eye wasn't bleeding yet, but it didn't look good.

Suddenly the Englishman lunged at Lee, bearing down with his great weight, striking down as if he were driving fence posts with a sledge hammer.

For a moment Lee thought he was done. The man was just too damn big. But he remembered what he was about and struck up into the Englishman's face with both fists, punching up into those bleeding eyes.

"Time!" called Tod Phipps. "Time!"

"Well, this is the best fist fight that I ever saw," the fat young cowboy said when Lee came staggering over to sit with a grunt on his bent knee.

Lee was worried about his hands. He couldn't feel them anymore. They didn't even hurt. He wasn't worried about the fight, they'd do for that, all right. But he hoped that no bones were broken. It was hard in a bare-knuckle fight like this not to break some bone in your hand if you were punching at a man's head. And he was certainly doing that. A broken bone in his hand would be very serious, especially in his right hand. Lee could draw and shoot quite fast with his left hand, but he missed as often as he hit with it. It could be trouble.

Tod Phipps strode out to the center of the circle, looking mighty neat and cool in his woven jacket. He had had somebody go get him a cold beer from inside, and he took a sip from it and called, "Time!"

Lee jumped up and walked out into the circle to meet Ashton coming in. Ashton punched Lee hard in the face, and that punch hurt Lee's head from front to back. It was a sharp pain that seemed to cut straight back from his forehead.

The Englishman's left eye looked like a broken plum, and blood was running down from it onto his cheek. He was blind on that side.

Lee stepped around to the big man's left, into that blind spot, and hit him on the ear as hard as he could. Ashton staggered and tried to turn to see Lee and swing at him, but Lee keep moving off around to the side, keeping in the blind spot, and hit the Englishman twice more across the side of the head.

Ashton staggered from the blows, then recovered himself, and spun fast to find Lee with his good eye and hit him.

When he turned, Lee struck at his right eye, missed with his first punch, then struck again and hit it. The Englishman grunted with pain, stepped into Lee, hit him in the body, and missed his face with another punch. They were both missing punches now, and Lee wondered if he'd ever manage to hit Ashton hard enough, to beat him.

He feigned a move to the big man's blind side, to his left. When Ashton turned to protect himself, Lee swung a hard punch at his face and hit him in the eye.

"Damn . . . damn!" one of the cowboys said. The rest of them made no sound at all. The women up on the balcony were quiet too. Lee could hear Ashton's hoarse breathing, his gasps for breath. The Englishman's red beard was stained and stringy with blood. His right eye was almost closed now, as well.

If I shut that damn eye, then I've won the fight, Lee thought. He could hardly remember what fight he was thinking about, he was so tired.

But he still felt fine.

Ashton spit and gritted his teeth and reached for Lee, punching at him twice. One punch hit Lee's side, and the other one, more of a push than a punch, hit the side of his mouth. Lee felt a tooth cut into his lip.

It's time to finish all this, Lee thought. If I can.

Lee stepped back away from the big rancher and stood for a moment sizing him up.

Ashton snorted and came for him again, swinging slow, pawing punches at him. Lee stepped back again. The Englishman had plenty of fight left and more strength than Lee.

Lee took a deep breath, stepped into the big man, brought up his hand with a short punch, and then hit him twice in the right eye as hard as he could hit.

Ashton went staggering back, two or three long steps, and Lee was right after him. As the big man tried to get his balance, to get set, Lee hit him in the face again.

Ashton seemed to stumble and fell down to one knee.

As Lee waited, the big Englishman struggled up to his feet again, the flesh of his eyes puffed black and broken, his face splotched and stained with blood.

There wasn't a sound from anyone in the alley.

No sound at all but the Englishman's harsh breathing and Lee's.

Lee felt dizzy, as if he could float away.

He swung his fist back as far as it would go and took a little skipping step. With a hoarse grunt he threw that fist into Nigel Ashton's face just as fast as it would go.

The blow landed with a sound like a dropped feed sack. Blood flew from the Englishman's face. He pitched forward into Lee. He tried to clutch at Lee's clothes, couldn't hold on, and fell out full length into the dust.

"Don't get up," Lee said to the man. "Don't get up."

But he didn't know what he would do if the man did get up. All the pleasure of the fight was gone: it had been hard work. Lee felt tired to death.

Nigel Ashton lay still in the dust for a moment, then he slowly drew his legs up and dug his hands into the alley dirt. His broad back bowed, and his arms trembled as he tried to push himself up so that he was sitting.

"Oh, dear heavens," one of the women said above them.

"Oh, shit," said one of the cowboys.

The big Englishman groaned aloud. He heaved and shoved himself so that he was sitting up. He sat staring around him, looking for Lee, and he reached up and wiped his eyes with his fingers, trying to wipe the blood from his eyes so that he could see.

Lee bent over before he thought and put his hand on the man's shoulder.

"The fight's over, Ashton," he said. His own voice

sounded strange to him. "It was a good fight."

The big man reached up a fumbling hand, felt for Lee's wrist, and held it. Lee thought the man was trying to pull himself up, but couldn't. He just sat there with his hand on Lee's wrist, and then he let go of it.

"Holy jumping Jesus!" one of the cowboys said.

Lee turned and walked through the crowd and on into the Arcady's back entrance. It was cool in there. It was so shadowy in the hall that he felt dizzy for a minute.

When he woke, the first thing he felt was something cool touching his hand. Then it burned.

A hoarse voice said, "Get it in there good and soak it all around."

Lee opened his eyes to a cool, quiet, dark room. An ugly, froggy little man was standing over the bed, looking at him. He was a familiar looking man.

Beatrice Morgan was holding Lee's right hand, dabbing at it with a wet cloth that smelled of horse liniment.

"That's it," the froggy little man said. "It doesn't do any good, Beatrice, unless it soaks in real good." He looked up at Lee. "Well, well, so our naughty boy is wide awake, is he?" He shook a stubby finger at Lee. "And you have been a naughty boy!"

"Who the hell are you?" said Lee, and his voice came out a rusty croak.

"My dear, you sound like I look," the froggy little man said. "I am Bud Martin, proprietor of my own sundry sundries and millinary emporium, enemy to the death of Greedy Kimble, the Mercantile King, and, to your very good fortune, a two-year medical student at Tulane College, which only happens to be the finest school of medicine in the entire South!" He pouted and preened himself for a moment. "Which establishment I

157

was forced to abandon due to my style of Universal Love.''

"You fainted out downstairs,'' Beatrice Morgan said to Lee, as she dabbed the liniment onto his hand. The hand was dark red and swollen.

"How long—''

"Oh, do try to be original, now,'' the little man said. "You've been in this sweetie's sweet bed for just three or four hours.'' And the little man patted Lee on the shoulder. "Handsome is as handsome does,'' he said, absently, staring into Lee's eyes.

"Don't be distressed,'' he said, "I'm not spooning. Just making sure you're not badly hurt . . . Beatrice, turn up that lamp and bring it here.''

When the girl brought the lamp over, Martin held the light up to Lee's eyes and then moved it back and forth.

"How many of these lamps do you see, Naughty One?''

"One,'' Lee said.

"Hmmm . . .'' The little man turned and handed the lamp back to the girl. "Well, I do think you'll survive, though your looks are certainly spoiled for the time being.''

"How is . . ?'' For a moment Lee forgot the Englishman's name.

"Yes?'' said Mr. Martin, looking interested in this lapse.

"Ashton.''

"Oh, Mr. Ashton prefers to forgo my medical advice. I believe he disapproves of my style—''

"—of Universal Love?'' said Lee, with a smile.

"Precisely,'' Mr. Martin said, and patted Lee on the shoulder again. "My dear,'' he said to Beatrice, "you appear to have better judgement than most of your sex. And now I'll leave you two together, to make any mistakes you wish . . .''

"Thank you, Doctor,'' said Lee, and the little man,

pleased, paused at the door to bow in a dignified fashion.

"He's nice," Beatrice said when the little man was gone.

"I guess he is," Lee said.

"He's as good as a real doctor when it comes to most things."

"I hope so," Lee said, and he smiled at the girl. It hurt his face; that Englishman had given him quite a walloping.

"He said you should just stay in bed until tomorrow." She blushed.

A blushing little whore, Lee thought.

"Well, I can be going now, I think," Lee said. "I feel pretty good. I don't usually go to fainting in saloons."

"No," she said. "No, you shouldn't go. Mrs. Chase said it would be quite all right for you to stay as long as you want."

She got up and went to a dresser and got a bottle of medicine.

"Does laudanum make you sick? I know it does some people."

Lee shook his head, and the girl carefully measured out two drops of the drug into a glass of water. When he reached out to take it, Lee could feel that his right hand was all right—stiff and sore with split knuckles, but no bones broken. As good with a gun as ever in a few days.

"Mr. Martin said you were very lucky your rib hadn't broken all the way. It might have stuck something inside."

Lee shifted on the soft bed. Sure enough, his chest was taped tight. Ashton had broken a rib on him with that punch just the way he'd thought. Or cracked it good, anyway.

The girl, Beatrice, came back to the side of the bed, picked up his hand, and began dabbing at it again with the liniment. It stung a little, and the smell reminded him of the stable on his family's old farm in Parker, Indiana.

Lee slept, and he dreamed that he was there, up in the hay loft, with Puss, the cat, waiting for James to come home.

He could hear his mother talking with Bertha May as they worked in the kitchen cooking dinner for all the people that would be coming to welcome James back home.

It would be a big welcome because James was a sergeant. He became a sergeant after he got a medal at Fredericksburg. Lee had been jealous for two years, waiting to be old enough to go. The war would have to last three more years for him and George Babcock to make it. They were both thirteen, and their folks wouldn't let them go, not even as drummer boys. It was unfair, because everybody knew this was the last war there would be. And it meant that James would have this over him no matter how old he got. And just for being born a few years too late.

He rolled over onto his back in the hay, smelling the stable smells—leather, and horse shit, and liniment. He'd got up early and done all his chores. There was nothing for him to do all day now but wait and see James and watch everybody make such a fuss over him that it made you sick to see it. What for? For doing what *he* would do if anybody gave him a chance. Give those Rebs pure hell, that's what!

Puss kept trying to get away. She had kittens down in one of the stalls. Lee thought of going to look for them, but it was a waste of time. She'd just move them away again.

He thought he heard his mother calling him. Yes, she was calling him to come in. She sounded excited. James was coming down the road.

Then he was out on the road, watching for James. It was a real hot day. And there was James coming along

160

in a wagon, and everybody calling to him. Waving his hand, James was waving to them all, smiling to beat the band. And Daddy was driving the horses.

CHAPTER ELEVEN

Lee woke late the next morning. It looked almost noon. The room was bright with sunlight, and there was a bunch of fresh flowers on the table beside the bed. Wild flowers. Bluebells and eglantine.

Lee lay still awhile remembering the fight. Then he threw the covers back and sat up on the edge of the bed. He was naked, and his side hurt him whenever he took a deep breath. He stretched both hands out and flexed them, working his fingers. The knuckles were sore and swollen and cut in a couple of places where he'd hit the Englishman in the mouth and got cut on a tooth. His hands were achy, but they felt all right. And his face was sore.

He got up and walked stiffly over to the washstand and looked at his face in the mirror. It looked pretty bad, puffed up and black and blue, especially on the left side where Ashton had landed with his right.

His nose didn't seem to be broken, though. There was a bump on the bridge, but it wasn't broken.

Lee bared his teeth. They looked all right. None of them even loose. All in all, not bad, not bad for a gentleman's fight with so big a man. And a man who'd had lessons with a professional for sure.

Phipps must be real disappointed—or pleased to see them both knocking the stuffing out of each other, win or lose.

162

Lee turned as the door opened and saw that it was that girl, Beatrice. For a moment he looked around for something to cover himself, then he remembered what the girl was and relaxed.

She seemed shy about it, though, and turned her face aside when she came into the room.

"I've bought your clothes," she said. She had his clothes all washed and folded over her arm, and she was holding his socks, washed and rolled in a ball, in her other hand.

She put the things on the bed and turned to go.

"Are you feeling all right?" she said. She still wouldn't look right at him. A strange girl.

"Yes, I'm fine." Lee said. "It was very nice of you to take care of me last night. You were a good nurse."

"Oh, that's all right," the girl said. "That's all right. I was glad to." She went out and closed the door.

Lee started to dress, then looked around for his gun. It was in its holster, hanging on the bedpost. As he finished dressing Lee tried to remember the dream he'd had. Something about his father . . . and James. Both of them in there somewhere. Well, there was some water under the bridge. Both killed the first year of the war.

Water under the bridge.

He finished dressing, buckled on the gunbelt, and went out and downstairs. He met Rebecca Chase on the landing.

She gave him a bright smile.

"Well, hello, Mr. Lee! How are you feeling this morning?"

"Well enough," Lee said. "Thanks for the hospitality of the house."

"Oh," she said. "Don't think anything about that. I suppose you know you've become quite a famous man. Mr. Ashton was thought to have had no equals!"

"He didn't get much the worst of it," Lee said and started to go past her. She reached out and put her hand

163

on his arm.

"I keep my bargains," she said in a different voice. It made Lee angry. She was still worrying about that fancy lawman of hers.

"So do I," he said to her and went on down the stairs.

"Listen," she called down over the bannister, "there's late breakfast served in the kitchen now . . ."

That sounded good. Lee walked around the staircase to the hallway door and went down the dark hall toward the sounds of women's voices. As he walked, he worked his hands, working the stiffness out of them.

The kitchen was a big, bright room flooded with sunlight. The old Indian woman and the big-mouthed barkeep were standing at the stove frying eggs and hamsteaks. The food smelled wonderful.

The long kitchen table was packed with girls. Ten or twelve of them, anyway. Lee saw the half-breed girl and her lover, Phyllis. Beatrice Morgan was sitting at the end of the table, drinking a cup of coffee.

The girls all looked up when Lee came in. They were as brightly colored as a field of flowers, each one in a pretty wrapper, yellow or blue or green, with stripes or flowers on it. They were a nice-looking set of girls, better than most saloon women looked. Rebecca had picked some good ones.

The girls sat looking at him, and Lee felt out of place for a minute. He knew how like a home kitchen a whorehouse kitchen was for the people who worked the house. It was a place they could go and relax from business and trouble, a family place for them.

"Good morning," he said.

"Good morning," the girls said back.

The barkeep at the stove just nodded and went back to cooking his eggs. Lee thought he was still worried about having tipped Ashton's men at the bar the day before.

Silently, the girls all shifted down to make room for him beside Beatrice Morgan at the end of the table. It annoyed him a little, but he went and sat down there anyway, so the girl wouldn't be humiliated in front of her friends.

"Good morning," she said to him. "Are you hungry?"

"As a grizzly bear," Lee said.

She got up and went to the stove, and he could hear her talking to the old Indian woman and rattling around with the pans there.

"You feel all right now?" one of the girls asked him. She was a fat, round-faced girl in a yellow wrapper with ruffles on it.

"Yeah, fine," Lee said.

"My," the fat girl said, "you were sure sick as a horse after that fight . . ."

"I guess I was."

Beatrice came over to the table and brought him a cup of coffee, black. He liked cream in his coffee, but he didn't see any on the table.

"You want some cream?" she said to him.

"If you have it," he said. She went to a sideboard to fetch the pitcher for him.

All around the table, the girls were looking at him over their coffee cups.

"You sure showed that high and mighty Mr. Ashton something," the fat girl said.

"And Mickey Slawson, too," said a strong-looking girl with a squint in her eye.

The girls murmured and sipped their coffee, looking at him.

Lee was feeling like getting up and going, when Beatrice came to the table with his breakfast. There were three fried eggs on the platter, a pile of pan-fried potatoes, four biscuits, and a ham steak an inch thick. When Beatrice sat back down beside him, the other girls

165

drifted back into their own conversations, chattering and giggling, sometimes making a loud remark about some Johnny they'd had the night before and what the fool had wanted. Then they would glance sideways just to see how Lee had taken it.

Lee hadn't thought he'd be able to eat that much food, but he did, and took another buttered biscuit with his second cup of coffee, too. The Arcady fed its people well.

Beatrice sat beside him, watching out of the corner of her eye as he ate. She didn't say much. Just talked a little about how fast the summer was going and how pretty it was out in the mountains.

"You have a horse?" Lee asked her.

"No. I had one last year, but he got sick." She seemed to be thinking of the horse. "His name was Jumper," she said. She sighed. "Rebecca drives us out in the buggy sometimes to take the air . . ."

When Lee had finished, he wiped his mouth with one of the red-checkered napkins and got up.

"Thank you," he said to her. "That was a prime breakfast." He wanted to thank her again for taking care of him and having his clothes washed, but that seemed like too much to say in front of all those people. So he just said thank you again, nodded to the girls and walked out of the kitchen into the hall.

He heard the girls giggling behind him.

It was a nice sunny day outside. There was a cool breeze blowing softly through the town from the mountains to the north.

Lee was crossing the street to get to Mrs. Boltwith's, when he noticed the sign for Martin's store. He crossed that way, climbed the steps to the raised boardwalk, and walked down to the store. His side gave him a little trouble on the steps; a muscle pulled there when he climbed up them.

He bent down to peer through the glass panes in the door and saw the frog-faced little man behind his counter, talking to an old farm woman in a poke bonnet.

Lee pushed the door open to the light tinkle of its bell and walked in.

"Calico, calico, calico!" the little man was saying. "Mrs. Simmons, I don't say that fine lawn is what you need—or plain muslin either! But you just have no excuse not even trying a dimity. We are talking about a wedding, aren't we? Not plowing the north forty!"

The old farm woman didn't seem convinced.

"Oh, God, Sarah, I give up on you. If you have to have something you can cut into shirts for that old fool Ralph, then you may as well take bleached denim to start with!"

"Well, maybe I should," the old lady said. "It won't look too coarse for the bridemaids though?"

The little man waved acknowledgement to Lee. "Oh, God, Sarah, you wear me out. Of course it's going to look coarse! Your girls are going to look like three cows in overalls! But it's your decision, not mine. Don't take *my* advice! What do *I* know? I was only born and brought up in the best circles in New Orleans, that's all. I don't know a thing about proper dress and elegance. Not me!"

The old lady seemed to be wavering.

"But it would do for shirting?"

"Yes, Sarah, it would do for shirting."

The old lady sighed.

"Well, then, I'd better have it, I suppose."

The little man turned to his shelves and pulled a bolt of heavy white cloth out to cut.

"Sarah," he said. "You are the biggest fool going. That Ralph of yours is just all take and no give. It would serve that selfish man right if you just up and ran off

167

with a man who'd appreciate you!"

The notion seemed to please Sarah somewhat.

"I mean it," said Mr. Martin. And he folded and cut a length of the cloth, and folded and cut it again.

"There, that's enough even for those three fat girls of yours, dear. Why in heaven's name you don't get some of that weight off them, I don't know. No handsome boy's going to look at them twice, I can tell you that!"

"Well, they're never sick at all," the farm lady said.

"That's not all there is to life, Sarah," the little man said. "As I'm sure an experienced woman like you remembers."

The farm woman laughed a surprisingly young laugh, counted out her money, and collected the tied parcel the little man slid across his counter.

"Good day, Mr. Martin," she said, glanced shyly at Lee, and walked past him out the door.

"Well, now, what did you think of all that?" the little man asked Lee. "I suppose you thought all that was just a lot of sissy nonsense, didn't you?"

Lee didn't know what to say, so he kept his mouth shut.

"Well, let me tell you, Mr. Lee, that that sort of 'sissy nonsense' will have more to do with civilizing this wild country than that ugly gun you're wearing ever will!"

Lee smiled. "I guess you're right at that," he said.

"You bet I am," Mr. Martin said. "Now, what can I do for you? I don't sell gentlemen's clothes, but you could certainly use a handkerchief or a bandanna of some sort to compliment that blue shirt. Not a bad shirt at all, as those sort of things go . . ."

"No thanks. I wanted to thank you for your services last night and find out how much I owe you."

The little man stared up at him like an astonished bullfrog. "Will wonders never cease," he said. "A ready offer to pay for anything is a considerable rarity in my experience." He stared at Lee for a while and blinked. "Let's say the bill stands paid in full by the sound thrashing given that pompous ass of an aristo. You do know that Ashton is the nephew of the Earl of Leicester?"

"I knew he was something."

"The nephew of the Earl of Leiscester, the son of the Honorable Winslow Manning Cooke."

"My, my," said Lee, who didn't know what else to say.

"That's right. Once a very great family, some of the best people in England. And now look what they've produced! A great buffoon. Now, I can tell you, I don't give that!"—he snapped his fingers—"for the Leicesters!"

"I guess not," Lee said.

"And off he goes," the little man continued. "Off to Helena to see some licensed quack who'll fiddle with that eye until it's really injured. And I can tell you I don't like the look of that left eye myself. Cleansing, cover, and rest, that's what the eye needs! And it's never going to get it, not in this world!"

He turned away to his cloth shelves and began sorting through some material.

"A nice dark maroon," he said. "That poor great silly. A cattle baron, indeed!" He sighed. "Well, handsome is as handsome does. If the big fool doesn't know a friend when he has one . . ." He pulled out a small bolt of dark red cloth. "Here. I'll give you a yard of this for a bandanna. And do tell that child Beatrice to double hem all round. I've forgotten more about sewing than that girl ever knew!"

Lee reached for his billfold to pay for the cloth, but the little man waved it away.

"Consider it a wedding gift," he said and leaned on the counter, his chin propped in his hands. He stared at Lee without blinking, exactly like a sleepy frog.

When Lee walked up the steps to Mrs. Boltwith's he found the usual crowd there waiting for one o'clock dinner. Mrs. Boltwith's dinners—always fried chicken or pan-fried steak—were even more popular than her suppers.

The hostlers and whiskey drummers studied Lee with care as he went up the steps. That old look; a fast gun . . . fist fighter too now. Well, better to have fist fought Ashton than killed him. Especially considering what he'd done to the man's sister.

Mrs. Boltwith was squeezed in behind her little desk at the foot of the stairs. She looked up as he came in.

"Do you feel as bad as you look, Mr. Lee?" she said.

"Not nearly."

"You're lucky," she said. "And I've got a note from Mr. Walker at the bank." She handed a folded paper to Lee and watched as he opened and read it.

"My bank draft has come," Lee said to her. "Is the bank open at midday?"

"Open all day long."

Lee turned to go out and she called after him.

"Are you going to be taking a room for tonight, Mr. Lee?"

"I don't think so." And he was off down the steps, the drummers moving fast to get out of his way. He walked back up along the high boardwalk toward the bank, anxious about whether the Don had sent the full amount. It would have been like the old thief to send a short account—and a courtly note of apology along with it.

But the old man had played it straight. Walker, the banker, brought out the draft for a thousand dollars, drawn on an El Paso bank, looked it over carefully, then accepted it for deposit and withdrawals.

Walker was an odd-looking banker. He had a feed lot

on the edge of town, and, squat and strong, dressed more like a hand than a businessman, he seemed out of place in his oak-paneled office.

"I suppose this will do well enough," he said to Lee. "Though those damn Texas banks do go in and out of business like barbershops, the damned fools!"

It was important money for Lee; it was his wintering money. Now he wouldn't have to sell a colt off for grain and supplies.

"Mr. Walker," he said, "I have a notion to get one of the farmers around here to plant some oats and timothy on my place. Maybe some man who's short on land down here in the valley. If he'd do that, I'd go shares with him on the crop and get my horse feed out of the deal."

"Now there's strange talk for a rancher," Walker said. And his hard gray eyes gave Lee a sharp once-over. That look said, What the devil kind of fellow are you, anyway? A saloon tough, a rancher, or what?

"It's a good idea, and maybe I know a farmer'd be glad of the deal, if he could find some suitable meadow up there. Damn short growing season. It's short enough in the valley."

"Well, you get sun up there longer than you do in the valley."

"Yes," the banker said. "But I don't think that makes the difference. Anyway, I'll have Virgil go up and see you on Sunday, if you're going to be out at your place."

"Yes, I will."

"Virgil Payson. He's a nice fellow, and supposed to know his business. And I know he's looking for more growing land, so you might suit."

"All right, I appreciate it."

"Well," the banker said. "I've found that it's good business to put businessmen together. Somehow, the bank always gets something out of it in the end." He gave Lee a minimum smile.

Lee left the bank with a balance in his account of fourteen hundred and seventy-three dollars. And with twenty dollars spending money in his billfold. A solid citizen, a square John, and a man with one killing, one rape, and a black and blue face to his credit.

"The wild West . . ." Rebecca Chase had said.

Wild enough.

He still felt a sharp stitch in his side while he was walking down to the livery. Two little boys walked beside him for a while, copying his walk, the way he held himself.

He didn't do anything to encourage them, and after a while they walked off. He'd had enough of that kind of stuff. He'd even liked it for a time when he was young. To have a bunch of kids hanging around, showing them how to quick draw their wooden guns. Hard to believe he was ever such an ass as to do that.

The livery was off a side street that passed behind Mrs. Boltwith's. It was run by a woman, too, a skinny spinster named McFee. Mary McFee. She had a half-wit boy named Alfred to help her with the chores and mucking out. Supposedly her husband or betrothed or whatever had been killed by Pawnees on the Platte. Though, in Lee's experience, most men supposed to have been killed by Indians had died of the pox or the runs or something unromantic of that sort.

"Great God in Zion!" said Miss McFee. "That Englishman must have put up a heller to mark an American like that!" She was referring to Lee's face.

"Yes," Lee said. And he went over to the dun's stall. The big gelding was happy to see him and whinnied and nuzzled at him.

"Handsome horse," Miss McFee said.

"Yes. What do you have for sale, ma'am?"

"You're not selling that dun!"

"No. I'm looking for a nice pinto." He patted the dun on the nose. The big horse wasn't usually so

172

friendly. "A pony for somebody else."

"Oh, I've got a bunch, all of them prime stock. I don't keep scrubs."

No, Lee thought. I'll wager you don't keep them. You sell them.

"Let's look them over then, Miss McFee."

They walked out to the corral behind the livery, squeezing past old surreys and dusty, broken-down buggies for hire. The place smelled strongly of sour old leather and fresh horse shit.

"There the beauties are," said Miss McFee. "I don't know where that half-wit Alfred's gone to. Alfred! Oh, Alfred! Abusing himself in the tack room, I suppose. If the Lord sends half-wits to hell, that poor boy is headed there on a racer!"

There were seven horses loose in the corral. Three of them were scrubs, galled cow ponies with all the run run out of them. Another was a big sturdy plowhorse, looked like some Belgian in him. There were two pintos and a pretty little mare, a light-built gray with black stockings.

"What are you asking for the young pinto?"

"Oh, that's a fine horse, best Chippewa blood in the state," Miss McFee said. "That's one in a thousand."

"How much?"

"Oh, my goodness, I couldn't let Lightning go for less than $300. Or, since you're a friend, say $275."

"That's a fair price, and I'd pay it too," Lee said, "if I was Andy Carnegie. But since I'm not, I'll offer $75 flat."

"Great God in Zion!" said Miss McFee. "You're a jokester, you are, Mr. Lee!"

And so it went back and forth for several times, until Miss McFee sacrificed Lightning at $97.50, plus an old rope halter and lead.

"Nothing else for you?" asked Miss McFee, noticing that Lee had glanced at the mare quickly, twice. "She is

173

a little beauty, isn't she? Manuela Ryan—the captain's wife up at the lumber camp?—she brought that beauty in here consigned to sale. Manuela's in an interesting condition now, and the captain won't let her ride. Won't hardly let her walk, from what I hear! You'd think a fine figure of an Irishman like that could do better that some dark little dab of a Mexican girl that don't know beans when the bag is open. But that's men for you . . ."

Lee climbed the corral fence, which made his side hurt more than a little, and went slowly up to the mare to look her over. She was a well-behaved, friendly little horse, and had obviously been a lady's pet. She came prancing shyly up to Lee and stretched out her soft muzzle to be stroked.

He slid his hand over her and found no whip weals or galls, no spavin or leg-splint. Her neat little hoofs were sound as stones.

"Two hundred dollars," he said.

"I like a man with a sense of humor," said Miss McFee.

A while later, poorer by $97.50, and by an additional $243.75 for one lady's horse, three years old, furnished with bridle rein, martingale, and a sidesaddle, slightly worn, Lee handed Miss McFee his bank draft for the full amount.

"These monies to be returned to me, Miss McFee, if either animal proves broken-winded."

Miss McFee sighed and said all right. She told Lee that Alfred would bring the dun and pinto around to Mrs. Boltwith's, ready to travel, and that he would then take a note to Beatrice Morgan at the Arcady, telling her that she now owned a fine riding mare named Belita complete with tack.

A half-hour later, Lee rode out of town, the fresh dun dancing, the pinto trotting along at the end of his lead, and Lee's side hurting like the devil. It seemed taped tight enough, but the horse's motion hurt the side anyway. Lee held the dun in and sat a little sideways in the saddle, turned to favor the broken rib.

It was a hot day, the first really hot day that Lee had seen since coming to the valley. The sun came beating down through the clear mountain air, making the brush and grasses gleam with the light. Lee felt the sting of it even under the brim of his Stetson.

He looked back, from time to time, as he rode, checking the paces of the pinto. The small horse had a nice even stride, and he stepped high. A good pony. Fair enough exchange for shooting the boy's out from under him. Fairer than that, when you consider that he'd have been within his rights shooting the boy, too.

And the horse for the girl.

Well, probably something he'd regret, doing that. She was bound to take it as a personal thing. Probably a waste of money there. Nothing wrong with the mare, though.

Once clear of the town, Lee eased his rein and let the dun find his way up the broad meadows. He turned him aside once or twice, but generally the big gelding knew his way after only a couple of trips to town. Good horse.

Summer partridge, looking ragged as chickens, flushed from the scrub as Lee went by, flying in swift angles away, then ducking down into the brush again. There was a day when, broken rib or not, Frank Leslie would have drawn and shot on them. For practice, or just for the hell of it. And probably would have hit one too.

It occurred to Lee then, as it had before, that he might be slowing up with a gun. Well, if he was, it hadn't been enough to do Mickey Slawson any good—and Slawson had been quick.

But had he been a shade off? He sure hadn't tried for Slawson's head. And that Tom Small hadn't been set for a fight; too busy showing off.

And if he was a little slower than when he'd been twenty-three and killed Bob Trout and those other two men, what of it?

Settling down was to be the name of his game now.

Settling down and maybe getting married. It made him uncomfortable to think about it. He saw Rosilie smiling at him every time he really thought about it seriously. Well, it wouldn't be a girl from the valley. Not many farmers or small ranchers would want their darling daughters matched up with a shooter and brawler from God knows where. No. If he ever did make up his mind to do it—and the River Ranch was going to get damned lonely as the years went by if he didn't—he'd have to get a girl from outside. Maybe go to Helena and see about that stock-haul contract on the lumber railroad.

He'd been thinking about that just for his own horses in a few years. But it might make more sense to borrow from the bank for a five-year contract for stock cars. That way every rancher in the valley, and maybe someday every farmer too, would be hauling in his leased cars.

If Walker saw his way clear to making the loan. *And* if the railroad wasn't interested in factoring that hauling business themselves. Maybe not. Maybe not. Those people were lumber people up there, not really railroad people.

A solid businessman in a pretty valley. What would Bob Trout think of that? What would poor Holiday think of it? They'd both probably think it was funny.

He'd thrown away $243.75 on that damn mare.

He was just coming in sight of the river, late in the afternoon, when he saw the Indians. Crees, he supposed. They were fishing in the river.

There looked to be about a half-dozen all together, and a couple of them women.

176

Lee was considering turning the dun and riding around. A lone man with two good horses was some temptation to poor Indians. He was about to do that when he heard children's voices.

They weren't likely to be wanting trouble with their kids around. Lee aimed the dun for their camp.

There were lots of theories and advice on how to approach wild Indians, and maybe they were useful with wild Indians. But Lee hadn't seen a really wild Indian since he'd seen some naked Commanches riding out of Mexico fifteen or sixteen years ago. And that was only that one time.

Nowadays, most Indians weren't wild; they were just flat broke and out of luck.

He spurred the dun out into the shallow river rapids, hauling the reluctant pinto along behind, and booted the gelding up the opposite bank.

Four Indian men were sitting around a smoke-rack fire, smoking split salmon and trout over a broad bed of coals. One had a pistol in his belt; it looked like a Webley. Some Canadian Mountie must have gotten careless a while ago.

And the man sitting on the near end had a shotgun lying beside him. A single-barreled nothing-much, but a shotgun just the same.

Lee reined the dun over to a larch sapling and tied both horses to it. They'd circle and tangle, but it would take a while.

He nodded to the Indians. A woman was looking out at him from some kind of willow shelter they'd rigged up. She didn't seem too happy to see him. Lee smiled at her and swung down off the dun, keeping his hand away from his revolver. The children by the river didn't even look his way.

He unfastened his saddlebag, dug into it, and brought out one of Mrs. Boltwith's pies, a little the worse for wear. He had two pies in there. She had given them to him to remind Old Bupp what a pie was supposed to be about. He had two, but one was a rhubard pie, and Lee supposed the Indians would prefer the sweetness of the peach.

He took the peach pie out, unwrapped the heavy brown waxed paper she'd put around it, and set it out on the ground beside the campfire. He waved to the woman, pointed to the two little girls playing at the edge of the river, then pointed down to the pie.

Then he sat down and waited for the fish to cook.

CHAPTER TWELVE

There had been no trouble at all from Fishhook. No
Fishhook riders had come over the line, and only a few
dozen stray Fishhook steers had had to be chivvied back
off River land.

Sandburg, Bupp, and Tom Cooke had heard about
the fist fight; a cowboy named Budreaux had ridden by.
And Bupp wanted to hear about every punch.

"It was just a hard fight, Bupp; let it alone."

"Just a hard fight! You call that telling a story!"
Bupp hadn't thought much of the rhubarb pie, either.
"Well, thanks for giving the peach pie to those
Indians—if there *was* any Indians and you didn't
devour all that pie yourself riding up. Peach pie just
happens to be the only pie she does proper, I can tell
you. And you give it away. A rhubarb pie is no pie at all
without strawberries. Every cook in the world knows
that . . ."

When Lee asked Sandburg how Bupp's cooking was
coming along, Sandburg had considered the question
carefully and said, "You still need a knife to get at them
eggs."

So Lee told Bupp he'd give him the complete history
of the fight with the Englishman the day Bupp cooked a
good egg.

The first three days after Lee got back they'd spent

cleaning out brush down by the river crossing. It was rough work, and it played merry hell with Lee's broken rib. After the first day, working with his jaw clenched, and more sweat than usual running off him, Lee had to give up the ax work. He'd driven the team of sorrels they were using to haul and stack the heavier stuff instead. His rib didn't like that much, either, but he could do it.

He was getting so that he liked the rhythm of hard physical work, of using his hands that way. If he could keep liking that, he thought he might make a reasonable rancher some day. He thought he'd be sure to find a good market for the appaloosas over in Helena. They were a special breed, a showy-looking kind of horse as well as being strong mounts. Those rich Mine Kings over there should be happy to buy them.

And he was glad to see Sandburg being more friendly with Tom Cooke. He might not like working with an Indian, but he didn't show it anymore; they seemed to get along all right. It was one of those things that Lee had to worry about, it seemed, until it was fixed or had fixed itself. This one had fixed itself.

The pinto had pleased Tom Cooke, as why in hell shouldn't it?

Late in the afternoon on the third day, it started to look like rain, so they all came up from the river bank, Lee driving the team of sorrels home.

There was a strange horse tied at the house hitching post. Strange for a second, then Lee recognized the mare.

Beatrice Morgan had come to call.

She was sitting in the porch chair. The same chair India Ashton had used.

Sandburg and Tom Cooke raised their hats to her and rode off to the corral. But Bupp stayed to say hello.

"How are you, Miss Morgan?"

"Fine, Mr. Bupp," she said.

"Now, there's a prime little mare . . ." He climbed

180

off his cob to have a look. "Yes, now, there's a prime little mare."

"Thank you," she said. "Her name's Belita."

"Very nice. Oh, very nice," said Mr. Bupp.

He stroked the little mare's slim legs. "Never thrown out a splint in her life," he said. "What did she cost you?"

"She was a gift, Mr. Bupp."

"Damned nice gift, I say," said Mr. Bupp, and he glanced up at Lee and then went stumping off to the corral, leading the cob behind him.

"Good evening," Lee said to her. "It was nice of you to come see us."

"Not very respectable, I suppose," she said. She was wearing a long riding dress, a blue one, and was holding her straw hat on her lap as she sat. There was no doubt she had nice dark eyes.

"Not very respectable, but I wanted to come and thank you for her. She's too much of a gift, I know . . ." She looked down and toyed with the blue ribbon on her straw hat. "It's embarrassing to have that much of a gift . . . for just nursing you a little. That was nothing at all." She raised her eyes.

"I can tell it embarrasses you to have done it. I shouldn't have come." She stood up.

Lee climbed off the wagon and left it for one of the hands to come and get it.

"Sure, you should," he said. "I gave it to you for that smile you gave me before the fight, not for the nursing."

She blushed like a child. What in God's name was he supposed to do with her?

"Come on inside," he said, "and let's see what we have for supper."

They ate an early supper; rabbit stew and potatoes, and a dry-apple pie. Bupp put extra effort into the pie,

181

and it was quite good, but a little juicy.

"This pie is delicious, Mr. Bupp," she said.

"Call me Tim," said Mr. Bupp.

They all hadn't talked much as they ate; the rabbit stew had been good. Tom Cooke had shot the rabbits on the ridge in early morning.

When supper was over, Bupp scrubbed the dishes, and Sandburg and Tom Cooke said, "Good evening," and got up and left.

"Like to see the place before it gets dark?" Lee said to her.

"Oh, I would," she said. "My father raised horses. We had Morgan horses on our place in Illinois. People used to make jokes about Mr. Morgan raising Morgan horses."

They were walking out behind the house.

"Well, come on up to the meadow and see my young ones," Lee said. "If you like horses, you'll like them."

He led her out around the bunkhouse. He could hear Sandburg in there singing "Hop Up, My Ladies." It was a favorite song of his, and he had a nice deep voice to sing it with.

"What a pretty song," she said. "I don't think I ever heard that song."

"It's a square-dance song," Lee said. "We danced to that tune when I was a kid."

"Not us," she said. "My folks didn't let us dance at all. And my mother would only let us sing church songs in the house, except at haying . . ."

She walked along for a while without saying anything more, lifting the long skirt of her dress to keep it clear of grass.

"I suppose you think that's pretty funny—strange, I mean," she said. "For me to have been raised that way and turn out to become what I have." She looked over at him. "How I make my living . . ."

"I told you before that makes no difference to me at

all. That's not my business," Lee said.

"Yes, you're right," she said. "I only mention it all the time to keep you people from thinking about it secretly." She smiled. "As if that makes any sense at all . . ."

It was just the sort of thing that Lee didn't want to hear. If she wanted to come up, all right. There was no need for her to harp on being a whore, or talk about what he was thinking, either.

"There are the horses," he said.

The evening light was going fast. The two colts and the little filly, Lightning Bug, were playing in the long grass, galloping, rearing, kicking like lambs. They usually slept through the afternoon or wandered beside their mothers through the meadows. But in the evening, when it cooled, they became as lively as in the morning and played together, chasing each other more like puppies than young horses.

The little filly was racing ahead of the colts, kicking up her spotted behind and galloping along, her short, feathery tail cocked straight up in the air.

"What a darling," Beatrice Morgan said. "What do you call her?"

"Lightning Bug."

They watched the young horses running for a while.

"Is there something wrong with his eye?" she said, pointing at the bigger of the two colts. "He shakes his head and turns sideways when he runs."

Lee watched that colt, a tall, black-headed colt he was thinking of calling Long Tom. It ran along with no changes to its gait for a few strides. Then, just when he was about to tell her it was nothing, Lee saw the colt quickly shake its head, as if a fly was bothering it. It cantered sideways for a few dancing steps before it dug in to gallop after the others.

"Goddammit!" Lee said. "What the hell have Bupp and those two been doing not to see that!" He looked at the girl beside him. "You have a good eye for horses," he said.

"It might be nothing," the girl said. "Just a scratch from some tree branch."

Lee went down to the barn for a rope, and when he came back up, he'd brought Bupp and the other men with him and had apparently been talking to them unkindly, because Tim Bupp had nothing to say.

Lee coaxed the colt in and roped him gently, then went up the rope hand over hand, talking soothingly all the while. Then he and Bupp went over the colt carefully. It was nearly dark by then, and Tom Cooke went down and got a lantern.

The colt's left eye was scratched.

"Nothing too bad there, Mr. Lee, I promise you," Bupp said. "I'll wash it out with a little salt water tonight, and in a couple of days it'll be healed right up."

"If the colt will stand a muslin cloth drawn over the eye, I believe that will help keep it from inflaming the next day or so," Beatrice said.

"He probably won't stand it," Bupp said.

"Do it," said Lee.

"Now—"

"Do it."

"Unless you feel a patch would be better, Mr. Bupp," Beatrice said.

"Yes, I do," Bupp said. "This calls for a patch, and that's flat."

"All right," Lee said. "Let's take him down to the barn and get it done."

The colt didn't like it, but he was patient enough as Bupp washed the eye out with mild salt water and made a patch and tied it on with torn strips of cloth. Bupp was working by the light of two lanterns in a stall at the end of the barn. The main thing worrying the colt was being away from his mother and the other horses. Beatrice stood by him and soothed him, and she had torn the cloth ties for Bupp. She congratulated him on the neat patch he made.

When they finished with the colt, they decided to let it loose with the others, and Tom Cooke led it back up to the meadows.

After the men went back to the bunkhouse, Lee took Beatrice up to the house. They didn't say much on the walk.

She'd intended to stay, at least for the night, for sure, or she wouldn't have come up so late. Lee supposed she'd intended to bed down with him, but he didn't feel like it. There was something uncomfortable about the whole situation for him.

"Do you want me to make us some coffee?" she said when they went into the house.

"All right; I could do with a cup."

They sat at the kitchen table after the coffee was made and didn't say much of anything. It was a quiet night, almost no wind at all, and the only noise in the kitchen was the ticking of the iron stove as it cooled and a moth's fluttering against a lantern's smoky mantle.

She cleared her throat. "You have such a pretty place up here, Mr. Lee. You must be very happy with it."

"I guess you can call me Lee," he said, "and drop the 'mister,' since you're a guest in my house."

"All right," she said.

"My first name's Frederick, but most people call me Lee."

"All right."

They sat for a little longer, until the first light of the rising moon shone in through the kitchen window. Beatrice leaned over to put the lantern out so the room was only lit by the moonlight.

After awhile, Lee stood up.

"It's time for bed," he said. "You take my bedroom; I'll bunk out in the office."

"All right," she said. "I'm sorry to have come up so

late and put you to this trouble." Her face was smooth and white in the moonlight; her eyes were shadowed and dark.

"No trouble," Lee said. He bent to light the lantern for her to take to the bedroom. "Do you have night things?"

"I'll seep in my shift," she said.

He woke to her singing the next morning. She had a sweet voice, but she sang a little off tune. She was singing "Shenandoah."

When he got his shirt and pants on, Lee went down the hall to the kitchen. Beatrice was out in the yard washing her dress and shift in a fire-blackened old wash tub. The tub was propped up on four big rocks, and she had gotten kindling and built a fire under it.

She was wrapped from neck to toe in one of the blankets, had it pinned in place somehow, and was scrubbing her dress and shift. Lee saw her stockings and underthings, too. She was singing away, a little off tune, and looked happy as a spring robin.

Seeing she was out of the house for a while, Lee stripped and washed at the kitchen pump, then went and got clean clothes in the bedroom.

She'd slept in it only the one night, but the room already smelled of a woman.

When he'd dressed and come out, Bupp was in the kitchen starting breakfast.

"You're a little late, aren't you, Tim?"

Bupp gave him a sly glance. "Better too late than too early," he said and went back to greasing the skillet.

Beatrice came in the kitchen door with her arms full of wet clothes.

"Have you a clothesline and some pins, Mr. Lee?"

"Just Lee."

"Lee?"

"No, I guess not. We have some light line in the barn, but I don't think we have any clothespins at all."

"How do you dry your clothes?" she said.

"Generally," Lee said, "well, generally we dry them over the porch rail."

"I'll call Tom Cooke to get you some line," Bupp said.

"No, no. I'll put these over the rail. They'll catch the sun fine there."

She hurried through the kitchen with the damp clothes, and Lee saw the slim, bare whiteness of her feet flash under the edge of the blanket.

"I'm cooking ham and eggs for breakfast," Bupp said.

"Eggs?"

"Yes, dammit, eggs. There's nothing wrong with my eggs."

"So you say. What about the colt?"

"That scratch is clearing already. It wasn't much, and it couldn't have been bothering him long, or we'd have seen him favoring it . . ."

"So you say." Now she had all the men winking at him and starting work late so he could fuck his head off, as they supposed. It annoyed him.

Then Sandburg and Tom Cooke showed up, also way late to be eating breakfast. At least they kept their faces straight and didn't favor him with any of Bupp's sass.

When they were all seated at the kitchen table, Beatrice still wrapped in her blanket, Bupp started frying the ham in a big skillet and the eggs in a smaller one. He fried them for a considerable time.

"Tim," Beatrice said.

"Yes, ma'am?"

"Would you do me a favor?"

"Well, I probably would . . ."

"You see, I like my eggs way underdone, and I would

187

appreciate it if you'd let me have mine before they're really full cooked."

"You like underdone eggs?"

"I like them next thing to raw, Tim."

"Well, if you can eat them that way, not hardly cooked at all . . ."

He slid a wide-bladed butcher knife under two of the eggs and put them on a plate for her. They were already pretty hard. Then he added a slice of the ham and two of yesterday's biscuits, warmed up, to soak in the ham's gravy.

"I'll try mine underdone too," Lee said.

Sandburg and Tom Cooke said the same thing.

"Now, come on! You can't all like them eggs raw," Bupp said.

"Serve 'em out," Sandburg said. "I'll try anything."

After breakfast, Lee went down with the men to knock out the beams of the old tool shed. They'd been spiked in wrong to start with, and water running down the posts had rotted their ends out.

They pulled what spikes and nails they could, starting on the door-end beam, then got a trace chain wrapped around it and hitched the team of sorrels to the hook. The beam came tearing out like a rotten tooth.

But the second one split, and they had to pry and hammer that one out the hard way. Lee was worried that if they got too rough they'd have the whole shed down, which, except for that run of beams, was in good shape.

The third one popped out easy, though, and it looked as though they had their method for doing it down pat.

Beatrice came down from the house to see that one go. Her clothes had dried in the morning sunshine by then, and she had her blue dress on again. She looked nice, but Lee thought he'd have to figure out a way to ask her when she intended to be heading back to town. Even though there was nothing wrong with her looks,

188

barring, maybe, that her nose was a little big.

A whore on a ranch.

Ladylike or not, I'll find her out in the bushes with Tom Cooke if I'm not careful . . .

A dirty thing to think. He didn't believe it himself.

Though she'd sure as hell got down on her knees in front of some lumberjacks down at Rebecca's. You could bet on that. Not so much of a lady at five bucks a throw!

They got the fourth beam hooked up, cleared the chain, and Sandburg started out the sorrels. The beam groaned and then cracked free like a gunshot and flew out into the dirt.

"Now that's something like it!" yelled Bupp.

They had the beam business down pat.

"Would you like to take a ride around the ranch, Beatrice?" Lee asked her.

"Yes, yes, I would; it's so pretty. But I don't want to interrupt your work. And I do have to get back to town."

"Oh, a ride won't take long," Lee said. "The boys can finish this out."

Lee saw Bupp give Sandburg a glance at that. Well, the hell with them. If he had to worry for them, they could damn well work for him. It's what he was paying them for.

The little mare was a good goer. She could keep up with the dun quite well on level ground, and she went up and over banks and scrub like a rabbit, with Beatrice hanging on for dear life and laughing.

"I love her," she said. "She's a brave little horse." She bent and stroked the mare's sleek side.

"You look well together," Lee said. It was true enough. No reason not to tell the girl so.

Lee hadn't intended to go that far, but they stayed

out the whole afternoon, ate cold ham and biscuits and two damp pieces of Bupp's dry-apple pie. They got all the way up to the river falls.

It was near the ford where Lee had hung the cowboy, and he didn't want Beatrice seeing it or asking questions about it. So he turned off short at the rapids and found a place where they could water the horses.

Beatrice took off her high-button boots and her stockings and sat on the bank splashing her feet in the water.

Afterwards he gave her the cloth Martin had cut for him so she could dry her feet.

"My, what a pretty color," she said.

"It's for a neckerchief."

"Mr. Martin gave it to you, I'll bet," she said. "My, but that man has fine taste! Did you know he was from one of the finest families in New Orleans?"

"So I understand," Lee said. "I believe, though, that he doesn't think much of the Leicester family, the earl's family over in England . . ."

Beatrice laughed. "Yes, I know. He's always talking about that. But I think he's very fond of Mr. Ashton, has sort of a crush on him, you know?" She blushed.

"Hell, yes I know!" Lee said. "And for God's sake stop blushing, Beatrice. You're a damned saloon girl!"

"Yes." She blushed and then laughed. "I'm doing it again, I suppose."

"Yes . . ." Lee said. "Well, I think we ought to start back."

When they reached the meadows above the east ridge, she wanted to race. They rode the horses abreast, she counted to three, and off they went.

The little mare was handy and quick, and for a few strides she kept up. Then the dun began to pull ahead. Lee held him in. He didn't want to widen the gap. They thundered over the ridge at a hard gallop, the little mare just behind. They jumped a low hedge of pitch pine,

190

threaded through some trees—the mare doing even that—and ran flat out down the wide bowl of the pasture, headed for the bunkhouse.

Tom Cooke was out by the corral and saw them coming. Lee could see that he thought for a moment there might be trouble. But a moment later, when the boy could make out their faces and knew there wasn't trouble, he called out a long, yodeling Indian yell to spur them on.

The dun was driving hard for the finish now, and Lee had the devil's own time to hold him up without the girl seeing it, but he managed it so they flew into the bunkhouse yard almost together. They were going so fast that they had to haul around the corner of the building before they could stop.

"Oh, oh," the girl called out, breathless. "You dog, you cheated! You pulled that poor big horse in!" She patted her little mare. "Never mind, Belita, we did very well!"

That night they had a very good dinner.

By the time the mare was rested, it was too late for Beatrice to get back down to Cree before dark. She asked to go, and Bupp offered to ride down with her. They needed more flour and a basket of eggs. And Lee had forgotten the horse liniment when he'd come up from town.

But Lee said no. There were Crees fishing the river, and it would be better if she rode in daylight. Bupp could go with her the next day. And so she stayed.

Tom Cooke had shot a deer, and Bupp baked a cake. That was where the last of the flour and eggs had gone. He'd baked the cake from memory, from seeing Mrs. Boltwith bake one for Chris Nasby's birthday. Old Nasby was foreman out at Bent Iron and as harsh an old man as there ever was. His cowboys had been hoping a real birthday cake would soften him up, and as it turned out it did. A cowpoker had come in the next day to thank Mrs. Boltwith personally. Said the old Tartar had broken down and cried.

This was the cake that Bupp tried to remember while he baked it.

It was just the cake part. He didn't have any cream or chocolate or vanilla for the icing. Sandburg picked him some berries. Blackberries and red raspberries were what he had.

The venison was fresh, but very good, and they had roast potatoes and carrots with it, all freighted up from town with the feed and seed.

The venison and vegetable were very good. The vegetables were a treat, not something that Lee could keep buying like that. Rather sooner than later, Bupp was going to have to start a kitchen garden.

Then came the cake.

It didn't look very good. Something had happened to the middle of it. It was sagged down. Looks were exchanged around the table, but nobody said anything. Beatrice had asked Bupp if there was anything at all she could do to help out, but he'd told her no.

Bupp sliced it for everybody, saying he didn't want it messed up. Lee took the first bite, and it was good. It was quite good. The taste wasn't exactly like cake; it was more like a big damp cookie. But it was very rich and good, especially with the berries poured over it.

Beatrice said that it was the best thing of the kind she'd ever had and that Bupp had better be sure and remember the recipe.

So there was nothing the matter with the dinner. Afterwards Sandburg brought up his checker set. His boy had been a bear at checkers, and they played by the lamplight. Tim Bupp beat them all. It was Bupp's evening.

When the men were gone to the bunkhouse, Lee and Beatrice sat awhile in the kitchen the way they had the night before. They didn't say much. Lee still felt uncomfortable about her. Just being with her in the kitchen made him restless. She was a difficult girl to figure out, and, like most women he had known, she worked at it to make the figuring more difficult.

It was hard to imagine her taking five dollars to do some of the things men liked. And that was her game, as he well knew, to make that difficult to imagine.

When they got up to go to sleep, she went to the bedroom as she had the night before. Lee went to the little office room.

He didn't know whether she wanted him to just let her come and visit and go away again like a decent girl or if she wanted him in bed.

He lay on the narrow horsehair sofa in the ranch office, watching the branches of a pine outside the window cast black, moving shadows onto the room wall. It looked like a big eagle's wing, a black wing beating slowly on the wall.

He waited a long time. Then he stopped thinking about what the girl wanted and got up and went down the hall into the bedroom.

CHAPTER THIRTEEN

She was awake. From the doorway, he saw her lying beneath the rough sheet, her arms and throat and face white, gleaming in the moonlight flooding through the bedroom windows. She was looking at him.

He went over to her without a word, reached down, and slowly pulled the sheet back. Her thin cotton shift was as white as her skin.

She lay watching him and didn't say anything.

He reached down, slipped his hand through her thick dark hair, and gripped her by the back of her neck. Then he took her by the arm with his other hand and pulled her up off the bed until she was standing there against him, barefoot and small.

When he took the material of her shift in his hands, she raised her arms like a child being undressed. He slipped the material up and off.

Then he took his hands away and looked at her.

She was almost thin, with narrow hips and slim legs. He could see the rippled outline of her ribs under the soft white skin. Her breasts were sharp pointed and heavy for her size. They sagged a little and swung slightly when she breathed. They cast shadows in the moonlight against her skin.

He reached out, took them in his hands, and squeezed gently, then harder, weighing them in his grip, tugging gently at her nipples. She swayed against him as he pulled and stroked and played with her until her long nipples were swollen and stiff. Then he put his arms around her, a hand under her buttocks, and lifted her up onto the bed.

He slid in after her, knelt over her, and put his hand over the warm thatch of dark hair at her groin. He rubbed her there until he felt her damp and wet. Then he pushed a finger into her. He left it in her for a few moments, then pulled it out, raised his hand, and held the moist finger to her lips, stroking her lips with it.

He felt her open her mouth. She licked at the wet finger gently, sucking and biting at it as delicately as a kitten.

"You like that, don't you?" he said to her softly. "You've taken some cunt, haven't you, in your time?"

She looked up at him. Dark eyes. And didn't say a word.

"I've got something else for you, little whore," he said. His cock was up and hurting him, it was so hard.

He knelt up higher, over her, took a handful of her hair, and pulled her up to it. She thrust her face up and took it, moaning, as if she were desperate, and licked and sucked at it, not caring what sounds she made.

After a few moments, he pushed her away, forcing her head back down to the pillow. She lay, panting, looking up at him.

"That's what you're good for," he said.

And she smiled up at him and shook her head, then lifted her slender arms to him and said, "Oh, my dearest . . ."

She took him in like a river.

Early in the morning they heard Bupp and the others in the kitchen, talking softly, getting their breakfast. Later they heard horses out by the corral and Bupp saying something to someone.

Then, in a few minutes, horses' hoofbeats. Then nothing at all but singing birds from time to time and the sound of wind in the trees around the house.

They fucked and made love, and made love and fucked again, and while they were lying still, resting in each other's arms, she told him how she came to whoring, what her family had been, and her life. And how ashamed she'd been of the pleasure that she'd sometimes got in whoring.

"The other girls would say they always hated it and got no pleasure at all. But I sometimes did. Sometimes, if the man was nice, or handsome, or somebody I could dream about. Then I got pleasure from it. I didn't care what they did, sometimes. Once four men took me up to a room and they made me do everything . . . and I liked it." She started to cry. "That makes me as bad as a girl can get, I guess . . ."

"Not for me," he said. "Or any other man who is a man."

But he didn't tell her about himself.

He told her some things, about where he was born and his family, and something about the horse work he'd done as a young man. He told her of hunting and riding guard, of getting into the sporting life and gambling. And he told her about Mexico and being a gunhand for an old man.

But he didn't tell her that he had killed more than thirty men face to face.

He didn't tell her his name.

They didn't eat breakfast. They took some biscuits and cold venison and went down to the corral and saddled their horses, standing the animals side by side. Beatrice knew what she was doing, but Lee checked the mare's girth just the same, to be sure she hadn't held her breath when Beatrice tightened the cinch ring.

Then they rode back up to the river and swam naked at noon in a pool. The running water made little eddies past a boulder. The water was cold as snow and the sun was hot.

They ate their venison and biscuits by the river and spent the rest of the day riding hard over the north boundary of the ranch. It was big-pine country up there, and Lee showed her the place he was planning to put in a line shack so that a small crew could cover the place better, with a man posted high on the mountain for roundups and drives when the horseherd bigged up. The line shack could come right out of that heavy timber, cut two-feet square so a little green warping wouldn't matter.

They talked about cabins and how they were best made. Beatrice described one her father had put up with nothing but an ax and an adz when he was young. The corners all stacked and fitted square, no notched logs at all.

Then they pushed the horses down into scrub country, the little mare jumping and bucketing along, with Beatrice laughing and hanging on.

They rode past the place where Lee had raped India Ashton, and Beatrice asked him what was wrong. He shrugged, and they went on by, Beatrice thinking she'd been mistaken. But he was quieter for the rest of the ride. Thinking about the Ashtons. Thinking what Rosilie would have thought of Beatrice. Probably wouldn't have liked her. Rosilie was red-headed with blue eyes. Beatrice was dark. And Rosilie was always laughing, even when something hurt her. She had had the courage of a brave lad about everything. Beatrice was a softer, sadder girl. She only laughed a lot when she was riding.

Wouldn't have liked her. Always mooning around about something, she'd have said. And she hardly has any legs at all . . . sticks, more like it . . ."

197

Rosilie had even laughed when she was dying. "That's one on us," she'd said. "But you're not getting out of a wedding that easy, Frankie, not that easy." And then she was dead. In his arms, just like in a storybook.

Oh, how he'd killed Johnny Deuce! And if he'd killed him a thousand times—a thousand *thousand* times—it wouldn't be the beginning of enough.

They rode in silence down to the west ridge, and Beatrice didn't ask him if anything was wrong.

They saw Sandburg working on the fence in the upper meadows. He waved, but they didn't stop.

At supper, Beatrice was very nice and told funny stories to them about her grandfather Zebedee, who captained a pig boat on the Mississippi. He had known Mike Fink well and said that Mike was nothing out of the ordinary in size, but was a fierce biter in a fight. Once he started to lose a fight, her grandfather said, Fink would start in biting like a bulldog. Some boatmen had got together once and bought Fink a collar and chain for his birthday. On the collar it said: *He Bites.*

Her grandfather had met Jim Bowie twice, and Bupp and Sandburg wanted to know about him. A tall, handsome man with good manners and black sideburns, her grandfather had said. A Kaintuck with New Orleans manners.

"What about his knife?" asked Bupp.

"Grandad never saw no knife on him. A businesslike gentleman," Beatrice answered.

"If you believe it," said Bupp. "That man was a devil out of hell in a fight!"

After supper—something had gone wrong with Bupp's berry pie; it tasted of salt—they all went out to the porch to drink their coffee. Tom Cooke stood at the rail.

The sun was setting over the mountains in a very fiery

way, all golds and greens and burning reds.

"The Assyrian came down like a wolf on the fold," Beatrice said, quoting from a poem.

They all joined in, except Tom Cooke: "And his chariots were painted in purple and gold."

The sunset looked just like that.

That night was as fine as the night before had been. They were very good to each other, and Lee felt more and more for the girl. It was getting to be a serious thing the more time she spent at the ranch.

In the morning, he asked her what trouble Rebecca might give her about missing work at the Arcady.

"The hell with her," Beatrice said.

Lee got back to work that day, and Beatrice worked with them, helping to load fence rails after Lee and Sandburg had cut them out and then driving the team down to the meadows. She had a natural way with horses, and the sorrels didn't make any trouble for her.

They worked hard all day because the upper pasture needed to be fenced before they could turn the mares out into it. Tom Cooke had seen mustangs near the Fishhook line, and, branded stock or not, Lee didn't want them at his mares. If there was a stallion among them, there'd be trouble with Shokan. The big appaloosa had crippled another stud the month before Lee bought him.

They got the south line finished before dark, had a cold supper with Bupp's salty berry pie, which didn't taste as bad as it had the night before, and went to bed.

Beatrice rubbed Lee's back to get the aches out, and then they started to play wrestle and so forth. They broke the bed. The side split, and the slats fell out on the floor. So they dragged the mattress onto the floor, too, and slept on it there.

Beatrice stayed up at the River Ranch for three more days and might have stayed longer. But on Friday morning, while Bupp and Sandburg were in the corral yard digging post holes, and Lee and Tom Cooke were down in the mud laying a new length of lead pipe to the trough, a man came riding up from the valley.

Beatrice had done her washing and was hanging her shift and dress out over the porch rail to dry. She'd taken to wearing one of Lee's shirts and a pair of his trousers rolled up at the cuffs and tied around the waist with a piece of cord.

She'd looked out over the valley and seen the man riding up some distance away.

She called down to the corral, and Tom Cooke climbed out of the ditch and up onto a fence rail for a look.

"Old man," he said to Lee. And Lee nodded and kept working. It might be that farmer Walker was sending up. What was the man's name? Virgil something. Payton? Something like that.

Lee climbed out of the ditch and wiped his hands on his new bandanna. Beatrice had hemmed it for him with a needle and thread he kept for sewing up the horses when they were hurt. He'd told her what Mr. Martin had said, and she'd double hemmed it.

He walked past the corral to meet the farmer coming in. An old man, somewhere in his fifties, maybe late fifties, in a rusty black suit. Neat white hair under a black slouch hat.

Lee stopped where he was and tried to think how he might get back to his gun. He'd left his gunbelt hanging on the fence when he started working down in the mud.

And it looked like that was going to kill him, because this old man was no farmer.

The old man rode closer, and when he stopped his horse about a dozen feet away, he turned it to clear his right side. The suit coat was tucked back, and the worn butt of a Colt Peacemaker curved up out of a tie-down holster. The old man's foot was out of that stirrup, hanging straight down so as not to cramp his draw.

His eyes were a pleasant brown.

"You'd be Mr. Lee," he said. He had a slow border drawl.

George Small, as sure as God made little green apples.

It felt strange to Lee. He'd thought of being killed, although never while he was gunfighting. He used to think about it afterwards. And here it was. This old man was going to kill him now. And he'd kill the others—no witnesses.

Oh, Beatrice, I did you no favor.

"That's right," he said. "And you'd be George Small."

The old man's brown eyes twinkled like a sweet grandad's. He glanced down at Lee's waist where his gun would be.

"White hair fooled you, didn't it?"

"That's right."

"Young men these days . . ." he shook his head, "just ain't raised right."

He was going for it. Lee saw the relaxation in his eyes.

"Good morning!"

The old man froze.

It was Beatrice, come down from the porch.

"My," she said, "you must have started from town real early, mister. Please to step down and have some breakfast with us."

The old man must have seen her standing up at the house, but he hadn't realized she was a woman.

And he wasn't going to kill her. The not-going-to-do-it look was in his eyes. Lee could see it.

Can't kill the woman, can't kill the rest. Can't kill Lee.

Lee took a deep breath. The morning air was sweet as

fine champagne.

"Do," he said to George Small. "Step down and have some breakfast with us."

The old man threw back his head and laughed like a boy.

"You're a tarnation fool for luck, Mr. Lee," he said. He swept his slouch hat off and made a bow in the saddle to Beatrice. "In more than one way that I can see." He smiled at Lee in a friendly fashion. "I don't have time to stop for breakfast, but perhaps if your lady will excuse us, we might talk some business."

"Oh, yes," said Beatrice, "I'm sorry. You're sure you won't have even some coffee, Mr.—"

"Small," he said. "George Small." He bowed to her again. "But I thank you kindly for the offer."

She smiled back and turned and walked away toward the house.

"If this matter is about your brother, Mr. Small," Lee said. "You're on a fool's errand. Your brother rustled some of my stock and then murdered a boy who tried to stop him."

"So I've heard, and I'm sorry to say I wasn't the least surprised," the old man said. "Tom was a rotten pup; bound to make a rotten dog. Though naturally I was a slightway curious who stopped his clock."

"If not over that then, why are you here?" Lee said.

The old man's eyes looked merrier than ever.

"Business," he said. "You have apparently offended a young lady. The young lady is rich and has engaged me to redress her injury."

He tucked his foot back in the stirrup, flipped his coattail over the butt of his revolver, and turned his horse to go.

"Mr. Lee," he said, over his shoulder. "I'll expect you in town tomorrow. Don't disappoint me, now . . ."

And off he rode, straight and easy in the saddle, and

fresh as paint.

Lee couldn't fight him. Barring that he didn't want to fight the old man, he just couldn't weather another killing. One more shooting and Tod Phipps would have to call him out. For if he didn't, and the cowboys got the notion that Phipps was afraid, his day as Marshal was done. Phipps was not the man to let that ride.

Win or lose, either way it would finish Lee in the valley. He'd be marked a cold killer.

The old man was downy. It should be possible to talk sense to him—or pay him off if it came to that.

He walked slowly back to the corral and took his gunbelt down and buckled it around his waist.

"Will he raise the hay?" Sandburg said.

"What's wrong?" said Tim Bupp.

Lee saw Tom Cooke come running from the bunkhouse. He had his old Spencer rifle. He slowed down when he saw the old man had ridden off and stood in the yard watching him go out of sight.

"What's wrong?" Sandburg said.

"Will Mr. Payson do the hay?" Beatrice said. She'd remembered the farmer's name.

"That wasn't Payson," Lee said.

He went up to the kitchen to get a cup of coffee and to have some time away from the men to think. Beatrice was making a berry pie. Bupp had said it was all right, since pies weren't serious cooking.

"Is something worrying you?" she said.

"That's Tom Small's brother."

"Oh, my God," Beatrice said. She put her hand to her mouth. "Has he put the law on you? There's a federal marshal in Helena."

"That's not his style," Lee said. "I hope you're not putting any salt in that pie . . ."

"No," she said, "I'm not." She was rolling out the dough with an old sarsparilla bottle. "Do you want me to go down to town now, Lee?"

"You're welcome here for as long as you like. You're about the hardest worker I've got."

She was reforming the dough, packing it into a ball, and then kneading it, squeezing it between her fingers.

"I'll go."

"Not to Rebecca's. Unless you want to."

She sighed. "No, I won't go back to Rebecca's."

"If she makes any trouble for you at all, Beatrice, tell her I said to leave you alone."

Beatrice smiled and rolled the dough out again.

"Rebecca doesn't pay much attention to what men say, except for Mr. Phipps."

"Just tell her what I said. She won't bother you."

Beatrice draped the dough down into the pie pan, crimping it around the edge with her thumb. Lee sipped his coffee and sat watching her while she got a tomato can full of raspberries from the food safe and poured them into the pan, stirring them with her finger to even them out. Then she sprinkled sugar over them.

"I never learned to make an open-top pie without it drying out," she said.

"You can come up again . . . in a while . . . when this blows over."

"Would it help if I talked to Mr. Small? He seemed like a nice old man. I'll bet he didn't know what that brother of his was up to."

She'd learn soon enough once she was back in town.

"George Small is a bad man, Beatrice. A gunhand. I suppose twice the man his kid brother ever was . . ."

She put the pie plate down, and he saw that her left hand was trembling. A nervous girl.

"But he . . ." she sounded breathless, "he could have shot you. You didn't have your gun! And he didn't!"

"Because you came down just then. He's an old-fashioned man, I suppose."

"Are you sure he's so bad? People change . . ."

Lee finished his coffee and stood up.

"When you put that pie in the oven, come down to the corral. We're going to pull that old pipe; I want you to drive the team."

The rest of the day was like the other days had been.

Lee stopped Bupp from talking about Small and what had happened and kept them all at the work. And that was hard enough. The water pipe had been of good quality. It was fine two-inch lead pipe. But it had been laid in thirty-foot lengths. They were more than one man—or four men and a girl—could lift, unless they wanted to be rough and lever it around and bend it, maybe break it.

Lee had an idea that it had been laid into place by a couple of drag teams from the lumber camp. It was the sort of work those people were used to doing.

So he had the men dig a dirt ramp to the new trench the pipe was to rest in, and then worked out a way to get two teams on the job, pulling together: one team to haul the pipe straight out, taking most of the weight, the other team to slew it sideways off the ramp into the trench. It was hard work. Just picking a second team from the riding stock and tacking up a harness for them took a lot of time.

If he'd had the braces, wrenches, and a man who knew pipe soldering, he might have sawed the damn pipes up into short lengths, laid them where he wanted them, and then rejoined the pieces.

If he had the braces, the wrenches, and the man.

They finally got it done late in the afternoon after two false starts that took an hour each to rerig and set up all over again. They got the pipe laid in, well supported, all the way from the pump-off pipe beneath the house, out across the yard, and down to the corral troughs.

Straight, easy flowing, and buried two feet deep. Counting digging out the ditch the day before, it was two days' work.

Lee had enjoyed every bit of it. He'd made certain of that, knowing trouble was coming. It was as if he were storing up the day, storing up the River Ranch, and Beatrice, and the men, to last him for a long while.

He'd decided to go into town and offer George Small a thousand dollars if he would give India Ashton back her money. She surely couldn't have paid him more than that, and probably a damn sight less.

It would mean selling a colt for sure, maybe the filly, Lightening Bug, to get through the winter. But it was the only way to stay in the valley as a rancher instead of as some shooter for the weeklies to come and write about, always figuring he killed the old man. That could fall out differently, too.

It would cost him the last of the Mexican money. But it might be done. The old man seemed reasonable enough.

And he'd had this good day of work and the pleasure of Beatrice being on his place. There were a lot of things not as good as all that.

After supper that night, they all sat out on the front porch and drank their coffee and ate Beatrice's berry pie.

"It's a good pie," Bupp said. "I'll say it before anyone else does. It's as good a pie as any I can make."

After the men went down to the bunkhouse, Beatrice and Lee stayed out on the porch awhile, watching the moon come up over the mountains.

After an hour, its light filled the whole valley below like silver in a cup.

They left early the next morning. Lee on his big dun, Beatrice on Belita. Beatrice was wearing her blue dress again.

"What are you going to do in town?" Lee asked her.

"I'll help Mrs. Boltwith with the maid work at her place, and maybe Mr. Martin will let me keep his stock . . ."

"Not serve his customers?"

"No," she said, reining the little mare in. "The ladies wouldn't take cloth from me."

"Beatrice . . ."

"Don't you say anything more to me," she said, "or I'll start to cry, and I know you don't like that about me." She spurred Belita and rode on ahead.

When they reached the valley at the lower river crossing, Lee had to turn back and wait until Tom Cooke came up behind them. He'd followed them all morning, with his Spencer rifle across his saddlebow. Lee looked back and saw some blackbirds rising from the scrub where the boy was following.

It took some doing to get Tom Cooke to turn around and go home, but he finally turned and went, walking his pinto out of sight into the dwarf willow.

Lee and Beatrice rode on across the river and out onto the valley grass toward Cree.

The town was quiet when they rode in, and they went to Mrs. Boltwith's first. The lady was in her kitchen, and she seemed pleased to see them together.

"Now, you two are showing a little sense!" she said. "Beatrice, Rebecca is fit to be tied. Miss High and Mighty isn't used to having a girl ride off on her like that." She glanced at Lee. "Do you know that woman tried to get Marshal Phipps to go out after her as a thief?"

"For what?" said Beatrice. "I never stole a thing in my life!"

"She said a silver bracelet."

"That makes me laugh," said Beatrice. "To hear a tale like that! She sold bracelets to me and Sally Betts and took the price out of our money every week. I bought that damn bracelet twice over!"

"What did Phipps do?" Lee asked.

"He had to go to Butte last week, or he might have come out after you. Those two are thick as thieves, and so they should be, for thieves is what they are. Silver bracelets!"

"I'm not going back to work," Beatrice said.

"Well, hallelujah!" said Mrs. Boltwith, and she glanced at Lee. "Child, that's good news. You come and work here at the hotel for me, and you'll be company, too."

Beatrice started to sniff and dab at her eyes, and Mrs. Boltwith hugged her.

"Have you got a man staying here?" Lee said to Mrs. Boltwith. "A decent-looking old man. He has white hair."

"The only old man I've got here is the minister, Mr. Pierce. And that poor man has got no hair on his head at all. Try over at Mrs. Foster's. Poor Reba'll take anything that moves and has two dollars to rub together."

Lee got up. "Well," he said, "I'll be going."

Beatrice looked at him, but she didn't say anything.

"We'll fix up your room for you, Mr. Lee," Mrs. Boltwith said. "My new maid-girl and me." She gave Beatrice a nudge with her elbow.

"Goodbye," Lee said.

Beatrice just looked at him and said nothing.

Lee went down the boardwalk to the bank. He had to wait for a farmer to finish business, and then cashed a hand draft for one thousand dollars.

Lee borrowed a piece of paper and a clerk's pen in the bank and wrote a note.

Mr. Small:

Enclosed you will find a thousand dollars

cash. I think it makes good sense for both of us, for you to take this, and go back home with it, in a peaceable fashion.

Frederick Lee

Then he put the ten one-hundred dollar bills in with the note and borrowed another piece of paper to fold it up in. The clerk sealed it for him with the bank's wax and stamp.

On the way out of the bank, Lee passed the land agent, Calthrop. The land agent nodded and passed on his way, still grudging from the way Lee had spoken to him about his loose tongue.

At Mrs. Foster's he asked for George Small.

"Mr. Small is out just now," said Mrs. Foster, who was a tiny lady with a milky-white blind eye.

"I would like to leave something for him," Lee said. "It's important that he get it personally."

The little lady bristled up like a porcupine.

"This is a respectable premises," she said. "If you leave a message for a boarder, then that boarder will get the message—unopened!" She gave Lee a hard look out of her good eye.

He handed the paper to her.

"I'm at Mrs. Boltwith's," he said. The one-eyed lady sniffed at that. "You can reach me there—if there's an answer."

Lee picked up the two horses in front of Mrs. Boltwith's and led them around to the livery.

Miss McFee wasn't there, so he handed the horses over to her half-witted hostler.

"Curry them down good and give them some grain."

The half-wit boy smiled and nodded, ducking his head again and again.

By late afternoon, Lee was thinking about going over to Mrs. Foster's to see if Small had come back and gotten the note and money. It was a lot of money just to leave somewhere.

Lee was in the hotel kitchen, drinking coffee and smoking a cigar a drummer had given him. The cigar had been made in Alabama and was supposed to be as good as the finest Havana. It tasted a little strange, though.

Mrs. Boltwith had gone out, and Lee and Beatrice were sitting in the kitchen, resting up from dinner. Beatrice still had the dishes to do.

Lee got up and opened the back door to throw the cigar out. He surprised a little boy, about ten years old, standing there with his hand raised to knock. He was a ragged kid with pinned-up overalls.

"What can I do you for sport?" Lee said. "Mrs. Boltwith's out of the house."

The little boy didn't say anything. He dug in his pocket and took out Lee's note.

Lee took it, but when he reached for some change to give the boy, the kid turned and ran off down the alley.

Lee went back to the table and sat down and opened the note.

His thousand dollars were still in there, but the bills had all been torn in half.

Something was written in pencil across the top of the paper. It said:

Young men these days just ain't raised right. I'm over at the Arcady. You come see me or I'll come see you.

Beatrice came and read it over his shoulder. She reached out and touched the torn money with her finger. Her hand was trembling.

"I suppose," she said, "I suppose you'll have to go and kill that old son-of-a-bitch, my dear . . ."

CHAPTER FOURTEEN

"I think that money is still good," Lee said. "I think Walker can exchange them for good bills at the bank, then send these to Denver and get them replaced." He folded the torn bills up and tucked them into his vest pocket.

He finished his cup of coffee and stood up.

Seeing Beatrice's face, he said, "I'll try and talk the old man out of it. It's just a lot of damned foolishness."

He left the kitchen without kissing her and walked down the hall to the stairs. Beatrice watched him from the door to the kitchen, until he turned out of sight to climb the stairs.

Lee went up to his room, sat on the bed, and shucked the old rounds out of his revolver and replaced them with fresh ammunition from a box he had bought at Kimble's. The weapon was clean, so he didn't fool with it, or oil it again. He found he did better by not fussing with the gun. He didn't even practice with it much anymore. Years ago he had practiced every day, sometimes for seven or eight hours a day, drawing and shooting whenever he could afford the cartridges.

He'd stopped doing that a while ago, however. He could draw the pistol and fire it, all in his head. And that seemed to tell him very well what he could do with it. His muscles appeared to follow his thinking.

The old man was probably still pretty handy. More

important, India Ashton had sent a lot of hate along with him. Lee wondered if the fact that he himself deserved killing for what he done would harm his shooting any. Probably not. He'd never seen a bad man die from being bad.

Of all times for Phipps to have gone to Butte, the one time he might be of use. Lee considered whether the marshal might be shy, happier to be absent from killing occasions. But it wasn't likely, not having worked for Hickok. Hickok had a nose for a frightened man, and any man who rode with him was anything but that.

Lee got up off the bed, opened his trousers, and tucked his shirt well down before buttoning them up again. He'd seen a man killed in New Mexico because his draw got caught in a loose shirttail hanging out. A silly thing to be worrying about. The look he'd seen on India Ashton's face had been a merciless look. Small was of an age to have been her father.

He strapped his gunbelt on, settled it on his hips, and left the room. He went down the stairs, back through the hall past the kitchen. He glanced in. Beatrice was washing dishes; she didn't look up at him. He went on out back to the outhouse and took a piss.

Either way it went, chances were he'd have to leave Cree. It would likely be one shooting too many for the valley people—and more than likely one too many for Tod Phipps.

Crossing the street to the Arcady, Lee saw that the afternoon light had turned to evening dusk. Some children were still playing in the street, chasing back and forth with a little yellow dog. The lamps would be lit in the saloon. Something to take care about. Shadows and shifty shooting. He didn't know why, but he sometimes fired a fraction to the left in uncertain light. Not much, maybe half an inch or an inch—just a little bit to the left. No telling why.

He went up the steps to the batwing doors. There

were people in there early, talking and laughing. No Fishhook riders, he hoped. He pushed the doors open and walked in.

He saw the old man right away. White hair. He was sitting at one of the tables to the side, talking with a drummer in a yellow suit. The old man looked to be telling a joke. The drummer was laughing and nodding his head. They both had beer mugs in front of them.

The old man looked up at Lee right away and nodded in a friendly fashion as if he'd been waiting for him to come and have a drink. Then he said something more to the drummer, got up, and walked around the table to stand about thirty feet from the door, looking at Lee in an amused sort of way.

There were cowboys at the bar pretty far down. From the quick glance he gave them, Lee didn't see any Fishhook men, at least none that he recognized. There were two lumberjacks playing cards on the bar, too. One-up, or some game for drinks of that sort.

Lee started toward the old man, keeping his hand well away from his gun. When he was close enough not to have to yell, he said, "Mr. Small—"

The old man shook his head as if Lee were showing bad manners and drew his gun.

He had a wonderful draw.

It was the prettiest, old-fashioned draw that Lee had seen in years. He'd seen Bill Longley draw that way once at a dogfight in Baton Rouge.

It was a smooth swift circle.

The hand circled back, hooking the black coat out of the way, and going on down to the gun without a pause, bringing it up level.

Nothing jerky or hurried about it. All smooth and swift.

Lee shot the old man in the chest, high, and drove him staggering back across the floor, his coattails flapping.

But the old man's Colt had come level out of that perfect draw—and went off with a blast.

The slug struck Lee in the meat of his left shoulder and spun him hard.

That spinning saved his life, because the old man, still stumbling back, shot at him again. Lee heard the bullet go buzzing like a bee just past the front of his chest. If he'd been standing, facing front, it would have killed him.

He shot the old man low into the belly, and that put Small down on the floor, hard.

Lee jumped as fast as he could to the left, scrambling. He knew he must look a panicked fool doing it, but he was damn glad he had, because that poisonous old son-of-a-bitch cut loose again from flat on his back on the floor. Lee felt the snap and tug as the round went through the right-side flap of his buckskin vest.

From there, there was only one way to go. Lee dove for the floor—something he hadn't done in a fight for ten years.

And damned if George Small didn't fire again.

The round burned Lee across the calf as he hit the sawdust. He shot into the old man's body for the third time and killed him.

There was a long, heavy silence in the Arcady.

Nobody said a word.

Lee rolled slowly over and then climbed to his feet. He was feeling sick to his stomach from the shoulder hit. The slug had hit him hard.

He felt dizzy, and his leg hurt like fire from that graze. The old son-of-a-bitch had shot him to pieces. What a gunman he must have been when he was young and riding the Missouri border.

What a gunman.

Lee limped over to look at the old man lying on the dirty floor. He looked terrible, the way they always did: small and beaten up. He had turned on his face when he died, and his tongue was hanging out onto the dirty sawdust.

Lee limped over to a spitoon beside the bar, bent over, and vomited into it. He felt sick as a horse.

None of the people in the Arcady had anything to say.

Mr. Martin probed and took the bullet out up in Lee's room at Mrs. Boltwith's. It didn't hurt too badly, because he'd gotten up there fast, and Lee's shoulder was still fairly numb. Lee's leg stung more from the graze than the shoulder hurt.

"You," Mr. Martin said, his frog eyes bulging, "have got what the penny-dreadfuls call a minor wound. Which means it will hurt like blazes soon enough, but will not cripple you, since it impacted the bone but did not break it. But it may well *kill* you if it becomes inflamed with infectious pus." He was washing out the wound with a permanganate solution.

"This is the second time," he said dabbing at the wound with a pad of boiled cotton, "that I have had to attend you following violence. You appear to be making a habit of it."

"Sorry for the trouble," Lee said. His mouth felt dry.

"Practice for me, trouble for you," Mr. Martin said. He put a new pad in place and reached for a roll of bandage. "I will warn you that Marshal Phipps has arrived back in Cree this evening and is very angry at this affair, undoubtedly as much for reasons of *amor impropre* as legal distress. He is calling you a dangerous man."

Mr. Martin tied the bandage with a neat, small double bow. Then he cut another length of cloth, folded it into a sling, and fitted it to Lee's left arm.

"Thank you, Doctor," Lee said.

"I'm a draper, not a doctor," Mr. Martin said. But he seemed pleased all the same. "Now, I'm going to give you a reasonable dose of laudanum—nothing to interfere with respiration—and you should wake tomorrow with a very painful shoulder, but feeling better in spite of it.''

"Should he have something to eat?" asked Beatrice, who'd been standing at the foot of the bed, wincing while Mr. Martin probed.

"A cup of sage tea or something of that sort before he goes to sleep. Nothing else tonight. Tomorrow, some soup, if he feels like it.''

Mr. Martin had brought up a big sewing basket with his medical things in it, and he started to put his instruments away and pack up.

"And the marshal may well be right about you, Mr. Lee," he said. "Miss Ashton has had to take poor Nigel off to Chicago." He concentrated on his sewing basket for a moment. "Poor Nigel . . ." Mr. Martin sighed. "He's lost the sight of that left eye." He closed the basket and walked to the door. "That sad, great fool playing cattle baron. And look what comes of it." He closed the door behind him.

That night Beatrice got Lee his cup of tea and sat by the bed talking to him about the ranch, Tim Bupp's pies, and the feud between Mr. Martin and Kimble. She didn't mention George Small, or what people in town thought of the killing.

That night Lee dreamed of horses.

Not appaloosas, though. Cavalry horses.

All bay, and sorrel, and black.

They were running in a great herd, at night, and all of them were bridled and saddled. Running at a gallop, jostling each other as they ran.

Thundering through the night.

They had someplace to go, a place they had to be by morning. They were smarter than ordinary horses: they knew where they had to be.

There were hundreds of them. No. He was rising

216

higher now. There were thousands of them. All dark horses. He could see the dark backs surging up and over the small rises in the ground.

He couldn't see the ground because the grass was too high, and it was dark. Now he was high in the air, high over them all. Horses as far as he could see, from dark horizon to dark horizon, the land was covered with running horses.

They were running away from him, but he wanted to go with them.

When he woke, it was afternoon.

He lay a long time quitely in the bed. His shoulder hurt him; that was what had wakened him.

He thought about George Small and the shooting. About India Ashton off in Chicago with her brother, seeing doctors for his eye. He wondered if she had bothered to telegraph Cree to find out if Small had earned his money and killed him. But how would she word a telegram like that? Some message to a friend, maybe, and ask at the end of it: Any news in town? Something like that, maybe. If she bothered at all. He remembered her face, twisted in rage, then twisted in pleasure as she struggled under him. He felt himself getting hard remembering it.

Poor Small was in the right, after all; Lee'd deserved killing.

But he was here thinking about it, and Small must be in a box at the carpenters. No more sunshine for George Small. No deep breaths of mountain air. No sweets of life for him at all.

He was in the right, and now he was in a box with the lid nailed down. And that was that.

Beatrice came in to see him all through the day. Early in the evening, Mr. Martin came back up to look at the wound.

"Proud flesh and no stink, as a surgeon of my grandfather's day would have said." He pulled fresh cotton bandaging out of his sewing basket, folded out a pad, and wrapped Lee's shoulder afresh.

"In those days, of course, no surgeon would have thought of even nodding to my grandfather on the street," he said. "Surgeons weren't received by any really fine family in the city. Same as barbers, exactly the same. You had one called when needed, and that was all." He finished the bandage with a neat double bow.

Mrs. Boltwith put her head in the door.

"Ah, Mr. Martin," she said. "I thought I saw you coming up. There's beefsteak and roast potatoes for supper if you're of a mind to stay."

"Well, maybe I will," he said. "Maybe I will."

"Mrs. Boltwith," Lee said. "Mr. Martin's dinner's on me. And an extra piece of pie to boot."

"Not necessary," said Mr. Martin, "but, I suppose, an acceptable recompense for an amateur physician. Where in God's name did you get that dress, Maria?"

Mrs. Boltwith seemed pleased at the notice.

"Oh, it's one of my old ones, Mr. Martin. Just an old thing from St. Louis days."

"My dear Maria," Mr. Martin said, "with all due respect to your then occupation in St. Louis, these are different days." He went nearer to examine Mrs. Boltwith's dress in detail. "And may I add that green has never been your color, whatever they might have told you in St. Louis. My God," he said, "there are ruffles on the ruffles!"

"There, you see," Mrs. Boltwith said, "that's fine work."

"I won't hear another word," Mr. Martin said. "You look like an artichoke in that thing, and if it takes an old friend to tell you so, then that's what it takes!"

Mrs. Boltwith's face got a little red when he said that, and she stepped out of the room and slammed the door lightly behind her.

"A heart of gold—and the good taste of a drunken hard-rock miner!" said Mr. Martin.

The next day Lee felt fine. It was just as Martin had said; the shoulder still hurt—gave him a real jolt if he tried to move his left arm—but otherwise he felt fine. The bullet crease on the calf of his leg had scabbed and didn't bother him at all.

He wanted to get up. When Mr. Martin came by to change the dressing, he said, "We'll leave this one on for two or three days; wound's doing well." Lee then asked him when he could get up.

"Tomorrow," Mr. Martin said. "Not before tomorrow."

Beatrice came up to visit with him when the draper left, and she brought a *Harper's Weekly* only two months old to read to him.

" 'Fishing on the Pushquohatten,' " she read, " 'is a tolerable occupation for a late summer day . . .' "

When she finished the article, Lee tried to get her to come into bed with him, but Beatrice said she was shocked just by the suggestion coming from an invalid and laughed, staying out of his reach.

Then she made him tell her about Mexico.

He told her some of it: the smoky untanned leather smell of the small towns; the look of the mountains, how dry and harsh they were; and how the quiet brown people lived up there and minded their own business.

He didn't tell her about the shootings he was in working for the old Don. He and Beatrice had had enough shooting to last them for a while.

After Beatrice went down to bed, Lee stayed up a little longer, reading *Harper's*. There was an article in there about how the South was coming-about from the damage of the war. More of the country than just the South had yet to come-about from that war, Lee thought.

He finished the article, leaned over to blow out the

lamp, and then settled himself carefully on his right side. He didn't want to injure the shoulder now, not when it was healing.

He had no dreams at all that night, or none that he remembered.

In the morning he got up and dressed.

He felt dizzy at first, just as he stood up from the bed, but it passed. When he looked for his shirt in the dresser, he saw that Beatrice had darned over the bullet hole in the shoulder so that it barely showed.

Beatrice came in while he was trying to get his boots on, and she helped him with them.

"Tod Phipps went out of town to the lumber camp last night," she said, "but he'll be back tomorrow."

"You tired of nursing me, Beatrice?"

"I was thinking I could drive you out to the ranch in a wagon today . . ."

"And get me out of town." He smiled at her. "When is Phipps due back?"

"Tomorrow afternoon, I think."

"Then I'll ride out in the morning, okay?"

She nodded and finished pushing the left boot on. She knelt there a minute looking up at him, her hand resting on the tooled leather. A lock of her long brown hair had come down while she wrestled with the boot.

Lee bent over and kissed her gently on the mouth.

"Thank you, Beatrice, for everything," he said.

Then they went down to breakfast.

Mrs. Boltwith's minister, Mr. Pierce, was down to breakfast, and so were two drummers, one with his sample case beside his chair.

Lee said good morning to them, and one of the drummers nodded back. The other two didn't say anything.

Breakfast was sausage and flapjacks and berries with honey, and for a little while, they all ate in silence.

Mrs. Boltwith came into the kitchen and went to the

stove to grind more coffee and put it on.

Then the minister, a little bald-headed man in a rusty suit, put his fork down on his plate and pushed his chair back with a scrape.

"I won't sit at this table," he said very loud. And he got up and walked out of the kitchen. One of the drummers, the one with the sample case, got up and followed him. The other drummer sat where he was and went on eating, his head bent over his plate.

"Looks like I'm costing you customers," Lee said to Mrs. Boltwith.

"To hell with them," she said, but her face was red with embarrassment.

"Tell me," Lee said to her. "What does the town think of that killing?"

"They don't mind," Beatrice said.

"Tell me," Lee said to Mrs. Boltwith.

"Oh, dear," she said, and she put the coffee on the stove. "If that George Small wasn't so old . . ."

"Yes . . ." Lee said.

"He was a murdering son-of-a-bitch!" Beatrice said.

"Yes, dear," said Mrs. Boltwith. "I'm sure he was. A Missouri man, I hear he was, probably rode with that dirty dog, Quantrell. But the people in this town have gotten so they don't like shootings all the time."

"Well, Lee's going back to the ranch tomorrow, and there won't be any more trouble," Beatrice said.

"I do think that's best," said Mrs. Boltwith, and she came over to pour them fresh coffee. She and Lee exchanged a look over Beatrice's head. It was a look from the old days for both of them, from the sporting life. It was a look of trouble.

Lee had wanted to take a walk after breakfast, maybe go back of town to the river with Beatrice, read out there, or have a picnic. Instead of doing that, though, he went back upstairs and lay down in bed for the rest of the day and read some more in *Harper's Weekly*.

He didn't go down for dinner, or for supper either.

Beatrice brought them up to him. She said the minister had stayed away for dinner, but that Mrs. Boltwith had baked rhubarb pie for supper just to draw him in, and he had come back and eaten supper for that.

That night, after she took the dishes away, Beatrice came back upstairs, got undressed, and came to bed with him. It was the sweetest night they'd had together, even with his sore shoulder.

But in the morning, he woke early, anxious to go. He was worried about the ranch and the horses. He'd been away now for three days, and Bupp and the others would be worried wondering what to do. From now on one of the men would have to come into town for the supplies and whatever. Lee would just stay the hell out of Cree for a few months. If he did that, just maybe all this would die down, and in a year or so, people wouldn't think so much of it.

And he was up early to avoid meeting Phipps. He didn't fool himself about that, either. If he fought Phipps, that was the end, win or lose. And he might damn well lose, too. His gun arm was all right; the rest of him wasn't.

And if he did win . . . well, from the smell of the town, he'd have to clear out damn fast, or they'd likely catch and hang him.

So he hurried. He roused Beatrice, kissed her awake, washed at the basin, and began dressing. She got up and helped him with his boots, and then helped him buckle his gunbelt on. Then she went downstairs to light up the stove for coffee.

The sun was just coming up when he walked into the kitchen. The house was quite. Mrs. Boltwith, drummers, minister—the whole lot still asleep.

Beatrice had the coffee on and corn cakes cooking in the pan when he came in and sat at the table.

They sat at the kitchen table without talking, drinking

222

their coffee and dunking pieces of corn cake into it. It made a good breakfast. For Lee, quiet times with Beatrice were as good as talking.

When he finished his coffee, he stood up and stretched, favoring his sore shoulder, getting the last of the bed stiffness out of his back.

"Do you want to go up with me, Beatrice?" he said. "To stay awhile, if you want."

She looked up at him. "Oh, yes. Yes, I would."

"Then go get your possibles. I guess you'll want more than that blue dress. But only bring what you can carry on Belita."

"Oh, yes," she said and jumped up and started out of the kitchen, then came back around the table to kiss him, then ran out again.

"What in the world is the matter with that child?" said Mrs. Boltwith coming into the kitchen. She was dressed in a Chinese wrapper and had a nightcap on with the strings tied underneath her chin.

"We're going up to the ranch together," Lee said.

"Are you?" said Mrs. Boltwith, giving Lee a glance. And she sniffed. "I suppose marriage wasn't mentioned in this," she said.

"No, it wasn't," said Lee.

"The more the fool you," said Mrs. Boltwith. "More coffee?"

She brought herself a cup and came and sat down.

"I suppose," she said, "that you thought that old Martin was right about my St. Louis dress the other night."

Lee had to think for a minute to remember what she was talking about. He sat down again, too, to be polite.

"No," he said. "No, I don't think he was just right on that. I think you look good in green."

"Well," said Mrs. Boltwith, with some satisfaction, "I suppose I'll take a man's opinion then on a lady's looks." Then she looked somewhat uneasy. "Still, Mr.

Martin knows fine things and good taste. He once told Miss Ashton she looked like a sofa in her purple riding suit. And, you know, she never wore that suit again.''

"Oh, he's right about most things like that, I'm sure," Lee said. "But he made a mistake about that green dress of yours, I'll tell you that."

"Well, you know," said Mrs. Boltwith, "I believe you're right. The light isn't much up in these rooms at night. It's a daytime walking dress really, and that's a different color green in the daylight."

"Well," Lee said, getting up again, "I'll be getting my own stuff together." He bent over the table and kissed Mrs. Boltwith on the cheek. "And thanks for being so nice to Beatrice."

"Oh, no, you don't!" said Mrs. Boltwith. And she grabbed Lee's head and pulled it down and kissed him on the lips.

"If I was ten years younger . . ." she said.

Lee went up to his room, packed his hairbrushes and razor case in his saddlebags, picked his Stetson off the bedpost, and went out, shutting the door behind him.

Beatrice was waiting at the bottom of the stairs. She had an old carpetbag with her and some cord to tie it on the saddle with. She'd packed fast; there was a corner of some white cloth sticking out of the closure on the carpetbag.

"I'm ready," she said, breathless.

"That can't be much," Lee said, looking at the bag. "If there's more that you want to take, go get it. We'll handle it on the horses."

"No, no," she said. "This is all I need. Let's go now."

"All right," he said, seeing she was worried. "Let's go."

They walked out the door of Mrs. Boltwith's, down

the porch steps to the boardwalk, and off toward the corner where the street turned to the livery. Beatrice gave a little skip to her step to keep up with him, and Lee shortened his stride.

"Is that bag heavy for you?" he said.

"No, it's fine."

There were some people on the street now, going to work in the stores and freight offices.

Lee saw Rebecca Chase standing on the boardwalk ahead of them in front of the bank. She was talking to a man on a muddy horse. He had a beaver hat and a yellow duster on.

In the next moment, Lee saw that it was Tod Phipps.

He must have ridden hard from the camp. Ridden all night.

"Let's go back!"

"No," Lee said. "Just come on and we'll cross the street. Don't look their way."

As they walked down the boardwalk steps, Lee saw Rebecca staring at them.

They were halfway across the street when Phipps shouted after them.

"You there! *Lee*! You there, damn you!"

Lee stopped walking and turned.

Phipps had gotten off his horse. The duster was spattered with mud from his ride.

Lee heard Rebecca say: "Oh, don't, Toddy!"

"Lee! *Lee*! You're under arrest for a fatal shooting!" Phipps shouted. "You throw up your hands and come over here to me!"

People had stopped all along the street. Watching. Some man was pushing a woman into a store doorway.

"Stand away from me," Lee said to Beatrice. He shoved her away to the side.

"Small pushed that fight, Phipps! And he drew his revolver first!"

"Throw your hands up, damn you!" Phipps called.

He started across the street.

"I'm leaving town now, dammit!"

Still a distance away, Phipps pulled the duster back to clear the guns in his sash.

Then Rebecca screamed, "Oh. Toddy, Toddy, *don't*! He's Frank Leslie! *He's Buckskin Frank Leslie!*" She stood screaming on the boardwalk. "Oh, he'll kill you! *He'll kill you*!"

Phipps stopped about forty feet away. He stood still in the middle of the street, his duster held back from his guns, staring at Lee as if he'd never seen him before.

A man shouted something down the street.

"Forget it, Phipps!" Lee called to him. "I want no trouble with you." It was all over now. If he and Beatrice walked down these streets for fifty years, people would say: "There goes the killer and his whore."

He felt a terrible desire to draw and kill Rebecca Chase.

"Lee . . ." Phipps said. His face was white.

"I'm leaving the valley, Phipps. You have no call to fight with me . . ."

Phipps just stared at him. The poor son-of-a-bitch didn't know what to do. Everybody was looking at him.

Lee slowly turned, walked over and took Beatrice's arm, and started to walk away. His left shoulder hurt like blazes, even though he hadn't moved it, hadn't taken his arm from the sling.

"Frank Leslie!" he heard a man shout across the street. People were running, either to get away or to come see.

Maybe that decided Phipps.

Rebecca screamed.

Lee shoved Beatrice away as hard as he could and turned to his left to get further from her. He saw she'd fallen as he turned.

It all took time.

Phipp's first round burned across his ribs and knocked the wind out of him. Lee'd turned to face him.

Phipps was standing up straight, his arm outstretched, taking good aim.

Lee shot him in the belly. He heard the slug thump when it went into the man.

Phipps took a stiff step back, but kept his aim and fired. The bullet cracked past Lee's ear.

The marshal was shooting for the head.

Lee shot for his belly again, and missed him clean. It was too damn long-range shooting.

He ducked and hurt his bad shoulder. The marshal fired again. The round popped the air over Lee's head and went on back into a store window. The glass back there smashed with a loud musical sound.

Lee took a little time and shot the marshal very near where he had shot him before, straight on in the belly.

Phipps was no George Small.

He screamed like a woman and dropped his revolver and turned away. He walked stiff-legged over toward the boardwalk where Rebecca stood, holding his stomach and screaming. The second round had opened him up. There was pink and blue stuff between his fingers.

When he reached the boardwalk, Phipps sat down in the dust. He wasn't making any noise now.

"Lee!" It was Beatrice.

Lee waved her back and walked across the street.

Rebecca had run down into the street and was hovering over Phipps, moaning and screaming little screams.

When she saw Lee coming with his pistol in his hand, she flew around in front of Phipps like a desperate mother bird to get between them. When Lee got closer, she began to shriek at him, her fingers curved like claws.

He tucked his revolver under his bad arm, took her by the hair, and flung her down in the dirt. Then he

227

stepped up to Phipps. The marshal stared up at Lee as wide-eyed as a baby. His intestines were coming out into his lap.

When he walked past Rebecca Chase, she lay still in the dirt. Her eyes were blank as slates.

Beatrice came to meet him, stumbling. He was reloading as he walked.

"Let's go," she said to him. "Let's go." Her face was white as flour.

"I have to go now and never come back."

"Yes," she said. "Let's go."

Men were standing on the boardwalks, looking at them. Soon, Lee thought, some of them will go get their shotguns. It's time to leave this town.

"Go back to Mrs. Boltwith's. I'll go get the horses and come 'round for you."

She started to say something, but he said, "Go on, do it."

She went a few steps and turned back and called to him, "You'll come for me?"

"Yes," he said. "Go on." She turned and went on across the street.

Lee watched her go, and then he walked over to the bank. People were watching him, but nobody said anything. Two men were standing over the marshal's body, and a woman was kneeling down beside Rebecca.

He climbed the steps to the bank, pushed the door open, and went in. The clerk was there standing beside the counter, and Walker was standing in the doorway to his office. They both looked at Lee in an odd way. He'd seen that look before.

They were afraid of him.

"Mr. Walker," Lee said—it occurred to him that they might think he was going to rob the bank—"I want to do some business about my ranch and give you some damaged bills to exchange."

Walker cleared his throat and said, "What business?"

"I've sold my ranch and my stock and transferred my bank account, too. I want that sale and transfer made right and proper."

"All right," said Mr. Walker. "I guess you better come on into the office."

Through the office windows, as Walker and his clerk drew up the papers, Lee watched what the town was doing. Some men had carried Phipps's body into the carpenter's shop. He had seen Mr. Martin and a woman bent over Rebecca where she lay in the street. Lee had not yet seen a man carrying a rifle, but he thought it wouldn't be long now.

"Well, there you are," said Mr. Walker, and he read from the paper:

" 'In consideration of the receipt of the sum of one dollar in U.S. currency, I hereby sell and transfer that entire property known as River Ranch and all its attachments, livestock, and land rights. I further do submit and assign my account in Cree Bank, as with the foregoing properties, to Miss Beatrice Morgan of this county, Cree County, Montana, on August twenty-third, eighteen-hundred and eighty-seven.' "

"Now, if you will sign, Mr. Lee, we will witness, though . . . though I must tell you . . ." Mr. Walker looked unhappy. "Well, damn it, it's a hell of a lot to give away!"

Lee signed the papers "William Franklin Leslie, also known as Frederick Lee."

"Will this stand in law?" he said.

"Yes," said Mr. Walker. "It'll stand, all right."

Outside the office window, Lee saw a store clerk walking down the boardwalk. He was carrying a double-barreled shotgun.

"Here's your copy," Mr. Walker said. "Signed and witnessed. And I'll send those damaged bills to Denver for her."

"Goodbye, Mr. Walker," Lee said, and he leaned

229

over the desk to shake hands with the banker and his clerk.

"I'll . . . I'll try and look out for her for you," Mr. Walker said. His face was red.

"I'd appreciate that," Lee said.

Lee left the bank by the back door and walked down the alley toward the livery. Two lumberjacks came walking toward him. One had a pistol in his belt. Lee could hear men calling to each other out on the main street.

"Hey, you!" One of the lumberjacks ran over to him. "Is it true the marshal was shot?"

"Yes," said Lee. "He was shot, all right."

"Hot damn," the lumberjack said. "Who did it?"

"I did."

"Oh," the lumberjack said. "You did?"

He stepped back and stood beside his friend. Lee walked away from them toward the livery.

"What do you think of that?" Lee heard the man ask his friend. "He was ribbing you," the other man said.

In the livery, Lee gave Miss McFee two dollars for grain and found, saddled the dun, and led him out. He was wondering whether he might make a stop at the ranch. Better not. They'd go there first if they got a real posse together.

He swung up on the dun and settled himself. His shoulder was hurting something fierce, and his side stung where the slug had grazed it.

He touched the dun with his spurs and headed down an alley, riding for the river bank and the way out of town.

By nightfall, he was high in the mountains on the far bank of Rifle River. He'd ridden the landline of the ranch, but he hadn't gone on in. He thought, from a rise above the west ridge, that he saw one of the appaloosas, maybe a mare, running the high meadow below him. But by then it was already getting dark and he may have been mistaken.

Bupp and Sandburg and Tom Cooke. They'd do their best for Beatrice. She was good with horses.

No future for a little dark-eyed whore riding with a killer.

The moon was coming up, rising like a slice of silver over the peaks of the Rockies. Its white light would fill the valley soon. Lee pulled the dun up on a stony ledge and sat his saddle to watch. Slowly, very slowly, as almost an hour went by, the moon rose high enough.

Its cool, bright light poured slowly down like milk running into a dark green cup, and filled the valley up.

What had Beatrice sung at River Ranch always a little off tune? She'd sung "Shenandoah," and once, "The Last Rose of Summer."

> It was the last rose of summer
> That bloomed all alone.

Lee turned his horse's head, spurred him, and rode away.